THE TRUTH KEEPERS

Also by June Hall McCash

FICTION

Almost to Eden

Eleanor's Daughter

Marguerite's Landing

Plum Orchard

The Boys of Shiloh

NONFICTION

A Titanic Love Story: Ida and Isidor Straus

Jekyll Island's Cottage Colony

Jekyll Island's Early Years

The Life of Saint Audrey
(co-edited and translated with Judith Barban)

Love's Fools

The Cultural Patronage of Medieval Women (editor)

The Jekyll Island Club: Southern Haven for America's Millionaire
(co-authored with William Barton McCash)

The Jekyll Island Club Hotel
(co-authored with Brenden Martin)

POETRY

The Thread Box: A Collection of Poems

THE TRUTH KEEPERS

June Hall McCash

MERCER UNIVERSITY PRESS
Macon, Georgia

MUP/ H1015

Published by Mercer University Press
1501 Mercer University Drive
Macon, Georgia 31207

25 24 23 22 21 5 4 3 2 1

Books published by Mercer University Press are printed on acid-free paper that meets the requirements of the American National Standard for Information Sciences—Permanence of Paper for Printed Library Materials.

Printed and bound in CANADA.

This book is set in Adobe Caslon Pro.

Cover/jacket design by Burt&Burt.

Print ISBN 978-0-88146-818-2
eBook ISBN 978-0-88146-819-3

Cataloging-in-Publication Data is available from the Library of Congress

"*The Truth Keepers* is a work of fiction. Names, characters, places, and incidents are either the products of the author's imagination or are used fictitiously. Any resemblance to actual persons, living or dead is entirely coincidental.

To my wonderful and complex family, past, present, and future.

You are responsible for all my joys and all my hopes.

MERCER UNIVERSITY

MERCER UNIVERSITY PRESS

Endowed by

TOM WATSON BROWN

and

THE WATSON-BROWN FOUNDATION, INC.

The Truth Keepers

PART I

AMELIA

CHAPTER 1

Brunswick, Georgia, 1850

Truth can be a lonely place, especially if you are the only one left who knows it. During these long days, as I've sat in the flickering lamplight beside the bed of my son Joseph, praying for his recovery, I've begun to think—too much perhaps—about why God has let it all happen and to wonder whether I could be the one to blame.

The bedroom door creaks open. Félicité, dressed only in her nightgown, has crept out of her room to bring me a pile of small towels and clean rags. "You will need these," she says softly, gazing with loving eyes at her husband's face.

I take them from her before she can enter the room and pile them on the bedside table next to the oil lamp. Even in its dimmed light I can see the tears on her cheeks.

"Thank you, my dear, but you're not supposed to be in here."

"I know," she replies, her words muted in sadness. Then, hearing her mother's insistent call, she gives Joseph a last tender look, blows him a kiss, and turns to go back to her own room. She wants to nurse him herself, but the doctor has forbidden it. She has only recently recovered from this same illness they call the "winter fever," and the doctor says she is still weak and vulnerable to a relapse. Her mother is adamant that she stay in bed a while longer, although occasionally she sneaks across the hall just to be closer to her husband for a few moments.

He had insisted on sleeping beside her and holding her while she was ill. I don't think he fully realized that he too could be afflicted, but he loves her so much it wouldn't have mattered. I had suggested to him that he shouldn't lie with her, for it might be contagious.

"But she needs me, Mama. Where else would I be?"

Unfortunately, his case is far more serious than hers was. Dr. Woodbridge has come twice, cupping my son's chest to draw out the infection and providing a tincture of morphine to ease his pain, but it has done little good. Sometimes he opens his eyes and looks at me as though he isn't sure who I am. Then, just as recognition seems about to take hold, his body is wracked with coughing and his face crumples in pain. At the moment, however, he is sleeping, albeit restlessly.

One particular deceit from the past has begun to weigh on me. To some it may seem a small thing, but it looms large in my memory. I have never revealed to my husband, children, or friends the truth about my life before I came to Georgia. I've never thought of myself as a liar, but, still, I have allowed them to believe false notions, which are now my burden to bear alone. It's far too late after so many years to go back and set them straight.

None of us, I suspect, is immune to small falsehoods. As I sit here daily and pray for Joseph's recovery, I tell myself, as I also tell his dear wife, that he will get better, though deep in my heart I know he will not. That is not the kind of dishonesty I'm talking about. That's just a gentle deception, meant to soften the pain and ease the heart, for we all want him to live. He is still so young, only thirty-six, with so much life before him, but I see the signs, just as I saw them in *Maman* as she lay in her final illness. I knew that she too was dying, even as I told my rational mind daily that she would get well again to keep myself going.

The deceit that causes me guilt stems from my willingness to allow others to believe things I knew to be a lie. It was never meant to harm anyone, but it troubles me to realize that my children will never know the truth about my past. At the beginning, even my friendship with Mimi was based to some extent on those—what shall I call them?—omissions of the truth. Once it was done, it seemed impossible to undo. I fear that if I told the truth now, she and my family would distrust me in everything else. I don't want to be like Henry, who lived a lie and would have kept his secrets forever if he could have. I have too many sins of my own to worry about those of others. Now, for some reason, during these long and painful hours with Joseph, watching him take short, rapid breaths as he burns with fever, those old deceits are crowding in—making me wonder whether perhaps I deserved all that happened.

Mimi, Félicité's mother, is here to help with the children, thank God, and she appears to be managing quite well. She is one of the first people I met when I arrived in America. We've been close friends from the beginning and even closer since her husband died so many years ago. He too was only thirty-six—the same age as Joseph now. An omen, I fear. They were married only two years, and Mimi never remarried. After his death, she and Félicité, their only child, moved from Savannah to Brunswick so she could be nearer her sister Treyette. We were able to see each other more often. Then, when my son Joseph married Félicité and we began to share grandchildren, our bond was sealed forever.

Our stories interlock even before that. Only hers is true. She never talks about it. For her it's too painful. I remember when she first told me about the horrors she saw in Saint-Domingue, when runaway slaves attacked her family's plantation.

"I grew up in that land," she said. "I was born there. It was my home." Her family was driven out by the slave uprisings and violence in that country they now call Haiti.

"Only *Papa* stayed to look after the place as best he could. *Maman* begged him to come away with us, but he was sure the uprising was only temporary. We left him there," she told me, tears streaming down her cheeks. "I never saw him again." She had witnessed such terrible things before coming to America. "I heard they took him to the river, along with other planters, tied his hands, and stabbed him all over with bayonets until he died." She put her face in her hands, and her shoulders shook. She could say no more. Even now, she doesn't like to talk about it. Nor do I, though for different reasons.

She thinks, as do my family and friends in Brunswick and on the nearby islands, that this is what happened to me as well. And I let them believe it. People I have known for more than forty years now have no idea of the real beginning of my story. Only my brother Bernard and my half-brother Pascal knew that part. But they are both gone now—like my dear brother Joseph, the one I was closest to and for whom I named my son. He was the one who helped me craft the deception in the first place. Now, only I remain—the keeper of the truth my children will never know. I risked the trust of my family and friends for a lie that proved to be unnecessary, for I soon realized that no one would have cared. But what's done is done. To reveal it now would cause everyone to wonder why I had failed to be honest in the first place.

As I wipe the drops of sweat from my son's face and neck, using one of the towels Félicité brought, I try not to think of the future. Instead, I let myself rake through all those little deceptions of the past and wonder whether God is punishing me—taking my dearest son just as he took my beautiful Louisa and the other two precious ones so very young. Now, remembering what really happened in the past seems to matter, for when I am gone, that truth will cease to exist forever.

It all started back in France, before we even came to America. I was seven years old when I first began to understand the direness of our situation. It was a cold day in Bordeaux that January afternoon in 1793, when my brother Bernard bounded into the house, red-faced and shouting, "*Le roi est mort.* They killed the king! They cut off his head!"

"What?" shrieked *Maman*, her eyes wide open in horror at his words. "What did you say?"

"They beheaded the king, *Maman*. Everyone's talking about it."

Tears sprang to her eyes. "God help us all," she said, dropping her face into her hands.

We'd never thought it would come to this. The beginning of the revolution in 1789 had relatively little effect on our family. We had no concerns about the looting and violence feared by members of the nobility, for no one wanted to bother with a poor widow who had four minor children to feed. We lost virtually nothing in the revolution because we had little to begin with. Our father had been a gifted *menuisier*, a master carpenter and a leader in his guild, before his death in 1785, only four months after I was born. He'd left behind three children from his first marriage, four children from his marriage to *Maman*, a house on rue de la Taupe in Bordeaux, and modest savings sufficient to keep us fed and provide some education. We weren't exactly poor, but nothing remained for luxuries, not even after Anne, Pascal, and Cadet, the children from Papa's first wife, were old enough to move out and support themselves.

As the youngest of the four children *Maman* had with my father, I had not yet reached my fifth birthday when it began. Bernard, my oldest brother, was about to turn fourteen. Some of it I can remember. Other parts I learned from my brothers. I do remember how Bernard used to beg *Maman* to let him go out into the streets and march with the revolutionaries, sing their songs and yell their slogans, "*Liberté, Fraternité, Égalité*." It *did* look exciting, but she always refused, especially when they began to add the dire warning of "*ou la mort*."

"You're far too young, and it's too dangerous. The king could send his soldiers to do you harm," she would tell Bernard. But I think she secretly hoped the revolution in France would succeed like the one in America. I think she wanted the revolutionaries to overthrow the aristocracy and make us all equal. I didn't understand much about it at the time, but now I know that, before the upheaval began, the nobles didn't pay taxes and yet had all the wealth and privileges that *Maman* so desperately wanted for us. It was one of the reasons she made sure we had as good an education as she could possibly afford. She thought, if we could speak proper French and knew the kinds of things the upper classes knew, we might rise to a higher social station when it was all over.

At first the revolution seemed to go well. The nobility was abolished, the king became merely Citizen Capet, and it looked as though we might be headed for some kind of rational resolution that would benefit the common people without bloodshed—a kind of constitutional monarchy like they had established in England. But then, in the summer of 1791, the king and queen were caught trying to escape to Austria to seek help. They were brought back to Paris under guard and kept as virtual prisoners in the Tuileries Palace. After that, angrier mobs began to take over. The following summer, a crowd of commoners stormed the Tuileries, and the king and his family were imprisoned.

It was not until two years later, when the king was beheaded, that our mother finally realized how out of control the situation had become. Then, the following October, when they cut off the head of the queen as well, it was too much for her. She broke down and wept. It was the beginning of her decline. I can remember how the shock seemed to jolt the entire city. All over the region, members of the aristocracy began to panic, trying to flee for their lives or go into hiding. They were arrested nonetheless and guillotined in droves, mostly men but some women as well. The revolution had turned truly ugly, and suddenly the world seemed a bloody nightmare.

From that moment on, there was little protection for anyone who stood in the way of Maximilian Robespierre, the man who virtually controlled the country as head of the Committee of Public Safety. It was a frightening time when, I would learn, almost 17,000 people were condemned to death, many of them either from our region in the Gironde, where the less radical ideas of Montesquieu, a native of Bordeaux, prevailed, or others who held Girondin beliefs.

By then Bernard must surely have been grateful that *Maman* had never let him get involved, but many people who met their deaths on the guillotine were guilty of no crime. Their thinking was just not extreme enough for Robespierre and his committee. If they did not embrace his views, he considered them a "danger to the Revolution." It was a bloodbath, a year of horror. Eventually people came to their senses and turned against Robespierre, who himself died on the guillotine for his savagery. His death in July 1794 ended the Terror, but people were still skittish, hungry for a new leader, and a young Corsican general named Napoleon Bonaparte began his rise to power.

As soon as he was old enough, Bernard came to *Maman*'s bedside one evening to announce his decision. I was there beside her, and I remember it well.

"I've come to ask your permission, *Maman*, to join the army and to help Napoleon make France a great power. This is what my generation is called upon to do. Our time has come," he proclaimed in a proud voice, his chin jutting out in determination at his first grown-up decision.

She did her best to rouse from her bed before she began to weep. "How can you think of leaving me in my time of greatest need?" Her voice was plaintive. "How can I give you my permission, when my illness makes you more necessary here than ever?" Her sunken eyes flooded with tears, and her chest was racked with sobs. But Bernard did not give up. Not yet.

"My brothers are here—Jacques and Joseph. They are here to help with anything you require. My country needs me, *Maman*," he pleaded.

"Your family needs you more. Jacques and Joseph are still boys. You are the man here now. You can't think of abandoning your family unless you are compelled to do so by the government. I fear it will happen soon enough. But please, do not put this burden on me—to give you permission to march off to your death. I could not bear it. Your little sister needs you. Who will protect her when I am gone? I need you to do your duty."

Her voice sounded desperate, and I could see Bernard's resolve crumble.

"How could you think of leaving me here, sick and dying?"

It was over now. The very mention of her possible impending death touched his young and tender heart, and he knelt in the lamplight by her side and took her hand.

"I will never leave you, *Maman*. Please, don't fret anymore. I'm here...for you...as long as you need me."

After that evening, he never again mentioned his desire to don that fine blue coat and felt bicorne that the soldiers wore. While I never knew anyone who was a greater supporter of Napoleon than Bernard, if he resented losing his opportunity to fight for the general, he never let *Maman* know. He never spoke of it again.

She died in 1799, the year before Napoleon won the battle of Marengo and proved the power of the French military. We buried *Maman* beside our father in the St. Rémi parish cemetery on a rainy afternoon. I remember returning to the house, our feet muddy. All I wanted was a quiet afternoon, but already my two oldest brothers, Jacques and Bernard, who had grown progressively restless, were debating our future with vigor.

"There's not much of an estate. We've got to find a way to support ourselves," Bernard said. "There's not one of us who is the *menuisier* our father was. Anyhow, the guilds have been dissolved, and we need to find a better way to make a living."

"I don't want just to make a living," Jacques said, his voice impatient. "I want to make a fortune, and the only way to do that is to acquire property. There are lands in the new world to be had. There's nothing for us here."

"There are a lot of confiscated lands from the decapitated nobles," Bernard pointed out.

"But powerful people are already squabbling over those. There's plenty of cheap land to be had in the new world if we're willing to take the risk. Lots of folks have already gotten rich over there," Jacques said, his voice growing louder, his hands gesturing with impatience. "There's Saint-Domingue...and America. We can't be cowardly and hope to get ahead."

Bernard frowned and then said with finality, "We know

nothing about those places. We shouldn't rush into anything." He was the only one of us who was over twenty, and he had assumed authority.

For the moment the conversation ground to a halt, and Jacques stomped away, fuming, as he would do many times thereafter. My brothers continued in their menial jobs to keep us out of debt until matters could be decided. I worried about their frequent quarrels, preferring to keep peace in our family, but there was nothing I could do.

As the debate erupted from time to time, Jacques became increasingly irritated by what he perceived as Bernard's "foot-dragging" and his imperious attitude as the oldest brother, who had assumed, as *Maman* had instructed, the role of head of the household. Thus, as soon as he turned twenty-one in February 1800, Jacques announced that he was moving out and planned to set sail for Saint-Domingue to seek his fortune as a coffee planter. He was excited about the prospect, for Paris was teeming with coffee houses, which had been popular meeting places even before the revolution began.

"What do you know about growing coffee?" Bernard asked.

"What do I know about anything?" Jacques replied. "I can learn. And I'll bet land is really cheap there, now that so many planters are running away in the wake of the slave uprisings."

"Well, if they're running away it's obviously not safe there. Anyhow, I'm not going and I think we should all stick together," Bernard argued. He felt that Jacques ought to stay home and help relieve him of some of the family burdens.

"The slave revolts will be crushed by the French army before long. You'll see. The people who fled are just alarmists." Jacques was not to be deterred when he saw the opportunities before him.

Thus, on a foggy morning in early March, we all trudged to the harbor to see him off when he sailed for Le Cap. As the foghorns sounded, Bernard said in a mournful voice, "They sound like a warning." Jacques just laughed and boarded the ship with a casual wave.

He sent us a single letter when he reached Saint-Domingue to let us know he had arrived safely. Although there were no details about his encounters there, he sounded enthusiastic about his prospects. But months went by, and there was only silence. What little we were able to learn did not seem promising. The French army was still trying to put down the revolts, but the slaves were determined that the Declaration of the Rights of Man and the abolition of slavery should apply in Saint-Domingue as well as in France.

While *Maman* lived, we had employed a young serving girl, but after her death, given the rising wages and the loss of Jacques's income, Bernard felt we could no long afford such a luxury.

"You're fifteen now, Amélie. Joseph and I work to support the family, and I think you should take on the household duties. We just can't afford a maid anymore."

I was not happy to hear that, but I mumbled, "I'll try." I hated cooking and cleaning as much as Bernard and Joseph hated carpentry, but they were making an effort, so how could I refuse? As time went on, the situation became increasingly insupportable for us all. We agreed that there had to be a better life than this.

Like Jacques, Bernard had heard tales of wealth to be made overseas. But he was cautious and did not want to take Joseph and me into what he feared was a dangerous and complicated situation like that in Saint-Domingue. Even though he didn't understand all the details and conflicts among the various groups there—the *grands blancs*, wealthy whites; the *petits blancs*, poorer whites of the working class; the so-called *gens de couleur*, free people of color, mostly of mixed race and often wealthy; the restless slave population who were demanding their freedom; and the maroons, renegade groups of escaped slaves—he pointed out that it was already a powder keg of unrest.

"Perhaps we should consider the new United States," he announced one day. "I hear land is not expensive there and that there is plenty of it to be had. Better still, *their* conflict is over."

He had begun to inquire of people who had gone to the new country and returned filled with tales of a society where everyone was said to be equal and land was readily available.

"Our country helped them in their war against the British. Surely we would be welcome there," he finally said. "I think I'll go to the new world and see what opportunities may present themselves."

"Couldn't we all go?" I asked. The thought of staying in Bordeaux without Bernard, whom I looked on as our protector, was daunting.

"We can't afford passage for all of us until we know for sure this is going to work," Bernard said. "I'll sail to a southern port, where the weather is good and slaves are said to be cheap. If I'm able to buy land, I'll send for you."

Joseph disagreed. He was almost eighteen now and wanted his voice heard as well. "I think we should first find out about Jacques's situation in Saint-Domingue. The fact that he hasn't returned suggests that he's making headway there."

Bernard frowned. "I'm not so sure. He could even be dead, for all we know."

"Or he could just be too busy to write. He's probably forgotten all about us here in France," Joseph argued.

"Tell you what," Bernard said, this time trying to appease his younger brother. "I'll go to America to look for opportunities. You can sail to Saint-Domingue and see what's happened to Jacques. That way we can compare the opportunities the two options provide. Just be careful."

"What about me?" I asked. "Are you going to leave me here all alone?" Bernard looked as though he had forgotten about me and thought for a moment.

"I'll ask Pascal to look after you while we're gone," he said. There was nothing I could say in reply. I knew that my half-brother, Pascal, who was older and more settled, would make sure I was well cared for in my brothers' absence. I had always worshiped him when I was a little girl, and I could find no flaw in their plan, though I knew I would miss Bernard and Joseph. We had all grown closer since *Maman*'s death. And Joseph had become my confidant and best friend.

By mid-summer of 1802, Joseph, who was almost as eager and impatient as Jacques had been, was ready to leave. The leader of the rebellion in Haiti, Toussaint Louverture, had just been captured and sent back to France. It seemed like a good time to go. Joseph got his passport on July 13 and set sail for Le Cap as soon as he could book passage. Bernard stayed on to make sure everything was in order before his departure and to ascertain how much money we could make by selling the house on rue de la Taupe. If he decided we would move, he could use it to invest in land in America. Then he too left in mid-August.

It was lonely without Bernard and Joseph, but Pascal took me under his wing and treated me almost like a daughter. He was, after all, the oldest of us children while I was the youngest, almost fifteen years his junior. He and I formed a special bond during those months while my brothers were away.

"Why don't you come with us when we leave France?" I suggested.

"You know the reason, *ma petite*. It's Agnès. I couldn't bear to leave her."

I wasn't surprised, for I knew that he was courting the baker's daughter. "Perhaps you should ask her to marry you, and then you could both come with us," I said. He was certainly old enough.

Pascal gave me a shy smile. "Perhaps I should."

But when he told Agnès of our possible plans to go to America, she was horrified. "Leave France and go to that godforsaken wilderness? I could never do that. *Papa* wouldn't allow it." So Pascal decided to remain in Bordeaux.

It was Joseph who returned first, with the bad news that Jacques, who had begun to work with a coffee planter to learn the trade, had been conscripted into the French army in Saint-Domingue not many months after his arrival. He had been killed in one of the battles against the rebelling blacks, determined to be free.

I wept on Joseph's shoulder as Pascal stood there, his hands on both our backs in a gesture of shared grief. How could such a thing happen? Our brother Jacques was so young, so eager for adventure, so impatient for life. He hadn't even wanted to join the army. Yet now he was gone. We absorbed the loss, realizing at that point that living in Saint-Domingue was out of the question.

"Most of the French planters there sent their families away years ago," Joseph said. "Jacques was right that land was cheap, because everyone is trying to escape—mostly to one of the British colonies in the Caribbean or to the southernmost part of the United States." That now seemed our best hope, and we eagerly awaited news from Bernard.

We finally received a letter written on January 10, 1804, filled with exuberance. "Yesterday I purchased a plantation of 300 acres!" he wrote. I could tell he was writing quickly, for the handwriting skipped lightly and a bit carelessly across the page. "I am calling it Marengo!"

I smiled, recalling the famous victory of General Bonaparte, now First Consul of France, known as the Battle of Marengo. I wasn't surprised at Bernard's choice of names, for if not for his promises to our dying mother, I think he would have been in Napoleon's army long before now. Thank God he wasn't, I thought, remembering poor Jacques.

"Get your passports at once and put the house up for sale," he wrote. "The soil here is dark and rich. There is a small waterway called Green Creek that runs along the plantation border. Great live oak trees are abundant, as are pine and cedar; and it's filled with game, mostly deer. The people nearby are friendly. I have met only a few of them so far. I bought the land from a man named John Elliott and have learned the names of owners of the farms that border us on two sides—John Fox and David Jeffrey. I hope we shall become good neighbors. Do hurry. Get your passports and come. Marengo awaits, and so do I."

CHAPTER 2

Joseph and I were a bit apprehensive when we came to Georgia in 1804. We weren't sure what to expect. We knew that a fair number of French people had already settled there. Many were wealthy aristocrats or members of the *haute bourgeoisie* who had arrived in the early 1790s in an effort to escape the revolution in France or, like Mimi's family, the slave insurrections in Saint-Domingue with their lives and their fortunes intact. We weren't like them, for we were neither aristocrats nor wealthy *bourgeois*. We'd been in no danger of being toppled from our social status or losing our wealth. Nor did we have reason to fear the guillotine, as many of our predecessors did. For us, coming to America meant instead that we could better our social position and make our fortune if we were clever enough. It could put us on an equal footing with people who would not have cast a sympathetic glance toward us back in France. We could recreate ourselves. That was our goal.

Bernard had written about other French people he had met, most of them living in Savannah, most of them of the nobility. He told us of one group of French noblemen who had tried to start a company on a Georgia island called Sapelo.

"But they bickered among themselves. One returned to France and was guillotined, one shot another, and one died of fever. Apparently, it didn't work out too well," his letter said. I could picture his wry smile as he wrote those words.

"One of those families eventually settled on a nearby island, just off the coast of Brunswick. I haven't met them yet, but I hear they have two sons about your age, dear sister. Perhaps you can find yourself a nice noble husband here in America and become a true lady."

Joseph laughed at that. "I think you are a true lady already, Amélie. But I suppose we must practice behaving as though we are of their social class. Who will know the difference? We too are *émigrés*, just for different reasons perhaps. Besides, we're all equal now, aren't we?"

He made certain that I packed only my best clothes, and before we left Bordeaux he insisted that I have two fashionable gowns made in the latest high-waisted style favored by Napoleon's wife, Josephine. He even bought himself a secondhand powdered wig, thinking it made him look more like a gentleman. It was cheap, considering that such wigs were already out of style. He also arranged for one of his friends, who fancied himself an artist, to paint miniature portraits of each of us dressed in our new finery. Such miniatures had been *à la mode* among nobles in recent years. He had two copies made of mine, one of which he kept with him at all times. The other was for Bernard, and that one he entrusted to me.

"It's something I can show to young noblemen I meet—a portrait of my beautiful sister to tempt them."

I laughed. "And what nobleman would give a second look at a carpenter's daughter?"

"They need not know we're not of their social class. We could be just like the others escaping the uprisings in Saint-Domingue. After all, we did have a brother who died there, and I've just returned to France. We are orphans now. Perhaps we can suggest that our parents also died in the slave uprisings," he said, getting into the spirit of the story.

"Shame on you, using our poor parents like that," I said. "Besides, if they died in Saint-Domingue, how did we get away? I think only our father must have died and our brother, of course, who was heroically fighting to save us. It was *Maman* who brought us back to Bordeaux."

He thought for a moment. "Well, I suppose that could work."

Together, joking at first, we developed an entire scenario. As time passed, it took on a more serious tone. The only true parts were that we *were* orphans and that our brother *did* die in Saint-Domingue defending French planters there. We didn't think our little fiction would hurt anyone. All we wanted to do was elevate our family to a higher social status than that of a simple carpenter. No matter how good our *papa* had been at his trade, it wasn't like being the children of a wealthy nobleman or even an upper-class *bourgeois* who could always buy a title.

Our story grew as we crossed the Atlantic. Joseph put in all the details, gleaned from accounts he had heard in Saint-Domingue. We would add to the tale and tell it to each other, especially when the weather was rough and we were trying to distract ourselves with our fantasy. It was a game that became more and more real as the voyage continued, a way to forget the ominous creaking of the vessel and the increasingly poor food on the journey. We had little worry that Bernard had disclosed anything about our past, for he was always taciturn and private. At most he might have revealed that our parents were dead, but Joseph and I doubted that anyone in Georgia would know even that much about our past.

When we weren't creating our story, we were learning English. Joseph had bought a grammar book before we left France, and we found a passenger from Southampton who was bored during the voyage and offered to give us lessons if we would help her improve her French for at least an hour each day. It was an excellent exchange, and by the time we arrived, both Joseph and I had made great strides in our English at no cost to ourselves.

I will never forget our exuberance the moment one of the sailors spotted land. We all cheered, and Joseph and I stood together on deck, eagerly studying the shoreline as the ship made its way up the winding channel of the Savannah River, past several islands, and to the wharf where we would finally disembark. It appeared to be a rather primitive city by comparison to Bordeaux, but it looked pleasant enough. We had expected Bernard to meet us there, but a message, delivered to us before we left the ship, indicated that he was detained and had arranged for us to be met by a Mr. John Couper, who would escort us to his own home at Cannon's Point Plantation on St. Simons Island until Bernard was able to join us. The message instructed us to wait at a nearby inn until Mr. Couper called for us. We waited at the inn for two days. By this time, Joseph had already decided to stay in Savannah until we could join Bernard.

"I would like to get a feel for the culture and prices of things and perhaps even make a few connections," he said. I was not happy at the prospect of going to Cannon's Point without him, but he was determined.

When Mr. Couper arrived the next day, he had a young lady with him. He seemed a most gallant gentleman, introducing her as Marie Anne Félicité Grand Dutreuilh.

"*Mais on m'appelle Mimi*," she said, telling me her nickname. She looked to be in her late twenties, and I could tell from her manner and accent that she was from an upper-class family. I silently thanked *Maman* for her concern for our education.

As I chatted with Mimi, I could hear Joseph telling Mr. Couper his recent decision. "My sister will accompany you to your plantation, but I have decided to remain in Savannah to acquaint myself with the city and its people. Things are so different here from either France or Saint-Domingue, where we grew up. Our father and brother died there, you know, in the slave uprisings, and we lost our coffee plantation. I need to make certain we will be safe here."

I could feel my face grow hot as he told our concocted story to Mr. Couper, who nodded sympathetically. "Then you have much in common with Mademoiselle Grand Dutreuilh. She and her sisters have had a similar sad experience. I don't think you have anything of that sort to fear from the slaves here, and I'm sure you'll find Savannah quite to your liking."

"I'm glad to hear that," Joseph said. As they talked, I began to chat nervously in French with Mimi, forgetting that I should speak English now. Without thinking, I asked a question of Mr. Couper.

He turned toward us with a smile. "Now, ladies, I'm afraid my French isn't good enough to keep up. I'm from Scotland, you know, and we're not famous for our skills in continental languages. So do be merciful. You'll have plenty of opportunity to get to know one another back at Cannon's Point." He smiled a most congenial smile and explained, "Mademoiselle Grand Dutreuilh and her two sisters have also recently arrived in Georgia. They are back at the plantation with my wife, but I brought Mimi along so that you would feel a bit more at home. We have reservations on a packet ship for Brunswick tomorrow morning. We shall collect you at your inn at eight a.m."

We agreed and bid them both farewell for the evening. When Joseph and I were alone again, I pouted a bit at his decision not to accompany me to Mr. Couper's plantation. He gave me a hug. "Don't be upset, *ma soeur*. I think this is our best option. You go with Mr. Couper, study the social situation and customs of coastal life, and I'll spend the time learning all I can about the people and businesses in the area. I can't do that stuck on some backwater plantation. Just go, relax, and enjoy yourself until Bernard gets there. I'll send him a letter as to my whereabouts, and we will join you shortly."

I protested, but he went on, "If I know you are safe somewhere and being looked after, I will feel more free to explore the area." How could I say no?

Cannon's Point, Mr. Couper's property on the north end of St. Simons Island, was anything but the "backwater plantation" Joseph had foreseen. It was a gracious home with many acres of land, a spectacular view of the river that separated his home from a neighboring island, and plantings of every imaginable type—lemons, oranges, olive trees, figs, anything, it seemed, that he thought might grow in the area. I was to share the room with the three Grand Dutreuilh sisters, a large airy room on the second floor. I liked all three sisters, who went by the nicknames of Mimi, Treyette, and Fortunée. It was a good thing, for their baptismal names, all including "Marie" and "Félicité," were so much alike that I could never have kept them straight. I was surprised to find that my English, though limited, was a bit better than theirs thanks to my recent shipboard lessons, but it was still a relief to be able to speak only French again.

Little by little, they told me their story. It was amazingly similar to the one Joseph and I had invented for ourselves. They had come directly to Georgia from Saint-Domingue. When the uprisings began, their father had sent his family away, though he remained behind to try to protect their sugar plantation. Their mother was still alive, but she had gone north to New Jersey to live with a distant relative, while the sisters remained in Georgia for reasons they did not disclose. The family had heard rumors from other refugees that their father had been killed, but they weren't sure until their brother, Louis, decided to return to Saint-Domingue to check on their lands and find out what really happened.

"He wrote to us of our father's terrible fate." Mimi's voice quivered. "One night…it was almost midnight, he said, *Papa* and five other men were taken by rebels to the river, where"—her eyes filled with tears—"where their hands were tied behind their backs. Then…they were stabbed to death with bayonets, struck down like dogs." She covered her mouth with her hands, as though to hold back the sob that caught in her throat. Fortunée, the youngest of the three, sat clutching Treyette's hand.

"How awful!" I said.

"But you lost your father too," Mimi said, taking my hand in hers.

"Our brother Jacques was killed in Saint-Domingue as well. He had joined the army to defend the planters." I knew that, by not setting the story straight, I was implying my father had died there too. "We spent our recent years in Bordeaux, where we lost our mother to illness." I knew I was walking a thin line between truth and falsehood, but I didn't want to betray Joseph, nor did I want to lie. "Now we are orphans," I added. That part, at least, was true.

"You poor thing. At least we still have our mother." Mimi reached out to take me in her arms. They all commiserated with me, showing such sympathy that I felt guilty at the subterfuge. I wished Joseph hadn't felt it necessary for us to concoct such a story about our family, but he wanted to better our social position and promote us into a higher social circle. He hadn't realized that in this new country, such matters no longer had so much importance. Still, it seemed only a small fabrication. It was true that both our parents and our brother were dead. What did it matter to anyone how they died? I was determined to remain faithful to Joseph's story, though I kept hoping that he would soon join me at Cannon's Point and help me sustain this myth of our past.

The Coupers could not have been more hospitable. Mrs. Couper—Rebecca, as she wanted us to call her—was grace itself. She was quite pretty and still looked fairly young, as she opened her home and her heart to us, hoping, she said, that we would all be able to stay for a very long time as we grew acclimated to life on "this precious island," as she called it. I had to admit that it was one of the most beautiful places I had ever seen. Although I found it rather hot in August, the breezes from the river cooled the veranda and kept the air stirring in our room.

I have never dined on more sumptuous dishes than those prepared by their incomparable chef, a black man named Sans Foix. We dined daily on exquisite dishes of wild game, fish, beef, and pork, seasoned to perfection accompanied by fine French wines—sauterne, claret, and champagne—and pastry dishes of various types.

"How did you ever find such an amazing chef here in the colonies?" I asked.

"No longer the colony, my dear, but now the state," Mr. Couper reminded me. "He's very smart, and he learned from the best—the chef of a Frenchman on Sapelo, a man named Jean Bérard, the Marquis de Montalet. His chef is called Cupidon, and he kindly came here to instruct Sans Foix in the culinary arts—at my request, of course. I went to Sapelo to welcome the marquis when he first came to Georgia a few years back. Like all of you, he was a refugee from Saint-Domingue. When he invited me to dine, I thought I was tasting the food of heaven. I begged him to allow his chef to come and instruct Sans Foix, who was already a fine cook. But the secrets he learned from Cupidon transformed his cuisine into something truly extraordinary—a real art."

"I had not expected a slave to be able to prepare such fine cuisine," I said.

"Oh, Sans Foix is not a slave," Mr. Couper said. "He is a free man of color. And a very fine fellow. We pay him well. Let me assure you that we are not barbarians here. I have always dined better at Cannon's Point than any of my peers ever did in Scotland." He laughed. We both knew that such a claim was hardly boasting, for the Scots were not famous for their fine food.

Although I was quite comfortable at Cannon's Point, I began to wonder when my brothers would come for me. Finally, after more than a week, following another sumptuous dinner, I put the question to Mr. Couper. "Did Bernard tell you how long he would be delayed?"

Mr. Couper cast an odd glance at his wife, Rebecca, hesitating a moment before he said, "Ah, I don't recall a definite time. Do you, my dear?" Mrs. Couper set down her fork and seemed to search her memory. She did not look at me as she responded. "There was no certain time, as I remember. Some sort of problem on the plantation, I believe. I hope for your sake that we will hear something soon." She wore a slight frown as she reached for her glass and took a sip of wine.

"I wonder too how long Joseph will stay in Savannah. Your hospitality is superb and most generous," I said, "but I don't want to impose."

Mr. Couper brushed his lips with his napkin and cleared his throat. "You are certainly not imposing, my dear. We enjoy your company immensely, as do the Grand Dutreuilh sisters. Many of our guests stay for months. One couple even stayed for well over a year." He chuckled.

Mimi smiled at me and said in her halting English, "We have been here far longer than you, Amélie."

"Yes," Treyette added, "and we have always felt welcome." I

smiled then, tried to relax, and just enjoy the pleasant company.

The entire month of August went by, and I still heard nothing from my brothers. I was beginning to think they had forgotten me altogether, when Mr. Couper made an announcement that set the entire household in a tither.

"We will have another visitor in a few days—Mr. Aaron Burr, the vice president of the United States. He is visiting a mutual friend, Pierce Butler, at Hampton Plantation, his nearby residence on the island. Mr. Butler is required in Philadelphia, and for personal reasons, Vice President Burr prefers to remain behind. We have offered him our hospitality during Mr. Butler's absence."

Like the Grand Dutreuilh sisters, I was excited at the prospect of meeting such an important man. At the time, I didn't know why he was in Georgia, and no one informed me until much later that he had killed the Secretary of the Treasury, Alexander Hamilton, in a duel. I was not really shocked by such an act, for dueling, although illegal in France since the sixteenth century, was still considered by many a satisfactory way to settle disputes. Personally, I thought it a rather primitive practice and was pleased to know that it was outlawed and evidently considered dishonorable in parts of this new country. Thus, Mr. Burr, I was later informed, feared indictment and felt compelled to absent himself from New York and the New Jersey area, where the duel had taken place. Although now it is also against the law in Georgia, dueling still goes on, and it was certainly common practice forty-six years ago when I first arrived in America. At the time of his visit to Cannon's Point, however, I knew nothing of Mr. Burr's duel. As it turns out, there were many things I did not know.

Aaron Burr's arrival at the end of August was the source of much fanfare in the household. Sans Foix outdid himself with his extraordinary dishes, and Mrs. Couper prepared a special cordial she called "orange shrub," concocted from the demijohns of brandy and bowls of oranges so readily available on the plantation. The drink was a bit sweet for my tastes. Nevertheless, I drank it and exclaimed over it like everyone else.

Mr. Burr was a stimulating guest and curious to know the reactions of French citizens to Napoleon's having been named emperor of France, which had occurred during Joseph's and my voyage to America. Though I was reticent to speak, I think I was more pleased about the new position than the Grand Dutreuilh sisters were. Although I know very little about politics even now, I knew that Bernard supported Napoleon and was no doubt beside himself with joy. Mr. Burr listened carefully and then went on to expound his own enlightened views of education for women and why, when he was in the New York legislature, he had vigorously supported the immediate emancipation of all slaves. We all listened with rapt attention, and I noticed Mr. Couper, although he was indeed a slave-owner, nodding from time to time.

Aaron Burr was by no means the only visitor to Cannon's Point during the six weeks I spent in the warm and generous household of the Coupers. Two weeks before Mr. Burr's arrival, they invited to dinner the French family of Monsieur Christophe Poulain du Bignon from Jekyl Island, which lay just south of St. Simons. I gathered from our conversations that this was the family Bernard had mentioned in his letter, who had once been part of the Sapelo Company and who had two sons about my age. The older of the two was named Joseph, like my brother, and the younger Henri. Monsieur du Bignon made it clear that he was quite delighted to meet so many young French women. It was obvious that he was looking us over and considering both myself and Fortunée, who was only three years older than I, as potential brides for his sons. I assume he ruled out Mimi and Treyette, who, though still attractive, were nearly a decade older than the two boys, who were both still in their teens.

Out of consideration for the Coupers, we all tried to speak English at the table. Treyette sometimes had trouble following the conversation, and Joseph would thoughtfully lean over and explain something to her in French. Of the two boys, I found him to be the more attractive. He was taller than his brother and had a casual insouciance about him that I found quite compelling. His dark eyes seemed to hold secrets and mysteries I was eager to know, though he seemed a bit stand-offish. Even so, when he looked at me, I felt he could see more than I cared to show the casual observer.

Henri, on the other hand, was like an eager puppy. He had an open face, an easy smile, and a clear desire to please. Compared to his brother, he seemed naïve and rather simple. But he was likeable enough. While Joseph's sandy locks tended to fall over his brow, his brother's dark hair was cut shorter and combed stiffly into place.

Their father observed them keenly and did not hesitate to correct them either verbally or with a stern look of disapproval if either stepped out of line. Joseph constantly did things that made his father glower in his direction. He toyed with his silverware, mumbled his words, and even sneaked a quick bite of his dessert before the hostess picked up her fork. Each time, Joseph would glance toward his glaring father, shrug, and grin as if to irritate him. Madame du Bignon, clearly aware of the interplay between her husband and son, made every effort to distract us with friendly words. "You must all come and visit us soon on Jekyl Island," she said with a smile.

Of the four, Joseph spoke by far the best English, with only a trace of an accent, but Henri had a bit of trouble with the *th* sound, as I did. They had been in America since 1792, they said, twelve years already, but they still spoke French at home for the most part.

"I met your brother Bernard only a month or so ago at the dock in Brunswick," Monsieur du Bignon told me. "He said he had a very pretty sister who would be coming to America, and I can see he was right. In fact, *quatre belles demoiselles françaises à la fois, une vision très rare en Géorgie.*" He made the four of us laugh with his fulsome flattery, and everyone else followed suit, whether they understood or not. Overall, it was an enjoyable evening.

Then, on the morning of the second Friday in September, while Mr. Burr was still in residence, Monsieur du Bignon arrived once again at Cannon's Point. He had come, I think, to meet the vice president, but also with a rather shocking offer for me. He asked to speak with me alone in the parlor, though he was careful to leave the door open.

"Madame du Bignon and I were delighted to meet you. We were both favorably impressed and hope that you will consider either of our sons as a prospective husband," he said without preamble. I was quite taken aback. It was a startling and precipitous proposal and one that I knew I would have to discuss with Bernard and Joseph before making any decision of that sort, especially so soon after my arrival. How could I choose between two boys I hardly knew, especially when I wasn't sure I wanted to marry anyone at all just yet?

"Joseph is a year older than his brother and a bit more clever," he told me. "But Henri is far more steady and reliable—a hard-working boy. I suspect he has a brighter future. But it's up to you. You may have your choice of either one." Clearly, diplomacy was not his strongest characteristic.

Of course I gave him no answer on the spot, but I thanked him for the lovely compliment and told him I would consider his proposal and talk it over with my brothers as soon as they came. I tried to be as gracious as possible, but I was so flustered I can't recall exactly what I said.

Once he had set sail again for Jekyl Island, I went back to my room to think. Later in the evening, I walked out to the veranda to clear my head. Where are you, Bernard and Joseph? I thought. Why don't you come for me? I need you. I may even have said this aloud, for I thought I was alone, until I heard a voice behind me.

"Good afternoon, Mademoiselle Nicolau. Are you all right? You seem a bit upset." It was Aaron Burr.

"Oh, Mr. Burr. No…no. I'm fine," I stammered. "I just needed some fresh air. It's rather windy this evening, isn't it?" I hoped to distract the conversation away from myself.

"Indeed, it is." He looked up at the sky and knitted his brows together. "It's getting rather dark as well. I fear we may be in for a bit of a storm."

As I looked toward the river, I could barely see in the darkness that the waters were riled. The surf sounded rougher than usual, and the gusts of wind were tearing loose a few tendrils of hair about my face.

"Perhaps we should go inside," he said, offering me his arm. He was not an unattractive man, perhaps a few years younger than Mr. Couper. Despite his receding hairline, he had a youthful face, though I deemed him to be in his late forties. He had even, well-spaced features that were quite pleasant. From earlier conversations, I knew he was a widower, and I had noticed Treyette casting admiring glances his way from time to time, even though he was almost twenty years her senior.

In the parlor we met Mr. Couper. "I think we may have a real blow. I expect it's going to be a rather nasty night," he announced.

As the wind continued to rise during the night, he ordered the servants to close and bar the shutters throughout the house. It was probably near midnight before the wind began to howl in earnest. No one went to bed. We sat together in a circle in the parlor around a single lighted lamp as far away from any window as possible, sipping some Madeira wine Mr. Couper had brought up from his ample collection. We all tried to carry on as though things were normal, but I would occasionally peer through the cracks of the shutters and see the trees bending in the gale, even in the darkness. It seemed that everything would blow away as rain came in wild torrents. I had never witnessed such a storm before. It went on throughout the night. None of us slept very much. Most of the time we just huddled together in the parlor, praying. Mr. Couper was clearly worried as the house shook and rattled in the high winds. At one point there was a terrible ripping sound, and when he peered outside he announced that part of the veranda had blown away. Water was flooding the lower floor of the house, where the wines and other supplies were stored, and before dawn there was a crash as a chimney collapsed. I was so terrified that my teeth were chattering.

Would this night never end?

CHAPTER 3

By dawn the wind was still howling, and we could see that the waters had risen above the riverbanks. The storm continued much of the day, but about four o'clock, an eerie silence fell and the sun came out. We were all relieved that we were alive and the house was still standing. Mr. Burr decided that he should leave at once to go and inspect whatever damage had been done at Mr. Butler's plantation, even though it would mean crossing the swollen creek that stood between Cannon's Point and his destination.

Mr. Couper and one of the house servants waded out toward the slave quarters to see whether everyone was safe. They were gone almost half an hour and had nearly reached what was left of the porch again when, without warning, the gale grew violent once more. Rebecca, anxious for her husband and peering through the shutters, gasped. As we would learn, a huge limb fell across their path, almost hitting them, but they were able to get around it, bend against the wind, and finally make it to the house.

"My God, what a storm! I've never seen such devastation," Mr. Couper said as he peeled off his wet boots. "I trust Mr. Burr made it back to the Butler plantation before this started all over again." The gale bore down and continued well into the night, when it finally ended for good. I had never been so frightened in all my life and hoped I never would be again. It was the next day before we learned that Mr. Burr was safe. Little did I know that I would endure even worse in the future, storms and trials that would affect me far more personally than this one had.

Two more weeks passed, and repairs were well under way before Mr. Couper finally received a letter from my brother Bernard. He and

Rebecca sent for me to come to the parlor. Their faces looked somber as I entered the room and sat down on the sofa beside Rebecca. She reached out to take my hand and looked into my eyes. "We have news about your brothers, my dear."

"What? Has something happened?" They exchanged glances and Rebecca nodded to her husband.

"First," he said, "I want you to know that we have heard from your brother Bernard. He writes that he will come for you within the next week."

"That's wonderful! Did he say why it has taken him so long?" I asked, still concerned that they weren't smiling at the good news.

"He has been ill, Amélie," Rebecca said in a solemn tone. "Very ill, and he asked us not to tell you for fear you would worry. But"—her voice grew lighter—"I am happy to announce that he is on the road to recovery and regaining his strength daily."

"Then why do you both still look so gloomy?" I asked. There was a long silence, and Mr. Couper took a deep breath. Rebecca's hands squeezed mine as he spoke.

"We also have sad news about your brother Joseph," Mr. Couper said, his tone grave.

I looked at him, wordless, waiting for whatever he was about to tell me. Was it Joseph who was now ill? I shudder to remember the moment when he finally spoke.

"He is dead, my dear," Mr. Couper said softly. "Just before the recent storm, he went sailing with a new friend in Wassaw Sound. They were caught unaware by the terrible winds. Their boat capsized and both men drowned. We didn't want to tell you until we knew Bernard was out of danger."

"I hope you can forgive us for deceiving you, but we felt it was best not to inform you until we knew your older brother would recover," said Rebecca.

I stared at them in horror. Joseph dead? No, it was impossible. I felt as though I were going to faint. Then I heard a wail, something unearthly, and it took me a moment to realize it was coming from my own throat. I felt Rebecca's arms close about me, and my body began to shake with sobs that didn't allow me to breathe. Then, suddenly, with a great gasp, I caught my breath, and it began all over again. I don't know how long I cried. I don't remember leaving the parlor, but somehow I found myself back in my room, lying facedown on my bed, wanting to die. The Grand Dutreuilh sisters hovered about in sympathy and dismay, not knowing what to do.

I must have slept eventually, for the next morning I woke up and just lay in my bed staring at the ceiling. Mimi washed my swollen face in cool water and urged me to sit up and drink the orange juice Rebecca had brought up. I'd felt grief before when *Maman* had died and when I heard news of Jacques's death, but it was nothing like this. Joseph was not just my brother. He was my best friend. My confidant. We had never been apart, except for the months he was gone to Saint-Domingue. He was like my other half. I tried to take comfort in the fact that Bernard was well again. Certainly I was pleased, but we had never been close like I was with Joseph. It was as though a part of my world had been ripped away. And he had left me alone with this awful story we had fabricated together.

When Bernard finally arrived a few days later, we held each other for a long time, grieving our losses. It was the first time I had seen him since Jacques's death, and of course, the death of Joseph was a fresh, raw wound for us both.

"I'm so glad you're here, Bernard, and that we're together again." He looked pale and thin, but he assured me that he was regaining his strength and vigor. He stayed the night, as visitors often did because of the distance and travel time between plantations, but the next morning we were both eager to be on our way. We thanked the Coupers profusely for their kindness and hospitality, which, I had learned, was legendary in the region. I hugged the Grand Dutreuilh sisters, promising that we would soon meet again, and even made a point to thank Sans Foix and the house servants for their kindness.

Bernard seemed quite taken with the Grand Dutreuilh sisters, especially Treyette, and shook their hands warmly. All of the family and guests walked us to the dock, where we boarded the long, sleek wooden boat carved from a huge cypress log in which my brother had arrived. They stood there waving as the four black oarsmen began to row. We had barely cleared the dock before the rowers began to sing. Their deep voices, keeping rhythm with the movement of the oars, echoed across the marsh river waters as we glided toward St. Simons Sound, toward Brunswick. Their singing expressed the same deep-souled grief I felt, releasing it into the air, where it settled on the waters with calm determination. It's hard to explain how those voices affected me, but I'd never heard anything that better spoke to the pain and resignation I felt inside.

"I hope you're going to like Marengo," Bernard said once we were in the open water. "It's not as fancy as Cannon's Point, and the food won't be as good, but it's got a nice big house with a wide porch, many live oak trees with Spanish moss, and a lot of peace and quiet, especially after all the recent chaos in Bordeaux."

I didn't much care what it looked like. I was just relieved to be with my brother again, though I missed Joseph terribly and knew I always would.

When we reached Brunswick, Bernard had a carriage waiting to take us to Marengo and a mule-drawn wagon to carry the oarsmen and the little boat. He didn't say much until we were seated side by side in the buggy. As the horses began their lively trot inland toward the new plantation, Bernard turned to me, trying to divert my attention away from my sorrow.

"I hear that Monsieur du Bignon and his family came to call at Cannon's Point, and I take it you met both his sons," he said. "Do you fancy either one of them?"

"I hardly know them," I said, surprised at the blunt question.

"Well, I don't think you should rush into it. You'll have plenty of time to make a choice."

"I take it that you and Monsieur du Bignon have discussed the matter already," I said, a little piqued.

"Only in a vague sort of way," he answered. "But I think he

would be pleased to have a pretty French Catholic daughter-in-law to give him grandchildren."

"But he doesn't know our lowly background," I said, and then I told him the story that Joseph and I had devised during our sea voyage.

"That wasn't necessary," he said, frowning. "No one cares much about that sort of thing here. So many of us are refugees of one sort or another."

"But it's done now. You won't give it away, will you? They would despise me for the lie."

"No, but I don't like it. It's not a good way to begin." He was silent for a moment, then went back to the previous topic. "Now tell me, which of Monsieur du Bignon's sons did you prefer?"

This was all moving far too fast for me, and I didn't respond.

"Tell me, what *did* you think of the du Bignon boys?" he persisted, determined to get an answer.

I thought for a moment. "I have only first impressions. Joseph is certainly the more attractive of the two, but his father seems to favor the younger son."

"So I've heard," Bernard said. He was silent for a moment, flicking the reins at the team of horses to make them go faster. We had already left the wagonload of slave men far behind.

"For some reason, everything his oldest son does apparently annoys him. He seems agreeable enough, but his father suggests that he has no interest in the plantation and that he tends to be lazy. Anyhow, I think I'm older than both of them."

Bernard laughed. "Not anymore. When their father asked about your age and disposition, I couldn't remember your exact age, so I asked him how old his sons were. When he told me, I said, 'Well, she's about the same age as Henri.' That seemed to satisfy him."

"How old is Henri?"

"He's seventeen, and the other boy is a year older."

"Well, I'm nineteen, Bernard, older than both of them."

"Now, don't you go making a liar out of me too, Amélie. It makes no difference anyhow. You're seventeen from now on. No need to get things off to a bad start. I wouldn't want such a minor point to be a stumbling block."

Off to a bad start on two counts, I thought. In any case, I wasn't about to choose one son over the other at this point...and maybe never, for that matter. I did like the insouciant look in Joseph's eyes and the way his forelock fell across his forehead. He was by far the more handsome, but he had seemed indifferent toward me for the most part, while Henri was attentive in a boyish sort of way. He had little *savoir faire* compared to boys his age in France, but who was I to judge? I wasn't all that experienced either.

"Did you not like either of them?"

"I'm too young to get married," I said, trying to avoid the issue.

"Lots of girls marry younger than you," Bernard countered. "But you don't have to decide until you get to know them better. They're fairly rich, I think, and of the merchant nobility. Neither of those boys would be a bad choice."

"The Grand Dutreuilh sisters aren't married, and they're older than I am."

"True, and they're all mighty pretty." Bernard looked thoughtful for a moment. "They're closer to my age," he added with a smile.

"Maybe I ought to be the one asking *you* to make a choice. I wouldn't mind having one of them for a sister-in-law. My favorite is Mimi, but I noticed that you paid special attention to Treyette," I teased, managing a grin and a sideways glance at his blushing face. Bernard had never shown much interest in women before, but he would be thirty in just a couple of years, well past an age to consider marriage, and Treyette had seemed to welcome his attentions.

He abruptly changed the subject back to the du Bignons and began to talk more than he usually did. "I think you could do worse than one of the du Bignon boys. They're nobles, you know," he repeated, "and, from all indications, their father is doing quite well on his plantation. They only came here about twelve years ago, but since then he's managed to extricate himself, relatively unscathed, from that disastrous Sapelo Company. He's the sole owner of Jekyl, and he seems smart and determined. He still has property back in

France, or so I hear. I think he'll succeed here in America."

I didn't want to discuss it anymore, so we rode the rest of the way either in silence or idle chatter, as Bernard pointed out various sights and landmarks along the route.

Life at Marengo was, to say the least, rather dull, especially compared to the cheerful atmosphere at Cannon's Point, where interesting people were always dropping by or in residence. I also missed the beautiful view of the river and the neighboring island from the Coupers' veranda. Bernard was seldom at the house, for he was trying to serve as his own overseer to save money. Of course, he knew less than most of the slaves about growing cotton and often consulted the older black men about various details. He had acquired one of the new cotton gins, but even with that, it took many people to do all the work, and he often complained that he had too few slaves.

I'd had no experience with slavery back in France, and, after hearing Mr. Burr's arguments against it, I was persuaded that it was an evil system, and I wasn't sure how to deal with the house servants. I had difficulty understanding their speech, but that became easier as time went on. One girl in particular was friendly and helpful to me. Her name was Adella, and she must have been in her mid-twenties. I thought she was pretty in a primitive sort of way. Her eyes were almost as dark as her skin, but her teeth were whiter than mine when she parted her generous lips and gave me one of her cheerful grins. She tied up her hair in a red cotton bandana to keep it out of the way, I suppose, so I had no idea whether it was long or short. Her duties included cleaning house, washing clothes, and helping to serve meals. I was grateful to her, for now I didn't have to do these things.

We also had a cook named Martha. I won't call her a chef like Sans Foix, for her cooking style was quite different. While he cooked like a fine French chef, using all the techniques he had learned from

Cupidon, her dishes consisted mostly of overcooked vegetables and fried or baked meats, without the delicate sauces Sans Foix was so proud of. We ate a lot of chicken, eggs, pork, and sometimes catfish the slaves caught in Green Creek. I missed the delicious seafood I had grown accustomed to at Cannon's Point. We would have it occasionally in the cooler months, but it wasn't safe to cart it all the way from the Brunswick docks to Marengo in the summer heat.

I discovered at Marengo how much I needed to learn. Back at the Couper plantation everything was done for me, and I lived a life of stimulated leisure, but here it was different and often lonely. I missed Joseph terribly, and Bernard wasn't around to talk with me most of the time. Adella became my best friend during those early months. Occasionally, Bernard would invite some of the people from neighboring farms to come for Sunday dinner, but most of the time it was just the two of us who took meals at the sturdy dining room table, with Adella and Martha serving us. Between meals, my brother was usually somewhere out on the plantation.

I spent a lot of time sitting on the porch, reading or rereading the few books Bernard owned. I wrote long letters to Pascal describing our life here in Georgia and urging him to join us. One day, desperate for a change, I persuaded Adella to walk with me to the slave quarters. I wanted to see what they were like. For perhaps a quarter of a mile or a bit farther, we followed a narrow path into the pine forest until we reached a clearing where a dozen or so small cabins stood.

Adella presented me to an old black woman named Bioula, who was sitting on a long bench cracking pecans with a stone and watching the children. The woman nodded in greeting.

Bernard didn't have many slaves at the time, compared to other planters in the area, and most of them worked in the fields. Bioula was obviously what the planters called "superannuated," too old for such labor. Her hair was thin and white. Her skin looked like dry, wrinkled leather, and she didn't have all her teeth, but she appeared to be a good-hearted woman, calling the children over at my request so I could talk with them.

As they approached warily, Adella said, "I bes' get back to work, Miss Amélie." She seemed nervous being there during her work hours.

"That's fine, Adella. I can find my way back. Thank you for walking me here."

At first the children gathered around me, curious at a white woman in their quarters. When they realized it was all right to talk with me, they began asking all sorts of questions, and they laughed at my answers and my pronunciation. I'm not sure whether many of the younger ones had ever seen a white woman close up before. I told them they could call me Miss Amélie, but their versions mostly came out as "Misamie." I rather liked it.

Eventually, their curiosity satisfied, they tired of me and ran off to play with each other while I sat beside Bioula on the crude wooden bench outside her tiny house.

"They're all so young," I said. None of them appeared to be more than six or so. "Are the older children in school?"

Bioula gave something between a snort and a cackle. "No'm," she said. "They ain't no schools for colored. Over five or so, they're in the fields, helpin' their mamas."

"Working in the fields?" I had heard of poor children being put to work in France almost as young as that, but I couldn't imagine such little children having to work in those hot fields all day long. "That's hard for them."

"Hard for anybody, I reckon."

"Did you work in the fields, Bioula?"

"Yes'm, 'til I got too old and feeble. Lookin' after these young'uns—that's my job now."

"Do you have a family?" I asked.

"Did." She nodded. "'Til my husband died and they sold off all my sons and daughters, the las' one when she was only twelve."

"How awful!" I was horrified. "My brother did that?"

"No'm. It warn't him. It was the ol' man that owned the plantation 'fore Mas' Bernard."

Bioula taught me a lot that day about the lives of the people in the slave quarters. It was all so unfair. I hated that there was nothing I could do. I thanked God I'd never had to live like that—crowded into a one-room cabin with five or six other people and working from sunup to sundown for no pay on somebody else's land. That afternoon helped me to understand what the slave uprisings in Saint-Domingue must have been all about. I'd heard it was even worse there.

When Bernard learned of my visit to the quarters, he made it obvious that he didn't approve, but he didn't forbid me from going back. When I mentioned the children in the fields and suggested that I thought they were much too young, he replied with a laugh, "Keeps them out of devilment."

"Well, I think it's awful."

He just looked at me and shrugged.

That encounter was my first real exposure to what slave life was like. I know it varied from place to place, but when I'd been at the Couper plantation, I had not ventured into the slave quarters or had an opportunity to talk with anyone except the Coupers, their guests, and the house servants—all of whom seemed devoted to the master and mistress.

When I asked Adella about her own situation, she assured me that working in the big house as a domestic servant even at Marengo was better than field work. "Better 'n most ever'thing else, I reckon. I sho don't wanna be no field hand. That life is mighty hard. I reckon I'se lucky to be here." Lucky to empty chamber pots and bend over washtubs scrubbing other people's clothes. It was unimaginable.

The days passed slowly at Marengo, and I found myself eager for guests—any guests—just to relieve the monotony. Thus, when Henri du Bignon began to call after several months, I welcomed him and appreciated the effort it cost to visit. The trip was not an easy one, for it took many hours to come by boat from the island to Brunswick and then drive by buggy the ten miles or so out to

Marengo. Bernard would often invite him to spend the night or even stay for several days.

Bit by bit, as the months went by, he began to grow into a sort of manhood. His boyish eagerness was giving way to greater self-control, and briefly he even sported a fledgling moustache. He and I were both being prodded, he by his father and I by Bernard, toward making some type of commitment. I also noticed that Bernard began to leave us alone together more and more often, which polite society would surely have considered improper.

Henri had been calling for more than a year before he truly shed his shy and awkward ways and began to make every effort to take advantage of the absence of a chaperone, at first just stealing a quick kiss or managing to move in such a way that his hands would appear inadvertently to brush my hips or breasts. Of course I would push him away—at least at first. But as more months went by, he stopped even trying to make such movements seem like accidents. I can't imagine where Henri learned such inappropriate ways to behave toward a young lady—perhaps from his brother, who he told me had fathered a child with one of the slave girls. Maybe this behavior is just instinctive with men. I don't know, but somehow Henri discovered that if he whispered his warm breath in my ear or fondled my breasts in a certain way, I would shudder with sensations I had not felt before. I am ashamed now to remember the liberties I allowed him to take.

Only later did I learn that these moments were, in fact, observed or at least imagined by someone. Whoever it might have been, our conduct became the source of rumors among our acquaintances. I soon discovered that news traveled rapidly along the slave grapevine and that chatter among the servants was often the source of gossip among their owners, especially when it involved their white masters.

Finally, Bernard confronted me. "I think you have put yourself in a position where you have little choice but to marry Henri du Bignon."

"What do you mean?" I asked, all innocence.

"You know perfectly well what I mean," he said. "Besides, he's been calling for more than two years now. I think it's time you made up your mind, and, frankly, I don't think there's anything more to debate."

His comments made me wonder whether it was he who had spied on us. As I look back on it from a more mature perspective, I think it may have been a plot from the beginning to leave us alone and compromise my reputation so that I would have no choice about the marriage.

Still I argued. While I had grown fond of Henri, I didn't think I loved him as a wife should love a husband. "How can I marry Henri du Bignon when there is no priest to marry us?" I knew that the nearest Catholic diocese was in Charleston, South Carolina. The refugees from Haiti who had settled in Savannah had organized some type of Catholic congregation, but even the priest who served there did not often come our way. There were so few Catholics in Glynn County that it was hardly worth his time. Surely the absence of someone to bless the marriage would buy me more time before I had to make a commitment. But Bernard was not to be deterred.

"We'll arrange for a civil ceremony and have a priest bless the marriage the next time one comes to the area."

I could think of no other arguments. I knew I must marry sooner or later, and Henri seemed to be the only choice at present. His brother Joseph, to whom I had been more attracted at first and who was nearer my age, had never really been an option. I rarely saw him, and he had obviously found better things to do than compete with his younger brother. I gathered he just didn't fancy me as Henri did. Or maybe it was because his father favored the marriage.

Eventually, I gave in to Henri's proposal, and negotiations between Bernard and Henri's father began. I don't know why it took so long to get all the legal papers drawn up for the betrothal, but things moved slowly in coastal Georgia then, as they still do. Finally, when everyone was satisfied and it was time to sign the agreement, Bernard and I drove into Brunswick. It was a beautiful day at the very end of April. I sat silent for most of the trip, just drinking the sweet spring air, the wildflowers blooming along the roadside, and the occasional flutter of a red-winged blackbird as we trotted along the dirt road toward town.

My last moments of freedom, I thought, knowing that I would soon tie the rest of my life to that of Henri du Bignon and hoping that we would be happy together. Even then, marriage was more a matter of pragmatic negotiation than it was a question of love. It is comforting now to know that the marriages of my children did not have to be like that. Joseph adores Félicité, as she adores him. While I liked Henri well enough and I wanted marriage and children, our union was, to a great extent, simply convenience. There were not so many choices when one lived the limited life I had lived after coming to America. I knew that Henri was eager for the marriage and the marital rights he would be entitled to, though I must confess I was a little apprehensive about his avidness.

When we finally reached the law office on Gloucester Street, the du Bignons were already waiting, as was my old friend and erstwhile host, a cheerful-faced John Couper, who was to be a witness. It seemed only fitting, since Henri and I had met in his home and as a result of his hospitality.

"You have been a hard young lady to win over," Monsieur du Bignon said. "It has taken my son more than two years to persuade you to marry him."

I smiled, though I had no response. What does one say in such a circumstance?

"The two of you will also begin married life with security, for your brother and I have agreed that, even though you bring little dowry other than yourself, I will provide you with forty acres of good cotton land on Jekyl Island and ten slaves."

Although I had misgiving about being a slave owner, I knew it was a generous offer and better than most married couples often had.

After all necessary parties signed the agreement, Henri and I stood side by side in the courtroom as the grim-faced judge performed the ceremony to declare us husband and wife. I had never expected my wedding to be like this—just a few words said in a stark, empty courthouse room, where the afternoon light slanted through the western window to duplicate its bright outline on the floor. For some reason, the details I recall most vividly are the specks of dust caught in the light and floating aimlessly in the air. I barely heard the words the judge said, and today I can't even remember his name. But at the end of it all, Henri and I were married. A new life awaited me at Jekyl Island.

CHAPTER 4

Our married life began in the old tabby house of Henri's parents at the north end of the island. The very day after the nuptial agreements were decided upon, even before they were signed, *Père* du Bignon had ordered his slaves to begin building a wooden wing onto the house for Henri and me. It wasn't yet complete, so we spent the first night of our married life in the room Henri had shared with his brother Joseph—just across the narrow hallway from their parents' bedroom. I'm not sure where Joseph slept, but it was awkward and embarrassing to be so close to their parents. I'm sure Henri's grunts and groans and the sounds of the shaking bed could be heard throughout the house. He was never a quiet lovemaker, though he was certainly an avid one. I say it now in the past tense. Although he still lives and he is still my husband, he will never again be my lover.

My son's breathing grows more shallow and uneven with each passing hour. My sweet Joseph. Sometimes he goes for long moments without breathing, and I fear it is the end. Then, he will cough or take a labored, ragged breath. Sometimes he shivers; at other times he sweats profusely. I feel so helpless. All I can do is sit by his bed with my hand on his shoulder for reassurance, wipe his brow, or cover him with blankets when his teeth begin to chatter. Sometimes I lean over to share my own warmth with him and whisper, "I love you." When I kiss his forehead, his eyelids flutter a bit. I think he feels my touch, but he rarely opens his eyes. He has stopped eating altogether. I continue to pray, but God does not seem to listen.

Joseph was not our first child, nor was he his grandfather's favorite. Those honors belonged to Louisa, who was born at the end of March 1808, just eleven months after our civil wedding and two months after our union's official Church blessing on the following January 18, a warm and sunny midwinter morning. That occasion was certainly more festive than the civil ceremony, and though I felt rather awkward, almost seven months gone with child, standing before the priest and saying my wedding vows, everyone assured me it was not an uncommon situation among Catholic families along the coast. Like other French planters, *Père* du Bignon would arrange to have a clergyman come to the plantation from time to time—at least once a year, if possible, though he would have liked it more often—to say mass for his family and slaves, perform weddings, and baptize any children born during the year. This was his annual visit, but we made it a merry one.

We whispered our vows to each other and had them blessed before an array of guests, which included the Grand Dutreuilh sisters, my brother Bernard, and, of course, other French residents of the island to whom Henri's father leased land—the Goupys and the Bernardeys. One English family, who had recently moved to the island—Captain Wylly and his wife Margaret—also attended, and, of course, John and Rebecca Couper, who were in many ways responsible for our union. I was delighted to see the Coupers again.

After the ceremony and the mass, despite the brisk chill in the air, there was feasting, with trestle tables set up for guests under the trees, and even dancing—almost like a country wedding back in France. I could see the sun glinting cheerfully off the waters of the marsh creek. The marshes had always seemed to me so melancholy, yet today they were alive with the swaying of grasses, the occasional plash of a fish, and the screeching of saltmarsh sparrows echoing across the vastness. On that day, even the marshes seemed joyful.

The slaves, all but those who cooked and served or helped with the festivities, were given a holiday, and many of them stood in the background watching, clapping their hands, and dancing. I was glad to see them enjoying themselves. I suspected that their world was so bleak that they grasped at any moments of pleasure—even those of the whites who enslaved them. Some of the field hands were also clever musicians who accompanied the dancing. One of the men played a fiddle, another a sort of flute, while another kept the rhythm on a little wooden drum he'd made himself. It was so festive that even Henri's parents joined in the dancing. Such events, when all the island people celebrated together, didn't happen very often, for *Père* du Bignon was a hard taskmaster. When it did, it was always a special moment, and that was one of the happiest days on the plantation I can ever remember.

While I was overjoyed to see Mimi again, my brother Bernard came, I think, more to see Treyette than he did to celebrate my nuptial mass or worship God. That was fine with me. I was encouraging their friendship, which, I hoped, was blossoming into courtship. The sisters were no longer at Cannon's Point but were dividing their time between Savannah and Brunswick. When they were in Brunswick, Bernard could visit them more often and, indeed, found multiple excuses to go into town. He professed a need for supplies or to make arrangements for cotton shipments to Savannah, or whatever other excuses he could devise. He danced with all three of the Grand Dutreuilh sisters during the celebration, but more frequently, I noticed, with Treyette.

When our first child, Louisa, was born just two months after the wedding mass, Henri's mother, Marguerite, rushed downstairs to tell the men waiting outside under the trees, "It's a girl." We both expected them to be disappointed, especially *Père* du Bignon, who'd said he wanted a grandson named for him. But he surprised us with his reaction.

"A girl! *Une petite fille*!" he chortled. "I have a granddaughter!" he shouted to the trees outside. Then he pounded Henri on the shoulder. "You're a *papa*!" I think Henri was so surprised by his father's enthusiastic reaction that he didn't dare express disappointment himself. Marguerite was certainly pleased to have a granddaughter to pet and nurture, but Henri's father was virtually giddy at the news. Louisa was a sweet-tempered child and utterly spoiled by him from the day she was born. In his eyes, she could do no wrong. Anything she wanted, she must have.

Those were such golden days. Louisa was the first of eleven living babies I would birth during my life with Henri—three of them dead before adulthood. And now I'm about to lose Joseph, whose life I can see ebbing away moment by moment. As hard as those other deaths were for me, I know Joseph's will be even harder. While I'm well aware that a mother should never have a favorite, Joseph has always been special. He was named for my dear brother, and he was always a happy child, filled with optimism and dreams.

He has grown into a fine-looking man who has fulfilled every expectation I had for him. Despite his father's shortcomings, he, like his brother Charles, has become a prominent young man in the Brunswick community. He followed in Charles's footsteps as representative of Glynn County in the state legislature and is a Justice of the Inferior Court in Glynn County, among his many proud accomplishments. He can even perform marriages, which I'm sure makes him quite happy, for he is a great proponent of marriage. He and Félicité (or Cité, as he calls her) have been man and wife for more than ten years now, and I've never known a young man happier to be a husband.

I have been able to observe their marriage firsthand, for he and Félicité lived out the early days of their marriage on the island, and they opened their hearts and their home to me when I needed it. Now that I live with them, as Mimi does, we can both see that their love and joy have not diminished. It has been a fruitful union as well. They have six children, the youngest of which, John Eugene, is only a year old. It was when we moved into Brunswick, however, that Joseph really came into his own and was able to establish his reputation and capability apart from that of his father. He's far too young to lose his promising life. It makes no sense. How does anyone ever understand the ways of God?

I lay my hand on Joseph's arm, resting now across his chest. It is warm to the touch, too warm, but even so I am glad for it, for I dread the hour when that warmth will be no more. I close my eyes and say another prayer. "Please, God. Give us a miracle. Let him live." There is no response except for Joseph's labored breath.

Sometimes I feel that I have lived most of my life between the peaks and valleys of births and deaths. There have, of course, been pleasant stops along the way, as on that December 5 following Louisa's birth in March, when Bernard and Treyette also became man and wife. Their wedding too was celebrated on Jekyl Island, for Bernard had no idea how to organize such an event at his own plantation. My mother-in-law Marguerite and I, as well as Mimi, were all delighted to join Treyette in planning the festivities.

The same guests, for the most part, came to that wedding as well, but the guest of honor was Treyette's brother Louis Grand Dutreuilh, who came all the way from New Jersey to visit his sisters and attend the marriage ceremony. He charmed us all. In fact, the du Bignons liked him so much that they tried to persuade him to stay, offering to help him set up a little store on Jekyl. *Père* du Bignon, in a good mood, even said he would purchase the first stock for him.

"You'd like it here on Jekyl, Louis," he coaxed. "You'll be closer to your sisters, and we'd all enjoy your presence."

"I'm tempted to stay, both for your good company and to avoid that winter snow up north," Louis replied, "but I still need to take care of my mother in New Jersey. She was very upset by the circumstances of my father's death and her daughters' decision to remain in Georgia. I think it would be even worse if all her children deserted her, but she doesn't want to live here. It reminds her too much of Saint-Domingue, she says—the weather and the slaves. She wants to live in a cooler climate—one more like the France of her childhood. She needs me there." The three sisters were all disappointed by their brother's decision, but they had long ago become accustomed to his absence, as well as to that of their mother.

Now that Treyette and Bernard were married, we two couples spent as much time together as the growing seasons would allow.

Sometimes Henri and I went to Marengo, taking little Louisa and her nursemaid along, but more often Treyette and Bernard came to Jekyl.

Treyette's younger sister Fortunée was married exactly one year later to a man named Pierre Rossignol de la Chicotte, who lived in Savannah. The same priest, Rev. Antoine Carles, performed both ceremonies. Only Mimi remained unmarried.

Life on the island with Henri was proving to be quite pleasant, even though we were with his parents most of every day. I liked Henri's mother very much, and we would sit under the trees together on warm afternoons, sewing clothes for Louisa or embroidering pillowcases as we chatted and gossiped about any shred of news that reached the island. In the spring, the sweet smell of jasmine and the song of the birds twittering through the trees charmed the days. I could sit for hours with Marguerite, gazing out over the tranquil marshes. Such happy afternoons.

Père du Bignon was away on plantation duties much of the time, but the first thing he always did when he returned home was to find Louisa and bounce her on his knee. He was like a different person when she was around. And she responded to his attentions with chortles of laughter and bright, sparkling eyes that began to dance whenever she saw him. It was fun to watch them together as they adored each other.

After Louisa's birth, I became a more willing lover to my husband, for now the new wing to the house was finished. We had more privacy at night for our intimate life, and I became less tense. He had also learned how to please me in bed, and he made efforts to do so. I considered myself lucky in that way, for most women, I'd been told, merely endured their husbands' arduous acts, while I was actually enjoying them. Even today, after all that has happened, I can smile at those early years we spent together, caught up in each other and in our daughter.

We filled our days, in the rare moments we were alone, with

discovery and delights. Henri taught me to ride the horses, a new pleasure for me. He even bought me a stylish sidesaddle, though I always felt more secure astride. We would ride together down the old Horton Road, named for the Englishman who built it, that led from the house to the beach. We'd let the horses wade in the water while we watched the horizon for an occasional ship or the playful antics of dolphins bobbing in the sea. Sometimes we would dismount and walk along the shore, leading the horses and stopping for a while to examine the colorful swirls of a perfect seashell, rubbing our fingers on the smoothness that led to its inner chamber. I was always awed by the beauty and perfection of the designs spawned by the sea. God was surely the great creator to have imagined all the exquisite variety of form and color found on that small, unspoiled island.

Until I came to Georgia, I had never lived outside the city of Bordeaux. Dwelling in the middle of nature was an entirely new experience for me. I grew to love the soothing sounds of the ocean and the earthy smell of the marsh, identifying them with my new home on Jekyl Island. There was almost always a fresh breeze blowing, unlike at Marengo, where the air could become so still and humid that even outside one could sometimes feel enclosed by the stultifying summers.

As Louisa began to talk, she called Henri's parents *Mémé* and *Papi*, nicknames we all began to use for them—except their son Joseph, who most of the time insisted on the more formal *Mère* and *Père*. Sometimes he would forget and address his mother as *Maman*, as he had when he was a little boy, always making her smile. For the most part, however, the distance between him and his father seemed to grow rather than diminish with each passing day. Even so, he was back in his old room now that Henri and I lived in the new wooden wing. At least that's where he slept when he was on the island, but he spent as much time as he could find excuses for elsewhere—in Savannah or Darien or Brunswick.

I began to see why his father showed such a distinct preference for Henri, who was always available to help on the plantation, riding out with him to survey the fields or helping oversee the workers. He was more respectful and compliant than his brother, who was most of the time morose and even defiant toward his father's authority.

"Have things between them always been this way?" I asked Henri once.

"Only since we came to America. I don't know what has caused it, but Joseph no longer makes any effort to please *Papa*."

It came to a head one evening when we were all having dinner together. Joseph, who like me hated slavery, was trying to convince his father to free the slave woman who had given birth to his child several years earlier. As Joseph's daughter, the child was baptized as freeborn at *Mémé*'s insistence. She didn't want a grandchild in bondage, but the mother was still enslaved. "I think we owe it to her," Joseph admonished his father.

"*You* may owe it to her. But she doesn't belong to you. She belongs to me!"

"She shouldn't belong to anyone. She should be free!" Joseph's voice grew louder.

"If it were left up to you, you'd have me free them all," *Papi* responded in a mocking tone.

"Would that be such a bad idea?" his son asked. "They *are* human beings, you know."

"Then who would do the work? You certainly don't help. You're useless around here." *Papi*'s voice rose too in his anger.

Joseph glared at his father for a long moment. "You've thought me worthless ever since I was a boy. Will you never cease your carping?" His eyes flared with fury.

"Perhaps, if you ever deserve it," his father growled.

Marguerite reached her hand toward her son, but before she could touch him he stood up, knocking over his wine glass. "I'm fed up with it. With this plantation. With slavery. And with *you*. You're not going to have to put up with me any longer." He flung down his napkin and strode out of the room.

Red-faced with fury, Joseph packed his few belongings and left the island the very next morning. As he was preparing to leave, he said to his weeping mother, "I love you, *Maman*, but I can't live with him any longer. I hope you can understand."

I sympathized with Joseph. I had not known slavery in France and was glad that I hadn't grown up, like Mimi and her sisters, with that brutal system in Saint-Domingue. I thought Henri's brother was right that no one should ever own another person. It was an unfortunate way of life here in Georgia, but, like Joseph, I was powerless to end it.

I put my arm around Marguerite as she watched her son go. She was furious with her husband and for the way he had treated Joseph, and it took weeks before things calmed down around the house again. She grieved bitterly over her son's absence and her husband's indifference, but eventually she got used to both. And my father-in-law never even asked where his firstborn had gone.

Henri and I both missed Joseph, for he had brought much life into the house with his outlandish tales and clever ways. We never knew what to expect from him next. He was full of funny stories and strong opinions. I admired him for speaking out as he did on the injustice of slavery. But there was a restlessness about him that could be disconcerting. I think life on the island bored him, and he used whatever excuse he could find to go into Brunswick or up to Darien or Savannah, where he would hang around the docks to get whatever news he could about what was happening in Europe from the sailors who had just arrived. Then he would return to tell the rest of us what was going on elsewhere in the world. His absence left a gaping hole in my life. And in Henri's too, I think.

His mother had a letter from him after a few weeks, letting her know that he was safe and living in Savannah, in the house near the corner of Liberty and Montgomery streets that his father had bought when the cotton prices were good. *Père* du Bignon used it only for visits to his cotton factors, the agents who arranged for the sale and shipping of his crop to other parts of the world, and the family stayed there on their occasional visits to Savannah to see friends or purchase needed goods. The rest of the time it sat empty. Joseph assured her that he would vacate if his father planned a trip to the city.

Papi was, however, not likely to travel in his current foul mood. He found much to complain about—not only his wayward son but also the drop in the price of cotton as a result of a recent shipping embargo imposed against England and France. Although Congress had already repealed the Embargo Act, cotton prices remained low. Georgia farmers, for now at least, had virtually lost the English market. I thought his moods couldn't get worse, but I was wrong.

I vividly remember the sunny day Marguerite and I walked to the dock together to see whether any mail had arrived on the small packet boat that had just docked. There was one envelope. It had come from France, addressed to my mother-in-law.

"Is something wrong?" I asked after she read the letter the bosun had placed in her hands. She was pale as a ghost and looked as though she were about to faint.

"*Mémé*, what's the matter? Are you all right?" I could see her eyes grow cloudy as she sat down on a nearby wooden bench and dropped her face into her hands.

"Oh, Amélie," she said. "How could this be happening?"

"What is it? What's happened?" I sat down beside her.

"Something that's going to set Christophe off again and cause a new uproar. There's no way to prevent it. I might as well tell you now because it's going to upset the household."

I listened silently as she told me that, before she met Christophe, she had been married to a seaman from Mauritius named Jean-Pascal du Jong de Boisquenay. When she met Monsieur du Bignon, she was a young widow with a son and two daughters. The children of her first marriage were grown now, married and with young ones of their own—all back in France.

"At least they were," she said. "Now my son has written to tell me that he is having financial difficulties and is sending three of his children for me to look after. Grandchildren I've never met. I'm sure I'll love them, but I dread telling Christophe."

"When are they arriving?"

"They're already on their way. My son didn't ask for permission.

He just informed me. They were to sail on a French ship, the *Méduse,* three weeks from the date of the letter, which means they're already headed for Savannah." Her son had obviously timed it carefully to give her no opportunity to refuse, even if she had wanted to.

"Why is it such a problem?" I asked.

"Christophe hates the children from my first marriage. He thinks they're greedy fortune hunters." She didn't elaborate on the reasons, and I didn't think it my place to ask. "So you can see why I dread telling him. He'll be furious."

She was right. She asked me to be with her when she broke the news to her husband.

"What?" he shouted. "He's palming his children off on us?" I'm sure everyone in the house could hear his ranting. "I won't take care of those bastards, and I won't allow you to spend one penny of my money on them. They will not come to this island. This is my home, do you hear? They are not welcome!" I had never seen him in such a vile temper before, not even with Joseph. He sulked about the house for days afterwards, making everyone's life miserable.

I would find Marguerite sometimes in tears, wringing her hands over what she should do. I had no answer for her, of course, but I would put my arm around her shoulder and try to comfort her as best I could. Henri refused to take sides in the matter for fear of angering his father, and the whole incident hung like a pall over the house for weeks.

Marguerite wrote to her son Joseph, asking for his help when the children arrived. Unlike Henri, he supported his mother vigorously and without hesitation, even writing to his father, denouncing him in no uncertain terms, and informing him that he was a selfish miser. We were all in the *salon* when *Papi* opened the letter. His face turned bright red, and I could swear he actually growled.

"That ingrate," he muttered. "Listen to how he dares address his father. '*You have plenty of assets to help Maman support those children,*'" he read aloud, imitating Joseph. "'*Give her my share of the estate if you're too stingy to help.*'"

He gave a bitter laugh. "Ha! What makes him think he's going to have any share of my estate?" he shouted to no one in particular. I can understand parents having a preference for one child over another, as he obviously did, but there was actual hatred in his voice. Henri studied the back of his hand, while his mother's eyes once more filled with tears.

I worried that all the tension in the household would upset our own children. We had three by now, one for every year we'd been married. In addition to little Louisa, our first son Charles was born on January 4, 1809, only eleven months after his sister. Then Eliza, our most recent, came along thirteen months later, on February 9. Although the littlest ones may have sensed the tensions, they were far too young to understand what was going on. Three-year-old Louisa was another matter. She had never seen her grandfather display such a temper in her presence, and her face took on a most concerned look. She approached him slowly and put her hand in his.

"Don't be mad, *Papi*," she said, her wide eyes pleading.

He looked down at her for a moment. I could see the anger draining away little by little and watched as his face softened. "Dearest Louisa, my special girl," he said, wrapping her in his arms.

"I love you, *Papi*," she said earnestly, looking up at him.

"And I love you." The fury was gone.

I wondered if she ever realized the magic she wove in that moment.

In any case, things quieted down, and he grudgingly conceded his wife's obligation to meet and care for her grandchildren, especially when he was also confronted with her newfound determination, which Joseph's courage had strengthened in her. But my father-in-law held strongly to his decision that the Boisquenay children would never be allowed to set foot on Jekyl Island.

"Find a place for them somewhere else," he insisted.

When the time came for their arrival, *Mémé* was ready. Two weeks before the scheduled arrival, she took a packet boat from Brunswick to Savannah, where Joseph met her to help make final arrangements.

She stayed with him at the house in Savannah, and he agreed that she could bring her grandchildren there when they arrived. *Papi* had considered selling the house during the cotton price slump but fortunately had not done so.

With his wife away for several weeks, Henri's father grew sullen once more, resenting her absence and the attention he thought she was lavishing on "those Boisquenay brats," as he always called them. He took to wandering off and telling no one where he was going, and he would return looking disheveled, almost intoxicated, and wearing a smug smile on his face.

Less than a month later, my mother-in-law returned from Savannah to tell us all that had happened during the trip. She and Joseph had met the ship *Méduse* together to welcome her three grandchildren, Marie Mélanie, the oldest at thirteen; her eleven-year-old brother Louis Alexandre; and Clémence, who was only nine. They spent a week together in Savannah before she took the girls to the boarding school in Charleston where she had arranged to enroll them. It was an academy for young ladies run by a Miss Julie Datty, and John Couper's daughter Ann was also a pupil there. Louis Alexandre remained in Savannah to attend a Catholic boys' school.

"The girls are very sweet," *Mémé* told me, "though they speak very little English and will have to study extra hard to keep up." She seemed renewed, even exhilarated by her time away from the island and her husband. "Louis Alexandre is a handsome lad," she went on, "but his health seems quite fragile. Joseph has agreed to stay in Savannah to keep an eye on him. Such a good son." I know she loved both her sons, but Joseph had definitively captured a special place in her heart with his support.

When I think of that moment now, I feel less guilty for admitting to myself that I too have a favorite, though I hope it doesn't show. They have all been good children, but my Joseph and I also have a special bond. Perhaps it's because he is named for the other person I loved most in the world—my brother Joseph. My son even looks a bit like him. I almost lost him once before to the yellow fever that killed his sister and brother when they were six and seven. That fragile moment and his miraculous survival made him all the more precious. I think I must have transferred to him all the love I had for my lost children, for Joseph was still ill, and I had no choice but to nurse him back to health.

So many Josephs! It must get confusing to anyone who hasn't known them. At least my son bears the name of two people I admired, for I couldn't help but admire Henri's brother in his courageous confrontations with his father, even though he could be disrespectful and brash. *Papi*'s nature was not a forgiving one. He ruled his roost with an iron hand. Only *Mémé* and my little Louisa could get away with occasionally defying him. But this period was the most difficult one I would ever see my in-laws live through together.

When one of the slave women gave birth to a mulatto baby less than eight months later, *Mémé* was furious—not at the slave woman, who had no choice, but at her husband and the fact that he would behave in such a manner, even in his seventies. He did not deny it.

"How could you do such a beastly thing?" she asked. "I thought you were a gentleman." Tears filled her eyes, as they often did in those days.

"You were gone for nearly a month. Serves you right," he grumbled. "Don't forget, when the cat's away...." It was all he would say. But it was shocking to me to think a man, especially one his age, would carry on like that.

How little I knew of men.

CHAPTER 5

During that year things were so tense in the household that my marriage was beginning to suffer from the depressing atmosphere. Finally I could take it no longer.

"Henri, I think the time has come for us to build our own house," I said one night as we were preparing for bed. "We have three children already, and you know there will be others. We need more space."

His eyes lit up hopefully. "Are you with child again? Another boy, I hope."

"No, not yet, but I'm sure it won't be long."

Although he was reluctant at first, I wore down his resistance little by little until, finally, one splendid spring day we found ourselves in our carriage, all three children in tow, driving down the sandy plantation road in search of a suitable spot to build our new house. Henri wasn't willing to be very far from his parents.

"They're getting old now, Amélie, and we need to be nearby in case they need us."

"Of course," I agreed. "But I shall go mad if I have to live in that gloomy atmosphere much longer." As things were, every day, every meal was an ordeal. I had no objection to limited visits, as long as we could have our own space at other times. We decided that we would need at least four bedrooms—one for Henri and me, one for the nursery, one for girls, and one for boys, when they were old enough to leave the nursery. We finally agreed on a pleasant site about a mile south of the tabby house on the marsh side of the plantation road. His parents weren't too pleased with the idea until they learned that we would still be close by and willing to visit nearly every day, and Henri assured his father that he would still ride each morning to the fields with him.

In the middle of all the household turmoil, one happy occasion lightened the tension briefly in April 1811. I wouldn't mention it here, except that it would become so important both to me and to my son Joseph in later years. Mimi, the last of the Grand-Dutreuil sisters, who would become my very best friend, got married. She was already thirty-four years old, and she had almost given up—assuming she would be a spinster—when she surprised us with a fiancé, a charming man named Charles Pierre Riffault, who lived in Savannah. He was, like her, a refugee from Saint-Domingue. The following year, Mimi gave birth to a daughter, whom she named Félicité—the baby girl who would later become the bride of my dear son Joseph.

If Mimi and Charles had been given more time, there would doubtless have been other children, but they had so few years together. He died only three years after their marriage, at only thirty-six, the same age as my sweet Joseph now. It broke Mimi's heart, but it brought her back to Brunswick to live, where she could be closer to her sister Treyette and to me. They had such a brief span of wedded life, but she never married again, remaining content to rear her daughter alone. Félicité has turned into such a wonderful young woman, and she and Joseph have had ten joyful years with one another. I wish I could give them some of *my* years of married life, for too many of them have been a waste for me. Certainly they could make better use of them.

I was delighted with the new house, and by the time Henri and I moved later that summer, I *was* expecting another child, to Henri's delight. He must have considered my pregnancies a sign of his virility, for he was always eager to have more children. Of course, he wasn't the one who had to endure the morning sickness, the fatigue of that final month or two, or the pain of childbirth. But this time it seemed easier. It was like a breath of fresh air to be in our own home, where we didn't feel the daily tensions between Henri's parents.

Around that time we decided to make some changes in our customs and habits. When we lived in the tabby house, we had always spoken French, the language his parents preferred, but now we agreed that it was important to speak more English with each other and with the children. They would, after all, grow up in a mostly English-speaking world here in Georgia and needed to become Americans in every way. Besides, they had never even been to France.

We decided that, henceforth, we would call each other Henry and Amelia instead of continuing to use the French versions of our names. Henry began to write his surname on letters and documents as "DuBignon" instead of separating the "du" and "Bignon," as his father always did. The separated *particule*, as we called it in French, denoted aristocracy, and Christophe was proud to use it. But we were Americans now, and we wanted to fit in with other coastal residents, not just those who were from France or Saint-Domingue. Then, when the new baby came, the first to be born in our new house, we chose to give him an American name. Thus he became the namesake of our benefactor, John Couper DuBignon.

We lived closer to the Wylly family in our new location, and I was able to pay frequent visits to Margaret and her daughter Susan. By this time, after eight years in Georgia, I was fairly confident with my English and always enjoyed speaking with those who knew more than I did. I knew that my French heritage set me apart to some extent from the English and Scottish ladies who mostly populated St. Simons and mainland towns like Brunswick and Darien, but I wanted to be more a part of the social life of the coastal area. Thus, when Margaret Wylly approached me about giving French lessons to her daughter Susan, I accepted eagerly, for the lessons were a way of getting to know them better. I also taught Anna Matilda, the daughter of William Page, who owned Retreat Plantation on the south end of St. Simons, a property he had bought from a man named Thomas Spalding the same year I came to Georgia.

Once a week Captain Wylly had his boatmen row Susan and me across the sound to St. Simons Island, and I would conduct lessons for both girls. I loved those afternoons, gliding across the waters in a pirogue, listening to the songs of the men as they rowed, feeling the salt breezes tugging at my bonnet, and chatting with Susan more like a young girl than what I was, a matron with four children. On those afternoons I felt free from all my domestic duties and ready to explore new vistas of my life.

I loved those splendid hours in the sunny parlor of Mr. Page's magnificent house with the young women, sipping tea, reciting French verbs, and teasing each other about their accents, which were getting better with each lesson. They always amused me with their clever repartee. Susan Wylly, only three years younger than I, was a pretty, dark-haired girl with a playful laugh. Anna was still in her early teens. She was not as pretty as Susan but was attractive nonetheless. She was the only surviving child of the Pages, who had lost seven others, one only recently, I heard. How could they bear such loss?

Although Anna must surely have been pampered by her parents, it hadn't spoiled her at all. She was charming, smart, and capable, and she worked hard on her French. Her father seemed quite pleased with her progress. Every now and then, he would appear at the parlor door to listen, a satisfied smile on his face. Sometimes I wondered if he was checking on us to make sure I wasn't teaching his daughter any naughty French things. He was so very proud and protective of Anna.

Those were marvelous days. Befriending the Wyllys and getting to know the Pages, even as their daughters' French teacher, began to garner more invitations for Henry and me to the various social gatherings in the area. Those lessons opened for us the window to another world as part of the up-and-coming generation of coastal residents. It was just what we had hoped for.

While I enjoyed those opportunities, I found life at our new house exhilarating as well. Despite the additional responsibilities, I was now mistress of my own household, with freedom to do things my way. My life brightened even more when my half-brother Pascal arrived on the island. I had written to him many times to suggest that he should join us in Georgia, for I knew that his courtship of the baker's daughter had not worked out, and she had abandoned him to marry a miller's son. In his letters he sounded depressed and in need of cheering up, so I urged him to come as soon as we finished our house. Finally, after a long wait, I was delighted to receive a positive response. I remember well the day of his arrival.

He was tired but eager to learn about this new country. "I decided that the best thing for me was to leave Bordeaux," he said, "and accept your invitation to join you and Bernard in Georgia. A new start, I hope."

"And I'm delighted!" I gave him a long hug. "Though I'm sorry your courtship turned out as it did."

He shrugged with what I took to be feigned indifference. It was good to see his lanky frame and his unruly dark hair again. He had been more like a father to me than a brother as I was growing up. Now we seemed to be on a more equal level.

Henry welcomed him, assuring him that he could stay with us as long as he needed and that, if he decided to stay for good, the plantation workers would build him his own house. After only a few weeks, he finally agreed, which pleased me very much. He would settle on Jekyl, acquiring a few slaves of his own and planting cotton on the thirty acres of land he leased on the island. I found it comforting to have him nearby, though we rarely saw him. He divided his time between overseeing his land at Jekyl and visiting Bernard at Marengo. As far as I know, he never courted another lady in his life. As a consequence, he never married and would lead a quiet life until his death thirty years later. I often wondered if he comforted himself with a pretty slave woman named Silvy. I suspect so, but I can't be sure, for Pascal did not confide in me. But I do know that she and her boy, Joe, took loving care of him until his death in 1844, and he freed them both in his will.

The year after Pascal's arrival was especially eventful, for it was in

1814 that my sweet Joseph was born. Then, only six months after that, something happened that would upset our lives for a good while. We woke up one morning to learn that English sailors were landing on the island.

It had all begun with an incident in which officers from a British vessel off the coast of Virginia illegally boarded an American ship called the *Chesapeake* looking for deserters. Despite protests, they captured four of the sailors and eventually hanged one of them. It was an outrage. It was what had brought about President Jefferson's embargo against England and France, which caused cotton prices to drop. By now the conflict had escalated into a full-scale war, which began in June of 1812, the year of our son John Couper's birth. We knew that British ships were patrolling our coast, but we never expected them to set foot on Jekyl Island. What could we possibly have that they wanted?

Big Peter, the plantation's burly driver, was always astride his horse at dawn to make sure the slaves were headed for the fields. He was the first to see the ship, the *Lacedemonian*, which dropped anchor in the sound at the north end of the island. When he saw sailors lowering their dinghies into the water to come ashore, he rode at once to our house to alert Henry. He knew better than to awaken his old master, Christophe, unexpectedly.

We could hear him hollering outside, "Mas' Henry, Mas' Henry."

Henry threw up the window sash and leaned out. "What is it, Big Peter?"

"Sailors with guns and swords is comin' onto de island."

"Who are they?"

"Don't know, Mas' Henry. But dey looks mighty bad."

Henry quickly put on his trousers and boots and, without even bothering to lace them properly, dashed outside and leapt bareback onto his horse to race to the tabby house. I would follow behind in the wagon. Our man Samson had already hooked up the horses to carry some of the slaves to the nearest cotton field, as he did every morning. Now, at my command, he took the reins once again and drove like the wind. Without my noticing, my two oldest children, Louisa and Charles, still in their nightclothes, had climbed into the back of the wagon. They didn't intend to miss such excitement, which was rare on our island.

We weren't too far behind Henry. When we stopped at the back door of the tabby house, I jumped out of the wagon and rushed in and up the stairs to make sure *Mémé* was all right, the children at my heels.

She was standing at the top of the landing, listening to what was happening below.

"You brought the children?" She was incredulous.

"Not on purpose," I said, giving them a stern look. I knew they would have been safer at home, for I hoped the sailors would not go so far as our house on foot.

There was no time to scold them. I could only hide them and try to keep them and *Mémé* safe. Who knew what those English barbarians were capable of? We hurried back into her room, where a silk dressing screen stood in one corner. I gathered Louisa and Charles into my arms and motioned for *Mémé* to follow. We stooped down behind the screen, hoping the sailors would not notice us. I could feel the children trembling with fear as we listened to the men's approaching footsteps, and I tried to calm the beating of my own heart.

"Shhh," I whispered, a finger to my lips, as we heard them enter the room.

"Well, well, what have we got here?" The gruff voice of a sailor said in a mocking voice. "Is this where the French whores live?"

He knocked the screen aside, and we saw two rough-looking sailors standing over us with swords in their hands. *Mémé* and I both huddled over the children to protect them.

"Pipe down, Silas. Can't you see there's young'uns here?" the older seaman said. I hoped he was the father of his own offspring. I thanked God that my other children were safe back at the new house, being watched over by Mammy Celie.

"Just 'avin' a little fun, mate. Besides, this one"—I realized he was pointing at me—"she's not bad looking. The older one...well, you can 'ave 'er. She's more your type." The man called Silas laughed a coarse laugh, then spit on the floor.

The older man didn't smile, but he moved to stand between our little group and the taunting sailor. "Be 'bout yer bus'ness," he commanded Silas. "Open those drawers and see what ye can find."

Silas turned his back on us then and started to go through a drawer that contained Marguerite's best jewelry and special keepsakes. I could hear her soft moan as she watched him stuff her mother's gold locket into his pocket. Most of it, she knew, could never be replaced, especially the miniature portraits painted of her and *Papi* when they were fairly young back in France. She prized them highly, but they too were crammed into Silas's pocket. At least the men lost interest in us as they began to rifle through all the chests, helping themselves to whatever they wanted and could carry. I could hear *Mémé*'s quiet weeping next to me. Finally, the sailors left the room and went back downstairs, but we didn't move.

After the sailors had left and we were back home taking our bearings, I learned from Henry that matters on the ground floor had been even worse.

"I rushed into the house," he told me, "just in time to see one of the men, an officer, knock my father down and grab his musket. He's an old man, for God's sake. I couldn't just stand by and do nothing. I helped *Papa* to his feet and started toward the brute, shaking my fist. He hit me in the face with the butt of his gun."

"So that's what happened," I said, as I gently sponged the blood from his jaw.

"Damned British," he muttered. "They took everything they could lay their hands on."

"Well, at least they didn't burn the fields or pillage *our* house." It was already picking time, and they would have robbed us all of our livelihood for the coming year.

"Yes, there's that, but I don't think it's safe to stay here until this war is over. *Papa* and I have already talked about it. We're going to take all of you into Brunswick for safety's sake."

"What about the slaves?" I asked, worried for their safety as well.

Henry scoffed. "What's left of them. We're still trying to get a head count of those who ran off with the British."

"Can you blame them, given the life they're forced to live here? The English promised them freedom. I would probably have tried to run away too if I were in their situation."

"Don't be absurd. It was the English who brought slaves to these islands in the first place. Some nerve they have, trying to free them now that they no longer own them. They took between twenty-five and thirty of our best workers. I think the greatest loss of all was Big Peter. I can't believe he went with them—as good as we've been to him. Now we don't have a driver, and we're going to have to hire an overseer to see that the rest of the cotton is picked and ready for shipment. Another damned expense." Henry's voice was bitter.

I understood his frustration, but I knew that he and *Papi* had worked the slaves especially hard this year to get the best crop possible. I couldn't blame them for wanting to escape.

"It could have been worse," I said, trying to placate my husband. "At least the British didn't bother any of the other houses on the island." Even as I said it, I knew that our income would be small this year. We were always at the mercy of the elements, but we had never expected a war to come to our very shores.

It wasn't easy to bundle up all the necessities Henry and I would need for an indefinite period of time, as well as things for the five children we had now, all under ten years old, but I did the best I could. We all moved into Brunswick, where we rented rooms in a boarding house until we could go back to Jekyl. It didn't appear to be a long exile, for within less than a month we heard that peace talks were underway. We hoped there would be a quick end to the war and we could get back to the island and the harvest. Although the Treaty of Ghent was signed on Christmas Eve, we didn't learn about it until nearly the end of January and immediately began to make plans to return home.

We were in the process of packing our bags and boxes when news reached us that, even though the war was over, the same British ship was back in the area and headed once more for Jekyl Island.

CHAPTER 6

Henry and his father rushed back to the island, but by the time they arrived, the British sailors had already come and gone. This time they had completed the devastation of the plantation. The fields were still burning. The cotton shed and all the bales readied for shipment were smoking embers. The cattle lay dead, and the house had been ransacked a second time. Had it not been made of tabby, it too would likely have been torched.

"There wasn't much left," Henry told me later when we were alone. "They took everything, and what they couldn't take, they destroyed. I think *Papa* was in shock. He held it in for a while, but when he realized they had even stolen the spyglass and quadrant from his seafaring days, he actually broke down and wept. I'd never seen him cry before. They seem like such little things, but I guess they meant a lot to him. I didn't know what to say. I heard him curse the Brits. 'They've even robbed me of my past,' he said. It tore at my heart to see the old man like that."

Henry and I just clung to each other for a long time. Words were not enough to express our feelings. We were, of course, concerned for his parents, but even more so for ourselves and our children. Even though the sailors had not burned our house, thank God, our livelihood would certainly be affected. We worried for our future.

It didn't take long for fury to replace *Papi*'s grief. Eventually he filed a complaint with the British government for his losses, which he valued at over $80,000. Although the Treaty of Ghent called for restitution, Henry was skeptical.

"I doubt we'll ever see a penny of it," he confided to me. For the first time in our married life, we were in real financial straits. "In a way, *Papa*'s luckier than some of the planters. At least he will still have some income from his holdings in France," he said. "It's a good lesson. We should never let our entire existence depend on income from the plantation. There are too many problems—storms, rot, vermin eating the crops, slaves running off. It's too risky."

I agreed wholeheartedly. However, we had no income of our own to make investments elsewhere. We depended on the plantation and on *Père* du Bignon, and so far, Henry hadn't been able to convince his father to invest in much of anything on the mainland. He was a sailor after all, accustomed to depending on the sea and whatever it brought him. I suppose that in some ways, living on an island plantation was like living on a ship. One was always at the mercy of nature and the loyalty of the crew—in this case, the slaves. He seemed to understand that way of life and even like its challenges. In any case, communications with France were cut off at the moment, and he didn't have any resources with which to branch out, even if he'd wanted to.

Those years of recovery after the war were difficult ones. For a while, no income arrived from the French properties, as we had hoped, and money was scarce. None of us had new clothes or shoes for several years, but it was the slaves who suffered most. The children were barefoot most of the time. The adults had only one pair of shoes each, which they wore every day to walk the sandy roads and work in the fields. Those had long since worn out, and many of the men and women were going about, even in the winter months, without any shoes at all.

We sacrificed what we could, cutting back on household expenses, giving up luxuries like coffee and sugar and anything else that was not essential. *Mémé* even took her Boisquenay granddaughters out of the exclusive academy in Charleston and enrolled them in a less costly school in Savannah, run by a woman named Luce Cottineau de Kerloguen, the widow of a Revolutionary War hero. As it turned out, years later she would prove to be a determined advocate for those girls in more ways than one, and Henry would come to view her as a thorn in his side. But at the moment, her less expensive lessons were a godsend.

It looked as though even the cost of Madame de Cottineau's

school would be lessened a bit when, in November 1815, Mélanie, the oldest of the Boisquenay girls, married another refugee from Saint-Domingue, a fifteen-year-old boy three years her junior, and moved to Charleston. But the reduction did not last long. Fifteen months later, another granddaughter, eleven-year-old Eléonore, arrived from France to take her place. Unfortunately, the only ease of the financial strain came with the death of their brother, Louis Alexandre, from yellow fever less than two years later.

In the midst of all the troubles, I discovered I was pregnant again, as I seemed to be most of the time. I gave birth to two more children, Bernard in 1816 and Anne Amelia a year later. Bernard, of course, was named for my brother and Anne for myself, though we called her by my first name to avoid confusion.

It's still difficult for me to talk about those two children. I loved them deeply, of course, but all too soon we lost them both to yellow fever—Bernard when he was seven and Anne at only six. They were inseparable, so close in age and so much alike. If Anne got sick, so did Bernard and vice versa. God took them within a week of each other. Even now I don't like to think about the awfulness of my children's suffering—the jaundiced skin, the yellowed eyes, the vomit, the blood that trickled from their noses. It's still a scourge that rakes the area every once in a while—one I hope I never encounter again.

Their deaths are still with me today like a cold stone in the pit of my stomach, for there was no time to dissolve it with tears of grief. I had no choice but to give all my attention to Joseph, who was suffering from the same sickness. I nursed him day and night, trying for the sake of my sanity not to think about the two I had lost, pushing those memories away and holding my grief at bay. My days and nights were given over to doing what I had to do for him and praying for his survival. "Oh God," was my constant prayer. "Please don't take another one. Please let him live." Just like now. That time, God answered my prayers.

I felt such joy at Joseph's recovery that it overwhelmed any manifestations of sorrow I might have allowed myself for my other two children. Even now, I don't like to confront that truth, that rock of guilt that still sits inside me, hard and indissoluble, over my failure to mourn them as I should have. The bodies of Anne and Bernard were buried the same day they died, each in small graves side by side, with hasty prayers and a fervent hope that they had not exposed any of the other children. I try not to remember those days. It hurts too much.

Although Joseph recovered from yellow fever, the illness left him weak and vulnerable, but he has managed to stay fairly healthy until now. We called in Dr. Woodbridge again yesterday afternoon. He came and once more cupped Joseph's chest and administered something for his pain, but afterwards he took me aside.

"Amelia, I can only tell you this. There's nothing else I can do. He's in God's care now." The doctor put his hand on my back to comfort me, but both he and I knew there was no real solace.

"I'm so sorry," he said, picking up his bag and stepping into the hallway to talk with Félicité and Mimi and to reinforce his earlier instructions that Félicité should stay away from the sickbed because of her weakened condition. I could hear her protests.

"But doctor, he's my husband. I need to be with him."

"You're highly susceptible to a relapse just now, Félicité. Think of your children. They need you to be strong and healthy."

I could hear her crying and knew instinctively that Mimi had taken her daughter in her arms to let her weep out her anguish. Félicité was torn apart by her dilemma, remembering what good care Joseph had taken of her. We all understood, but the doctor was right. She needed to stay well for the sake of their six children. The youngest, John Eugene, was not yet a year old. It would devastate them all to lose both parents.

I went back to my vigil beside Joseph's bed and let my silent tears trickle down my cheeks. He was no longer waking up at all now, and I knew he would never see me weep.

Joseph's father has not tried to visit him, though he must know of his son's illness by now. I'm not sure Mimi would let Henry in, even if he did knock on the door. Perhaps he doesn't want to take a chance on that rejection. If it were up to me, I'd let him see his son. He was a good father for many years. But he is still a man who is not unlike his own father. And this is not my house.

Once things settled down from Mélanie's marriage, Alexandre's death, and Eléonore's arrival, I had no reason to think of the Boisquenay grandchildren for several years. Then late one morning in the fall of 1819, I saw in the distance a white man and woman trudging down the sandy plantation road toward our house. It was almost noon when they approached. I was sitting on the porch, rocking my most recent baby, Sarah. Louisa and Eliza sat on the floor nearby, playing with their rag dolls, as we waited for Henry to come home for dinner. There was such a glare from the midday sun that I couldn't make out who it was at first.

Finally, as they came closer I realized that the man was Henry's brother. I had never seen the woman before. She wore a wide straw hat and a pretty muslin dress with puff sleeves, a high waist, and a close-fitting bodice. The dress looked quite stylish, with its beige background and generous sprinkling of soft blue cornflowers. I took special notice for, compared to hers, my faded cotton dress, which I had worn for the past five years, looked shabby. I stood up and came to the edge of the porch.

"Why, Joseph!" I called. "How good to see you, and who is this charming young lady?"

I had asked the question in English, but Joseph responded in French. "*Amélie, permettez-moi de vous présenter ma femme, Clémence.*" I smiled and nodded, and the woman did a little half-curtsey.

"Your wife? Why, you rascal, you didn't even invite us to the wedding. Come up on the porch, and let me send Louisa for some lemonade." The woman's name had not struck me yet. "Sit down and tell me how you two met."

I thought she looked familiar. At first I couldn't place her. Then, suddenly, I recalled where I had seen those rich brown eyes, those gently arched eyebrows, and that chestnut-colored hair. She looked just like the miniature portrait of a young *Mémé* that the English sailors had stolen. Surprising even myself, I blurted out, "Oh my God! You're Clémence Boisquenay, aren't you?"

Joseph laughed. "Not anymore. She's Clémence du Bignon now," he said, still in French. His young bride blushed and smiled sweetly, reaching for Joseph's hand. I heard my own breath draw in suddenly. This was one of *Mémé*'s granddaughters!

My mouth fell open, and I could think of absolutely nothing to say. Louisa saved the day by returning from the cooler darkness of the parlor and announcing, "Sudie is making some lemonade, but she says to remind you it's almost dinnertime."

"Oh, yes, thank you." When I finally recovered a bit, I said to Clémence, "These are two of my daughters—Louisa and Eliza. And this"—I looked down at my baby—"this is Sarah."

"Another one already?" Joseph said with raised eyebrows. Then he smiled and gestured toward the older girls. "They're really growing up." Louisa was eleven now, and Eliza nine.

"Have you been to see your mother and father?" I asked him.

"We stopped there first and got the reaction from the old man that we should have expected. *Maman* was happy to see us, I think, though perhaps a bit shocked. Needless to say, we weren't invited to stay for dinner."

"You're welcome to dine with us," I said. "Henry will be here shortly. I know he'll be happy to see you."

"Henry?" he said. "No longer 'Henri'?" We had all switched back to English, which I was determined to speak.

"We're Americans now, Joseph," I reminded him.

"True. Perhaps we should do that, Clémence," he said, squeezing his wife's hand.

"It would work for you, but what is the English equivalent of Clémence?" she asked, her French accent still detectable, though she spoke her new language quite fluently.

"Hmmm… Is there one, Amélie, or should I say Amelia?"

"That's what Henry calls me now."

Just at that moment, Henry trotted up on his new horse, Cracker. "Joseph," he called, eagerly dismounting to greet his brother. "How've you been?"

"Pretty good, *mon vieux*. I want you to meet my wife, Clémence."

Henry's mouth dropped open. "Clémence Boisquenay?" he said in disbelief.

"The very same," Joseph said.

"Does *Papa* know?"

"He does now. He's still seething, I expect." Joseph's laugh was bitter.

I could see that the answer made Henry uneasy. He didn't like to go against his father, but I knew he also loved his brother. Clearly perplexed at what to do, he finally said, "Well, you're welcome here." His words sounded convincing, but I could detect uncertainty in his voice. "And welcome to the family, Clémence."

"I was already in the family, though you'd never know it," she replied without warmth.

"Run ask Sudie to set two more places for dinner, Louisa," I told her. "Tell her not to bother with the lemonade. If she's already made it, she can serve it at dinner."

"Are you sure we're not too much trouble?" Joseph asked. "I'd have let you know we were coming, but I knew you'd tell the old man and he would forbid it. I just decided to surprise him."

"I can imagine his reaction," Henry said, as he ushered Joseph and his bride into the dining room.

"I'm not sure why, but somehow I had hoped our marriage might soften his views. Of course, I was wrong. I should have known."

I hardly remember what we had to eat that day, but I do recall that Clémence was quiet and reserved throughout the meal. Henry and Joseph, however, chattered like the long-lost friends and brothers they were. I suspect Henry would have behaved differently if their father had been there, but it was one of the advantages of having our own house. We could entertain whomever we pleased, though in these hard times we entertained almost no one.

In mid-afternoon, Henry told Joseph and Clémence he had to get back to his duties. Since *Papi*, now in his late seventies, could no longer ride to the fields, he had relinquished all his plantation oversight to my husband, who was now fully in charge and busier than ever. Joseph took this as a signal that it was time to depart.

"We need to get back to the mainland before dark, and it comes earlier this time of year," he said.

Henry had Samson drive them back to their boat in our wagon. Before he mounted Cracker to return to the fields, he hugged his brother and Clémence as well. So did I, but we didn't urge them to spend the night.

When I next saw my father-in-law, I realized that he was almost apoplectic about the marriage, so enraged that out of spite, he decided to put the island up for sale and return to France, even though he no longer owned the fine house he and *Mémé* once had there. I don't know what he thought he would accomplish by leaving America, but all his announcement did was to upset *our* family. Henry was furious when he saw the ad in a Savannah newspaper. Neither of us wanted to uproot our children and move back to France. At the moment, we had little other source of income besides the forty acres of cotton land granted to us when we married. I thank God to this day that *Mémé* was able to calm her husband eventually, so that he took Jekyl off the market. But he had evidently been quite serious about it.

When we later learned that Clémence had given birth to a baby boy named Joseph Alexander, nothing changed. *Père* du Bignon made it clear to us all that he wanted nothing to do with his new grandson. He was growing more and more crotchety as he aged. I could see that his eyesight was failing and that he had begun to think of himself a helpless old man. Only Louisa could draw smiles and hugs from him. He liked my other children well enough, but his heart had always belonged to Louisa. Her death two years later, in the winter of 1824, undid him completely.

When Louisa died, however, I left the job of consoling him and everyone else to Henry and gave myself up, for once, to my own grief. I had no strength left for anyone else. Still weak from recently giving birth to yet another daughter, Catherine, I recovered barely enough will to care for Louisa to the end. Her death was too much to bear. My grief, suppressed for so long, may have been more intense than normal, and I had little energy to spare for anything else.

The entire family was deeply affected and our mourning intense, for she had been a favorite—a loving child, a beautiful and promising daughter in her prime at only sixteen, when she contracted one of the fevers that struck the island all too often. It wasn't yellow fever, with all its horrible symptoms, that took her, thank God, but one of those miasma-borne illnesses that plagued the coast and caused a person to grow weaker and weaker until there was no life left.

After several weeks, I was finally able to pull myself together enough to focus once more on the seven children I had left. Henry's father, on the other hand, made no effort. He seemed unable or unwilling to think or talk of anything but Louisa. Even before she took ill, he'd been already depressed—not only because of his son Joseph's marriage but also because of another hurricane that had devastated the island in mid-September, right at the peak of cotton-picking season. Once again, our income was reduced for the coming year. Calamity had piled on top of calamity, but with Louisa's death, her grandfather behaved as though the grief was his alone and he had nothing else to live for.

He had hovered by her bed day and night, and I had to push him away to tend to her needs. I worried that he would catch her fever and get sick himself, adding yet more to my burdens, for *Mémé* was too frail to care for him as I had cared for Louisa. While that didn't happen, I don't think it would have made much difference to him. He thought only of himself, growing more despondent day by day and losing his will to live. Then, one September morning a year to the day after the last hurricane, *Mémé* went to wake him for breakfast and found his lifeless body. He appeared at long last to be sleeping peacefully. I would never say this aloud, but I must confess I felt a great relief.

We were all there for the burial. *Mémé* had gathered her family around her, sending for Joseph and Clémence, who came to the island with their son, Alex, to attend the simple funeral. It seemed to please her to see all of us, both her sons and her grandchildren, including one Boisquenay granddaughter and even a new great-grandson, all standing together around the grave. My children, the six of those old enough to walk, were lined up like a staircase, holding hands. Henry held little Catherine in his arms, while my new baby girl, Eugenia, born only a few months before the funeral, slept on my shoulder. *Mémé* had tears in her eyes but a smile on her face as she looked around at her reunited family. There seemed to be an unusual feeling of togetherness among us.

The good feeling would not last long, for in his inimitable way, *Papi* struck a final blow at our unity. We were all gathered in the parlor of the tabby house to hear the contents of his will. At one point Joseph, who was reading it aloud to the rest of us, became suddenly silent, then flung down the document and left the house. Clémence followed him, and I could see shock and anger on her face when she returned and told us what had happened. I can only imagine how she felt or how I might have reacted if my husband were the one so insulted and slighted by his own father.

Henry continued the reading after Joseph's abrupt departure. It was shocking to learn what *Papi* had done. The will left Joseph only eighty dollars a year, the same amount he had bequeathed to Maria Theresa, the slave woman with whom he had fathered a daughter. In fact, he left her something far more valuable, freedom and a slave of her own. He had also freed the daughter she bore him. She would no doubt be delighted, but for Joseph, the eighty-dollar legacy was a deliberate and cruel insult. We were all aghast.

The will provided for *Mémé* during the remainder of her life-time, precisely what the law required, nothing more and nothing less. The one surprising request was that "my old Negroes be treated with all the humanity & kindness necessary to their comfort." Who knew he'd ever cared a whit about how they were treated? But his oldest son—that was another matter. Everything else of value—the plantation, the island, his holdings in France—he left to Henry.

I'd like to think that my husband had the same mixed feelings about the will as I did. While we learned that he had just become a potentially wealthy man, I felt bad for his brother. I know *Mémé* loved her husband, though for the life of me I never understood why. Nevertheless, his death was hard for her, and to my relief, Joseph, Clémence, and little Alex came to stay with her for a time on the island. I would, of course, have welcomed them into our household, but I was grateful that they had lightened my load somewhat and taken the opportunity to share their lives with her. Despite their lov-ing care, however, she lived only a few more months, long enough to surround herself with her family at Christmas—all of us together one last time.

On December 29, she passed peacefully away. We buried her beside her husband near a big oak tree, as she'd requested, to lie there for all eternity. We would miss her. She was a good mother to her sons, a good grandmother to my children, and a woman with love to spare for all the rest of her family, even me, whether I deserved it or not.

At the new year, Henry and I visited Joseph and Clémence, who were still at the tabby house. While we were there, Joseph an-nounced their intention to leave within the week.

"It's your island now," he said to Henry.

"You're welcome to stay on, Joseph," my husband told his

brother. "You can live in the tabby house. I want to deed it to you, along with some land." I nodded and smiled at Clémence, hoping they would agree.

"No, thanks, Henry. Staying here, in sight of the old man's grave, would depress me every day for the rest of my life. I want to forget I ever had a father and work at being a better parent to Alex."

"If you don't want to stay now, you can come back whenever you like."

"To be candid, I've never felt welcome here. It would only bring back bad memories."

"We can make new ones. I could use your help here on the plantation."

"You know I'm not a farmer, Henry. I don't ever want to own people and force them to work in the fields. I'd rather starve first."

I looked at Henry and watched his face redden at this remark. He seemed to consider it a judgment on his own moral shortcomings as a slave owner.

"I'm sorry you feel that way," he said. I think he took it more personally than he should have, letting Joseph's statement create a new tension between the two brothers. When I looked at Clémence again, I saw her take Joseph's hand in solidarity. *Good for her*, I thought, hoping I could have the same courage they both showed in that moment.

They left the island the next day. I was sorry to see them go, but even then I did not realize they would never return.

CHAPTER 7

I remember all too well the ominous April morning the following year when I felt so sick to my stomach that I had to lie down. I knew it was early in the season for those summer sicknesses that so often swept the island. Mostly, I feared what else it could purport. I felt better later in the day and went about my normal activities, but when it happened again the next day and the day after, I was more depressed than ever. I had not had my monthly bleeding. It hadn't worried me at first because it had become less regular in recent years. But when I realized how tender and slightly swollen my breasts were, I could no longer deny the fact that I was in the family way yet again.

I stood that morning gazing at the miniature portrait that my brother Joseph had made me sit for before we left France. That girl was pretty, so young and innocent, her long dark hair lustrous and curled softly about her face. Her eyes were bright and eager, ready to take on the world. Then I looked at myself in the mirror of my dresser, and I wondered where she had gone. The woman gazing back at me looked nothing like the young portrait. I could see a few strands of gray hair, all of it dull and dry, folded into a tight bun in the back of her head to keep it out of the way. Her eyelids sagged, her skin was dry, and the corners of her mouth had begun to droop, except on increasingly rare occasions when she smiled.

In the past seventeen years I had given birth to ten children, seven of whom survived. As much as I loved all my children, I had to confess that I was worn out. My body had grown flabby, and I looked and felt even older than my years. At that moment I decided, for my own health, that I had no real choice but to take no more risks. Finally, when I was absolutely sure of my condition, I worked up the courage to raise the subject with my husband.

It was late in the evening. We had finished supper, kissed the children good night, and retired to our bedroom. I put on my nightgown, brushed my hair, and sat on the edge of the bed. Just as Henry started to lean forward to blow out the flame of the lantern on the bedside table, the words came to me.

"Henry, I can't do this any longer. I'm exhausted. I love all our children, but I don't want to have any more after this one."

He paused, the candle still lit, and raised up to his full height with an astonished look. "What? And just what do you think we can do about it?"

"I only know of one sure remedy to prevent it."

"Surely you don't mean…" His voice trailed off as I watched his face. He was not quite angry but clearly shocked and flabbergasted that I would suggest such a thing.

"I'm afraid I do." I felt guilty, but it was true. I could barely recover from one birth before I found myself once again expecting another child. Henry's appetite for conjugal relations was limitless. While I didn't hate the act, I had long since ceased to enjoy its frequency and was always fearful of the possible results and the dangers of giving birth. My oldest living child, Charles, would be eighteen on his next birthday, while my youngest was not yet six months old. I was forty-one, though Henry still thought me thirty-nine. That was his age as well, and he considered himself a man in his prime, but it was different for women.

"I know you think it's unfair, but you don't have to go through the morning sickness and the pain and risk of childbirth, not to mention the lasting effects it has on my body. I just can't do it anymore."

"Do you expect me to become a hermit?"

"No, just a father and, I hope, an understanding husband."

"What I understand is that you don't want me in your bed anymore."

"Of course I want you in my bed. I just don't want to make more children, and there's only one way we can be sure to prevent it."

"You want me to go to the quarters?" he asked.

"Certainly not. Can't you live without…that?" I didn't say the word *sex*, which wasn't a proper word for a lady to speak, but he knew what I meant.

"You make it sound like a bad thing. Men have their needs." His voice was growing louder.

"Shh…the children." I motioned toward the rooms across the hall. "Surely grown men can control their…urges. And can't we talk about this more calmly?"

"I don't know what there is to talk about. You seem to have made up your mind."

"Let me get through this next birth, Henry, and we can discuss it again."

When he finally came to bed, he turned his back to me. He couldn't seem to separate affection from the physical aspects of marriage. I knew I was being punished, but I could not give in. For now, though, since I was already pregnant, I thought he might as well have his pleasures for a while longer. I lay there for a few moments, thinking about the situation and sensing his growing anger. That was when I snuggled up to his back and put my arms around him. I was his wife, after all, and it was my duty to comfort him. After only a few moments, I felt his stiffened body relax as he turned over and took me in his arms.

Our last child, a boy, was born on November 19. Since he knew there would be no more, Henry insisted on naming the child for himself, Henry Charles Jr. He was a hearty baby, a darling, and I think I took more time with him than the others and perhaps even spoiled him a bit at the beginning, knowing he would be my last unless my husband decided to force me. But I thought it was beneath Henry to do so and that he'd make no such efforts, just seethe in what he chose to consider his rejection.

I knew Henry was unsatisfied and suspected that, from time to time, he did go to the quarters to relieve his frustrations, but I had no proof and no reasons to accuse him, however much I might have objected. Perhaps, I hoped, he was learning to control himself instead.

More and more, he began to busy himself with business matters, settling the final details of his father's estate, learning about the family's holdings in France from his attorney René Peltier, and casting about for other, less risky ways to invest his new wealth so we wouldn't have to depend entirely on the cotton harvest.

Some of his time was spent in countering the demands of Luce de Cottineau, the former Savannah teacher and self-appointed champion for the Boisquenay children, who had not been named in the will. She insisted that, before her death, *Mémé* had drawn up some kind of contract to see that Joseph got his share of his father's estate, but Henry and I both doubted it, first of all because she could provide no proof and second because none of it was his mother's to bestow. What *Mémé* received in his father's will was only a lifetime benefit, *her* lifetime, which, as we all knew, had been very brief after *Papi*'s death.

At first, Henry had planned to share some of the estate with his brother, now that it was his to give. However, what he saw as the machinations of Madame de Cottineau made him dig in his heels. Besides, he had made the offer, and Joseph had rejected it. Henry was now reluctant to give up what he felt he had justly earned by being the good son. Some of his father's anger at the Boisquenay girls had also evidently rubbed off on him, and Madame de Cottineau's efforts on their behalf only made it worse.

"I understand now why *Papa* thought they were gold-diggers," he would say. "I think he was right."

I kept my opinions to myself, for the wealth was not mine. Everything belonged to Henry, and he was not in a mood to be particularly generous, even to me, though he did occasionally spoil the children with little gifts—things like pocketknives or slingshots for the boys and bracelets or dolls for the girls.

The cotton harvest was good that year, and for the first time in many years we made a comfortable profit and felt financially secure. We finally had enough money for him to begin to seriously consider other commercial investments. He was spending more time away from home, mostly involved in new Brunswick undertakings and making friends with important men in the community. Although I missed him, I was happy to see him using his energies constructively and not moping around the house, sour-faced and blaming me.

Instead, he was setting himself up to become a man of substance in the city of Brunswick. He already served as a commissioner in the public school system, and by 1818, he had been selected to serve as treasurer of Glynn Academy, where four of our children were enrolled in school, even though it meant a long boat ride for them every morning and afternoon. Often I spent my time with the younger children, too small yet to go to school, and the few house servants we had. I can't say that I was exactly lonely in those days, but I missed adult conversations with my peers. We had fewer neighbors on the island at that point. The Bernardeys had long since purchased their own land on Cumberland Island and moved away. The Wyllys, whom I had visited so often and with whose daughter, Susan, I had frequently crossed the sound for French lessons with Anna Matilda Page, had also left the island to make a permanent home at an eastern area of St. Simons known as The Village.

Thus, my life had become rather monotonous, especially as more of my children went to school. I remembered with longing the conversations I had shared with *Mémé*. We had visited back and forth and spent many hours together sewing and chatting under the live oak trees and the tall pines that grew around both our houses. I especially missed my oldest son, Charles. Only recently, he had gone north to further his learning. It was his goal to get a solid education and involve himself in government in some way. When he returned to Georgia, he planned to study law with a successful Brunswick lawyer named W. W. Cuyler, the same man who had recently persuaded Henry to invest in a new enterprise, the Central Railroad and Banking Company, where Mr. Cuyler himself served as president. He claimed he saw a great deal of promise in Charles and had agreed to take him under his wing.

I was very proud of my firstborn son. He had grown into a

handsome and intelligent young man, perhaps the most attractive of all my boys. He didn't have the narrow face and pointed chin so typical of the DuBignon men. Instead, his wide-spaced eyes and the broader contours of his jaw gave him a solid, honest appearance that people seemed to find trustworthy. His good looks and sharp mind would, I felt sure, serve him well in the years to come. Still I was sad to think he had probably left the island for good, for he was old enough now to stand on his own two feet and eager to broaden his horizons.

The day he left to go north, I couldn't help but weep a bit.

"Don't worry, Mama, I'll be back, and I'll make you proud."

"I'm not worried, son, but I will miss you terribly."

We had spent many afternoons together during his father's absences and while the younger children were in school, just sitting on the porch in quiet conversation as we watched the birds flit back and forth among the trees. He knew how much I loved the birdsong and the flocks that passed over the island in the spring, pausing for a while at Jekyl before continuing their trip north for the summer. I remember the day we caught sight of a painted bunting perched on a nearby branch. We saw them only rarely and usually in flight. This one was solitary, and we gazed silently, amazed at the varied, bright colors of his plumage. Charles watched him, a pensive expression on his face.

"Someone should write a poem about him," he said.

"Or her," I suggested.

"No, I'm sure it's a male. They always have the brightest plumage."

I knew he was right. It was always the males that were the most beautiful birds. The females were more drab and faded into the background, *as I have done*, I thought. I recalled my early life in Bordeaux before the Revolution, when the noble ladies wore such magnificent garments, trying to outshine each other. I'd had very little interaction with them, but I could see them ride by in their open carriages. The men dressed in finery as well, but I always thought the women were more beautiful. Here on the island, however, things were different. I gave little thought to fashion. Only when I went into Brunswick or to St. Simons, or when we entertained here on the island, which was not frequent, did I pay much attention to my appearance. But I made sure that, when Charles left, he had an adequate wardrobe, sufficient to look like the son of a wealthy planter among the offspring of those New Englanders.

Suddenly, I become aware that Joseph, who has been stirring restlessly for the past hour, is now quite still. I watch him carefully for a sign of breath, but I can see none. I feel a moment of panic. His hands are cooler to my touch and his skin has taken on a bluish tint. I lay my head on his chest to see whether I can still hear his heartbeat. It is there, faint and irregular, but it is there. Suddenly he catches a ragged breath and I feel his chest rise. *Thank God*! I think. I'm still not ready to accept the inevitable, still clinging to my feeble, false hope.

As I sit through the night, holding his hand, I remember how, even as a little boy, he always toddled around after Charles, trying to do everything he did. His oldest brother, five years his senior, was his idol. I had always assumed that he would follow in his brother's footsteps and, like Charles, head north to continue his education as soon as he was old enough, but as time passed, I learned I was wrong.

Through most of the 1830s, we enjoyed relatively happy times and even a fairly lively social life. Now that I no longer faced the constant threat of pregnancy and Henry had found fulfillment in his new business endeavors, we lived in reasonable harmony. He seemed to have accepted and adjusted to our marital situation. Although I suspected he still found relief from time to time with women in the quarters or a bawdy house here or there, I had no proof except for once, when in 1836 he acknowledged fathering a daughter named Charlotte with a woman named Margaret, a free woman of color. When I found out about it, Henry didn't deny it. I was upset, of course, but I didn't know the woman or anything about her. Henry was surprised by my reaction and seemed to think it was perfectly normal.

"A good number of respectable planters around here can claim mulatto bastards," he said. "Everyone knows that."

It was true, though it was never talked about in polite society. But he promised me it would not happen again. At my insistence, he settled a small sum on the child, made sure she was properly baptized, and declared the matter at an end. "We'll discuss it no more," he said with finality.

The incident did not appear to mar his reputation in the town, for Henry continued to enjoy increasing distinction as he became more involved in business enterprises in Brunswick. He had become more sociable and eager to attend gala events both in town and on St. Simons, where life was often festive, given all the plantations. Overall he seemed quite pleased with himself. And I benefited as well. Our life had not been so pleasant since those very first years together.

He had become friends with a number of the other area planters. James Hamilton Couper, for example, served with him on the Glynn Academy Board of Trustees. Henry was popular enough to get himself selected as a commissioner for the town of Brunswick, and he worked alongside many distinguished members of the community to promote the new Brunswick Canal and Railroad Company. He even got involved on the fringes of the political world when he was selected to attend a state convention in Milledgeville with other notables like Thomas Butler King and Urbanus Dart. The rise in cotton prices had motivated them all, and they were determined to promote the city's interests, which led to a sort of "boom" in the mid-1830s.

I was pleased with the way my husband was distracting himself with so many worthy undertakings. It eased my burden of keeping him happy, and he didn't just sit around being surly, as I had feared he might when I had denied him his "conjugal rights," as he often reminded me. For me, it was a new lease on life. Several years passed, and I did not have to go through another pregnancy and birth. My health was improving, and I was able to focus better on the children and my other duties.

If there were any doubts about the esteem in which Henry was now held, it became even clearer in 1838, when the new Bank of Brunswick was established and he was chosen to be its first president.

"Listen to this," he said, reading to me and the children from a copy of the *Brunswick Advocate* he had brought home. He was beaming as he read. "Col. Dubignon," he began, proud of his militia rank, "is extensively known and highly esteemed, and is every way qualified to discharge the duties of the office." I swear he walked around like a peacock for a week.

I was pleased as well. His new rise to prominence caused us both to be invited more frequently to special dinners and parties in town. As the wife of the bank president, I too gained a certain status in the community. It was the life I had hoped for in America, though I now felt a bit too old to enjoy it as fully as I would have if I were younger and less worn down. Still, I basked in it almost as much as he did.

Perhaps the greatest pleasure for us both was his newfound interest in the local boat races. Like his father, Henry had always been interested in boats, not so much the sailing ships that had been the older man's passion, but smaller, sleeker ones that could navigate both the shallow waters of the marshes and the deeper sounds between the islands. His closest friend in the boating community was a man named Charles Rinaldo Floyd. Henry often visited at one of the two Floyd plantations, Fairfield, which belonged to Charles, and Belleville, that of his father, General John Floyd. Charles Rinaldo was somewhat younger than we were. I liked him very much and I too enjoyed his company. He was feisty and handsome, with a head of thick dark hair that curled around his ears and an insouciant moustache that curved upward. He'd had many talents and adventures and was not at all embarrassed that he'd been expelled from West Point for insubordination.

"It was a point of honor," he proudly proclaimed. I knew these men understood what that meant. Gentlemen, they thought, were willing to risk everything, even their lives, for what they considered to be "honor" but which I think was only hubris. They did not hesitate to fight those infernal duels to preserve their pride. As far as I know, Henry fought only one, though there may have been others I never knew about.

The only reason I knew about this one was because my oldest son was involved. He had returned from New England by then and was indeed reading law with Mr. Cuyler, working as a court clerk, and living at a boarding house in Brunswick. A doctor from Darien, H. D. Holland, made some passing remark that offended my Charles, and in a huff he impetuously challenged the old doctor to a duel.

"That young fool," Henry steamed when he heard about the challenge. "What does he know about dueling? It's idiotic!"

I assumed his anger was the result of our mutual worry—our oldest and most promising son, risking his life for some trivial comment. I was beside myself.

"Henry, we can't let this happen. Suppose he is killed."

"It's a matter of principle, Amelia. He can't back down now. He's asked me to deliver his formal challenge to Dr. Holland."

"Henry, you can't."

"I must."

And he did. I was frantic until he came home again and informed me that Dr. Holland had declined the duel. "That's wonderful!" I said.

"I'm not so sure. He called Charles a 'young whippersnapper.' Said he had his whole life ahead of him and didn't need to risk it in a pointless duel."

"What did you say?"

"I informed him that my son was a man of honor and that he, Dr. Holland, was a coward."

"Oh, Henry! How could you? It was kind of Dr. Holland to refuse."

"It was cowardly," he replied.

He could keep his opinions, but I was relieved. It meant that my son would not lose his life over some silly comment that everyone would forget about in a week. But Dr. Holland didn't forget Henry's insult, for three months later in September, Dr. Holland, who had apparently fumed all that time, delivered a challenge not to Charles but to Henry.

"Oh, good Lord, you foolish men," I said when Henry told me of the challenge.

Charles was also upset. "It was my quarrel that started all this," he said. "Let me fight in your place, Papa." Henry refused, of course.

Why are men always so eager to fight? I begged Henry to decline, just as Dr. Holland had declined.

"So he can call *me* a coward? Don't be silly, woman. At least I get to choose the weapons, and I'm going to select short swords." But when he heard that Dr. Holland knew nothing about swordsmanship, he relented. "I guess it wouldn't be a fair fight. As a fair-minded man, I'm willing to use a rifle instead."

I knew that Henry considered the sword the nobler of the two weapons, and I didn't think the sword was quite as dangerous as the rifle. Needless to say, my opinion did not matter, and Dr. Holland seemed quite satisfied to use a gun.

The duel was to take place on Thursday morning, October 2, on the north end of Amelia Island, just over the border in Florida, for dueling had been outlawed in Georgia since 1809. Henry selected our son Charles to be his second, though his friend Charles Rinaldo lent him his special rifle and went along to make sure it was conducted appropriately. He too was quick to duel and had once invited Henry to serve as his go-between at Fairfield Plantation during another quarrel, but I later overheard Charles Rinaldo tease him that he had drunk so much brandy he was unable to carry out his duties.

On the day of Henry's duel, I sat at home, surrounded by my anxious daughters, wringing my hands, fearful for what could happen. I think I held my breath most of the day, until my husband and son finally returned later that evening, safe and sound.

"Papa was splendid!" Charles announced. "I think he handled the rifle far better than Dr. Holland, and of course he had the advantage of using Mr. Floyd's famous dueling rifle."

"So what happened? Was anyone hurt?" I worried about a possible killing, even though the intent of a duel was not necessarily to kill but to show that one was willing to risk his life for honor. Still, sometimes things went amiss. I still remembered the awful duel Mr. Burr had fought and all the problems he'd had after Alexander Hamilton died of his gunshot wound.

"I'm afraid Dr. Holland got the worst of it. I shot him twice," Henry said in a jaunty tone. "I didn't aim to kill, but he won't be walking around for a while, because I hit him in both thighs." He nodded with a satisfied smile.

"Oh, Henry," I said. "The poor man."

"Stop your fretting. It's all over now. I don't think he'll be challenging anyone in *this* family again any time soon." He laughed and Charles laughed with him. My husband seemed quite pleased with himself.

All of that happened more than ten years ago, when things were still relatively happy between Henry and me. His new friend, Charles Rinaldo, seemed to be involved in almost everything Henry did during that time. In some ways, I suppose he was a bad influence on Henry, as in the case of the duel, but in other ways, he was a good influence, more frequently directing him toward less deadly endeavors—like boating. Whatever his influence, Charles Rinaldo's family, the Floyds, were quite distinguished on the Georgia coast, and he thrived on his family's reputation and his fine breeding. He had done a grand European tour and even had an artistic nature. In fact,

I'm looking now at a delightful sketch hanging on the wall, a drawing of Félicité he did during one of his many visits to Jekyl. It's a good likeness.

He was in his mid-thirties, and after the death of his first wife, he had taken a second bride, a sixteen-year-old named Julia Ross Boog. She soon became friends with my daughters, especially Eliza and Sarah. I suppose I was the mother figure of the group.

Thanks to Charles Rinaldo, who was a master boat builder, Henry decided to take up boat racing in earnest. They competed in the sleek dug-out vessels so common on the Georgia coast, and our two families often attended races and regattas together. Those were fun days. Sudie and her young kitchen helper Julia would pack us the most delicious picnics for the event. We took all the children, as well as a wagonload of the male slaves, who were the best rowers in the quarters. Sometimes there were simple races along the Satilla River, not far from the Floyd plantations. At other times, the men organized more elaborate regattas.

Henry's favorite boat was called the *Goddess of Liberty*, which Charles Rinaldo had built for him. Another one he named the *Sarah and Catherine* for two of our daughters. I was not happy about that choice, and I reminded him that he had two other daughters—Eliza, who was the oldest now that Louisa was gone, and Eugenia, the youngest.

"Don't you think it imprudent to name a boat for only two of your daughters?" I asked. I was afraid the others might be jealous, and above all, I didn't want any more discord in our family.

Henry looked at me as though I'd lost my mind. "I'll name my boats as I see fit. And don't you think a boat named *Eliza, Sarah, Catherine, and Eugenia* might be a bit cumbersome? I doubt it would even fit on the hull."

"But you might call it *DuBignon Daughters*," I offered.

"That's not much of a name. Besides, I'll name my boats as I see fit," he repeated, and turned away.

I said no more and just hoped that the girls wouldn't feel hurt by their father's omission. But if they were, they didn't say anything, and they all still came to the races. I assumed it was a minor matter, and we all let it pass.

Sitting on the riverside watching the rowers, I felt like a young girl again. In some ways, those all-too-brief years in the 1830s were even better than our early days when Henry and I were both young, carefree, and eager to be together. They were certainly among our best times as a family. Henry seemed happy, and I, no longer having to worry about being pregnant all the time, was able to relax. Our children were old enough to enjoy such outings with the other young people. Many folks, islanders and townspeople, white and black alike, came to those races, whether they had boats in the competition or not. My friend Mimi and her daughter Félicité often joined us, as did Bernard and Treyette with their family. It was a grand social occasion.

We were all proud of Henry's boat *The Goddess of Liberty*, which often bested whatever vessel Charles Rinaldo was racing. He never took offense at the *Goddess*'s victories, for, after all, he had built her. I had to admit that she was fine-looking boat, dug from a single cypress log, like the pirogues of old. She was perfectly symmetrical and sleek, painted white with a blue band of twenty-four stars, one for each state, around her hull, and she was considered the "Belle" of local waters.

Sometimes Henry raced against Mr. Floyd's younger brother Richard, whose boat *The Devil's Darning Needle* would occasionally win. There were so many avid boaters in the area that they decided to organize into a group called the Aquatic Club of Georgia, with both Henry and Charles Rinaldo serving as officers. They considered their vessels to be the best in the land and believed that their Georgia boats could defeat virtually any other rowing vessel. They were so sure of themselves that they decided to challenge the Whitehallers, a well-known rowing group from New York, to a race.

"Why bother with boaters so far away?" I asked Henry one night.

"They think they're the nation's best. In fact they're so cocky that they once challenged the British Hussars, and they won. I have to admit they're good, but I think our Georgia boats can best them. They race with traditional Whitehall wherries, but we think our boats are faster, and we want to prove it."

A few weeks later, Henry came home and announced that the Whitehallers had declined the challenge. "They claim that they're gentlemen and won't row against what they called 'crews of black servants.' Charles Rinaldo and I and plenty of others are certainly willing to man the oars." Even with that assurance, the Whitehallers refused to compete. Henry was growing frustrated.

"They're just afraid we can whip 'em," he said with a laugh. "Cowardly Yankees."

Finally, the challenge was taken up instead by the Lower Creek Boat Club from Savannah, who were willing to race in their place using a northern-made wherry of the type the Whitehallers used.

How well I recall that day! It was one of the best in my life. I think half the population from Savannah to Brunswick must have turned out, for there were so many people. Even slaves and a few free people of color settled upriver from us for their own picnics. The day was sunny, the air clear and bright, and everyone was in a jubilant mood. Ladies sat on blankets spread on the grass and twirled their parasols to keep the sun off. All the planters' families were chattering, sharing pies and cakes with one another, comparing recipes and the latest gossip. There was plenty of time to socialize, for it was a four-mile race, and we were all gathered at the finish line to see how it turned out.

After a long time, someone yelled, "Here they come!"

We all stood up and craned our necks. I could barely see them at first. They were just small specks on the river. As the boats drew closer, the shouts grew louder. From a distance the two boats appeared neck and neck, but as they rowed toward the finish line, the crew of the Aquatic Club's *Lizard* suddenly spurted forward in a last-minute effort to take the lead. The men in the challenger, the Savannah *Star*, also seemed to be rowing harder, but little by little the *Lizard* pulled more and more ahead, as we all yelled, "Come on. You can do it!" or some such. It was clear that the *Lizard* would win, and in fact, they glided across the finish line with a hundred feet to spare.

We all cheered as though it had been a tight race, but it was all good-natured, and when it was over, the Aquatic Club donated the *Lizard* to the Savannah club. After that, club members of both teams and their wives, including Henry and myself, all proceeded to the newly built Oglethorpe House, where there was a grand dinner, along with much drinking, back-slapping, rivalry, and comradery among those present.

It became an annual event for a while, and the following year, the Savannah club actually defeated the Brunswick team, rowing the *Lizard* itself. As a gesture of good will, the Lower Creek Club donated to Charles Rinaldo another vessel, which they had had especially built for him and which they had named the *Floyd*. Those were good times.

But times were changing.

As the decade neared its end, cotton prices were falling again, and though planters held out hopes, it looked like the good days of cotton production might be over, at least for the time being. Fortunately, thanks to Henry's recent efforts, cotton was no longer our only source of income, though it was still an important factor. But the boom time for Brunswick also seemed to be ending. I wasn't terribly worried, for we had weathered such situations before, and now, I thought, we were in a much better situation. But the drop in income affected Henry's moods to a greater degree than I realized at the time. Or maybe that wasn't the reason at all. But something in him was changing. It was not until the very end of the decade that things really began to go awry.

The only thing that kept my spirits up was an announcement by my son Joseph, who came to me one warm September afternoon in 1838 to say, "Mama, I'm getting married."

"Who's the lucky girl?" I teased, as if I didn't know. It certainly came as no surprise, for he had been in love with Félicité Riffault ever since she was twelve years old. It was the reason he'd chosen not to go north to continue his education, for he could not bear to be so far from her. Although he waited until he was twenty-four to propose, I think it was already a foregone conclusion that they would one day wed. Mimi did not object, and both she and I thought it a good idea for them to wait no longer. Anything could happen.

They married the following January 22 and decided to make their home on the island. Joseph bubbled over with joy and urged every young man he knew to get married as soon as they could.

"I never knew what it was to be happy until I married," he told me. I don't think I've ever seen a couple more in love. I was, of course, delighted, as was Mimi, who came to the island to live with them. Joseph and Cité, as he called his wife, did everything together—fished, hunted, rode on the beach, went on picnics. In some ways, they reminded me of Henry and myself when we first married.

Even before their wedding, Joseph had started building a house on the island for his prospective family, with sufficient room for any children they might have—and for Félicité's mother, Mimi. Their presence was a great comfort to me in those years, and it was wonderful to have Mimi nearby. The young couple's babies started to arrive within the first year, and they occupied a lot of my time and thoughts, taking my mind off myself and my problems. I had not held a newborn of my own blood for more than a decade now. These grandchildren were a blessing during the painful years that followed, the worst time in my marriage to Henry. I thanked God for my son's new family and their willing hospitality and compassion when I needed it most. Without Joseph and Félicité, without my grandchildren and the compassion of Mimi, I'm not sure I could have survived all that was to come.

CHAPTER 8

Those dreadful days as the decade drew to a close are painful to remember. Perhaps they seemed even worse in contrast to the better days we'd so recently enjoyed. To avoid where I know my memories are inevitably going, I stand up to stretch. I am weary, tired to the bone, and my body aches with stiffness from sitting so long beside Joseph's bed. I know it will not be much longer, and I don't want to leave my post. I don't want him to pass without someone he loves beside him.

Once again, as she has done more than once each day, Mimi comes to the door and offers to take my place for a while.

"You need to get some rest," she urges. I know she's right. To lie down and put a cold compress on my aching head sounds like a true luxury, but it's one I can't afford. Not yet.

"No. Thank you, Mimi. I truly appreciate your offer, but I'm his mother. I need to be with him. I confess to dozing off in my chair occasionally, but I want to stay right here." Each time she brings me a plate of food, like this evening's butterbeans, corn, and fried chicken, she tries again.

"I understand, Amelia, but you can't keep this up. You haven't left his bedside for days."

That's not entirely true, for nature calls from time to time, a summons I must obey, but other than those occasional trips to the outhouse, she's right.

"Just as you didn't leave Félicité's side when she needed you," I reply. "How is she doing?"

"Grieving and holding her children close. I know what it's like. I can only hope she can be strong for them when it's all over. She's going to have a rough time, with six children to raise."

"But she has you—and me. She's as dear to me as a daughter, and I know how much Joseph loves her. We'll both be here for her."

"It's amazing, isn't it," Mimi says quietly, "how close we've grown over the years. So many things have brought us together. I'm closer to you now than I am to my sister Treyette. She's had a rough time too since her husband's death."

The recent deaths of my brother Bernard four years ago and my half-brother Pascal just two years earlier had been hard for me as well. I still miss them. They had both cared for me when I needed it most. The memory of Bernard's fatherly protection after *Maman*'s death is especially sweet, and there is an ache in my chest whenever I recall all the good times our two families had together—Henry and I, Bernard and Treyette, as we visited back and forth on our two plantations. Our children played with each other, and together we celebrated happy events like weddings and mourned sad ones like funerals.

The only period of tension between our two families came about when my son John Couper apparently overstepped himself in the company of their daughter Fannie. I knew he fancied her, but I had no idea that he would be so bold about it. Whatever he did, Fannie clearly thought it was inappropriate.

They had always spent a fair amount of time together, which seemed only natural. They were cousins and had known each other since they were children. I wouldn't even have been surprised if he had wanted to marry her. Cousins marry fairly frequently in Georgia, and he was, after all, the nephew of a man who had married his niece. Still, I would have expected John to go about it in a proper way, but something he did offended Fannie, and rumors about the incident reverberated throughout the family. No one ever told me directly what his indiscretion had been, implying only that it was something unspeakable. John had never been particularly comfortable around girls, so I can only assume that whatever he did, he did from ignorance or a lack of understanding about what is permissible in polite society. I wish I knew so I could help. Perhaps he was just being his father's son.

When I tried to talk with Treyette about the matter, she assured me only that Fannie held no ill will, for she had always felt for John the friendship "of a kind sister." Despite my efforts to find out the truth, Treyette didn't want to discuss it further. In confirmation, Fannie wrote to my daughter Eliza that she just wanted to forget the whole thing, to let it "forever rest in oblivion." So many secrets, so many untold truths we'll never know. But the tension between our two households was palpable for a long time.

Nevertheless, if that were the worst thing that ever happened to upset family harmony, my life would have been much happier. Just thinking about what occurred in the 1840s has caused my headache to intensify, but I can't seem to steer my thoughts in another direction. It's as though I must think it through and consider whether at least some of the fault might lie with me. The children all blame their father for what happened, and I let them, whether it's fair or not. But they don't know the whole truth about that either, and they never will. I wonder if it would make any difference.

At first I thought the new dourness Henry displayed at home was related only to the economic downturn. But apparently, unbeknownst to me the real problems had started in the summer of 1838 when Henry came home and told me, "I'm taking the children out of Glynn Academy this fall and hiring a private tutor to teach them. It will be far more convenient, and they will no longer have to get up so early to get ready for school. No more rowing into Brunswick at dawn."

I didn't object much, for I thought this would make the children happy, even though they might miss their friends. They always complained about rising in the winter dawn and the chill of those early-morning boat rides.

"What made you come to such a decision?" I asked.

"I have encountered a well-educated English woman, a widow who needs employment and who is willing to move to the island and tutor the children for a very reasonable fee."

"Where will she live? Not with us, I hope."

"Certainly not. The Bernardey house has been empty for years. I thought she could live there and bring some life back into the place."

"You said she was a widow. Does she have children?"

"Two daughters. They're younger than all our children, I think, but old enough so that they're not babies anymore."

I thought about the arrangement, and it seemed to make good sense if her services didn't cost too much. I knew Henry well enough to know that he would not have hired her without some assurance that her work would be quite reasonable. I just hoped that she was sufficiently well educated to teach my two youngest, Eugenia and Henry Charles Jr., the only ones still in school, whatever they needed to know. It wouldn't be long before they reached an age when they would no longer require such tutoring, so the widow's time on the island would be limited, and it would no doubt help her get back on her feet. I looked forward to meeting her.

She and her daughters arrived unexpectedly on Jekyl one week later. When I reached the front door, she introduced herself. "I'm Sarah Aust, the new tutor. And these are my two daughters."

"And what are your names?" I asked the children.

"I'm Mary," the oldest girl said with a small curtsey. She was a pretty little thing, with blond hair that would likely darken with age.

"And I'm Fredonia," announced the younger one, the very image of her raven-haired mother. "I'm four years old," she said proudly.

Mrs. Aust seemed nice enough, very polite, appearing to be about thirty or perhaps a bit younger. Her dark hair was caught up in a well-groomed chignon, which made me feel rather frumpy. I had pinned my own hair in an untidy bun rather quickly that morning, noticing in the mirror the conspicuous threads of gray that dulled its once-rich color. *I must make more of an effort on my appearance*, I thought, but she seemed not to notice. Her words and her self-deprecating manner suggested that she was focused on her own feelings of inadequacy and embarrassment at her situation.

"I could not get a position at Glynn Academy or anywhere else, for there was no opening for my services," she told me, her tone apologetic, "so I really appreciate Mr. DuBignon's kind offer. There aren't many opportunities in Brunswick for women, you know. I was a bit desperate."

I nodded. "I'm afraid the salary isn't much," I began.

"But it will provide a roof over my children's heads and a steady income. Your husband says we can plant a garden and buy eggs and game at good prices from your workers. If that's the case, it should be sufficient, and I'm very grateful for it. I wasn't sure what we were going to do. My husband left us with almost nothing when he died so recently."

Henry was out inspecting the southernmost fields, so I was the one who accompanied her to the old Bernardey house to see what needed to be done and how I could help.

"As you can see, you won't be living in luxury," I said, "but I'm sure you'll get by. Let me know if there's anything I can do. One of the servants can help you with the cleaning, and I'm sure you'll want to make some changes."

She looked about the house, silently appraising its cracked plaster walls and meager furnishings. "Thank you. It will be fine with a little sprucing up. Mr.. DuBignon also said he would be happy to help. He is such a good man," she said.

I made no response other than a smile and turned to her two daughters. "I hope you will both like it here," I said. They nodded politely and chorused *thank you* in unison.

"Well, what did you think of her?" Henry asked as soon as I was home again and he learned of her arrival.

"She seems nice enough, well-bred and courteous. Let's just hope she can convey the necessary knowledge and values to our children. Only time will tell," I said.

He nodded but did not reply.

As months went by, I saw little of Widow Aust and her two daughters. Although she had offered to come to our house to give lessons, Henry thought it best for the children to go there.

"It will disrupt our day less and give us more privacy," he said. Thus, Henry Charles and Eugenia walked the two miles down the sandy road each morning to her house, where she held classes in her parlor. On rainy days, Henry or Samson would drive them in the buggy. It seemed a satisfactory arrangement all around, and as the days passed, it had little effect on our daily lives. Just as before, the children would report on their studies each afternoon when they returned home, and as we had hoped, they arrived earlier than they had when they were enrolled in Glynn Academy. They also appeared to be making suitable progress.

I assumed all was well until one Saturday afternoon in mid-October of 1839 when Joseph and Félicité dropped by with their month-old daughter, Mary Amelia, to bring some squash from their kitchen garden. I wrapped the child at once in my arms and cuddled her, placing a kiss on her sweet-smelling cheek. It had been a long time since I'd had a baby of my own, and glad as I was not to have a constantly swollen belly, I was delighted to have a little one to hold. In fact, I was far happier to see my granddaughter than I was to see the squash, which they had begun to deliver far too often.

"We've had so much of it," Félicité explained with a laugh and a shrug, "that Joseph is threatening to run away if I feed him squash one more time this week. I can't get rid of them fast enough. Do take some of these." Joseph grinned and set the basket down without waiting for my reply.

"They shouldn't last much longer," I offered. "I suspect that Widow Aust could use some of these as well. You might drop a basketful off at her house."

Joseph and Félicité glanced at each other. Félicité pressed her lips together and looked down at her hands.

"Well," Joseph began in a hesitant voice, "we had planned to take some by her place this afternoon, but as we drew near her house, we saw that she had company, so we decided it might be best not to stop."

"Company? Someone from the island?"

"I couldn't say for sure, but it looked a bit like...Cracker tied up at the hitching post."

"Cracker? Oh, it couldn't have been. Henry rode him to the south end this afternoon to see if he and Samson could round up a new horse or two." This was not unusual. They would occasionally ride out together to see if they could catch some of the marsh ponies that roamed the island. Félicité wrinkled her brow and reached for Mary Amelia, who was beginning to whimper.

Joseph frowned thoughtfully. "That so? Well"—he hesitated—"I hope he has some luck. Those wild ponies can be difficult to catch, sometimes a little dangerous and hard to break, even if you can rope one. Tell him to let me know if he succeeds. We're going to be needing a new horse one of these days just to keep up with Mary Amelia."

We all laughed, though their amusement seemed a bit forced. After they left, Joseph's comment nagged at me. Could it have been Henry's horse at Widow Aust's place? Probably not, but I did wonder.

When Henry came home and peeked in the basket that Joseph had left on the dining room table, he laughed. "More squash?"

"You're looking chipper. Did you have any luck? With the horses, I mean."

"Not this afternoon. We spotted a small herd not far from the beach, but when we got closer, they ran off, and we couldn't catch them. We'll keep tryin'."

"I heard you might have stopped at Widow Aust's place this afternoon."

Henry looked at me sharply, then said, "Well, I just stopped by for a few minutes to see how she and her girls are gettin' along and whether they needed anything."

"And did they?"

"They seem to be doin' just fine," Henry said with indifference, then changed the subject. "What time's supper? I hope we're not having squash again."

"I'll ask Sudie," I said.

It was apparently not the only time that Cracker was seen tied up at the widow's place, though I knew nothing of it then. Instead, I decided to take Henry at his word. After all, he had promised to help her whenever she needed it. It wasn't until the following month that I really began to worry.

I was consulting with Sudie about a Sunday dinner for November 18, the day before Henry Charles's thirteenth birthday. All the children would be with us—even our oldest, Charles, who led an active life in Brunswick and rarely came to the island these days. It was always a special event when every single one of our children was home for a big Sunday dinner, and they were eager to be together to celebrate their youngest brother's birthday.

"I think we'll start the meal with roasted oysters," I said. "Henry Charles adores them. And then, perhaps a glazed ham would be good. Maybe a spinach soufflé, green beans, and some kind of potato dish, and a dessert, of course. What would you like to make?" Sudie had become quite a good cook over the years, and she loved to bake cakes and pies. I thought I'd let her decide.

"Well, I reckon I could make pecan and chess pies and that chocolate cake the birthday boy likes so much."

"They all sound delicious."

"And I 'spek you gon' want rolls with dinner. How many people you gon' have?"

"Just the family, I suppose. And Félicité's mother, of course. Perhaps we also could invite Widow Aust and her two girls if that's not too many." It *was* a special occasion for one of her pupils.

"I heared she ain't gettin' out much nowadays," Sudie said.

"Why's that?"

"Well"—she hesitated—"dey say she startin' to show."

"Whatever do you mean?"

"You ain't heard? Dey say she be in de fam'ly way."

"What? But she's a widow. You must be mistaken."

"Yes'm," Sudie said, avoiding my eyes. "Maybe I is. 'Scuse me, ma'am. I best get back to the kitchen. I got biscuits in de oven." She headed for the dog trot that led to the kitchen.

Surely she's wrong, I told myself as I watched her go. *How on earth could that be true?* I wondered how long Widow Aust's husband had been dead and whether she could have been already expecting when she came to the island. *No, that would be too long*, I thought, reminding myself that she'd been here for more than a year. She would already have delivered by now. *Perhaps it's not even true, just one more rumor for the grapevine.* But I really wanted to know, and there was only one way to find out for sure. I had Samson hook up the buggy and drive me to her house that very afternoon. It would be an occasion to invite her to dinner, if it seemed right.

She answered the door wearing a faded dress with a pleated bodice and a drawstring waist that allowed for expansion. It was not new. The dress had seen wear, and I suspected that she had worn it during her earlier pregnancies. It was hard to tell from the ample garment whether she was with child or not, but given the style and the way it fit certainly suggested it. *But maybe she's just gained weight and can't afford to buy new clothes*, I told myself. There was surely not enough income from her meager salary to provide many new dresses for her and the children, who were growing rapidly. I had given her some of the gowns my girls had outgrown. While she looked less tidy than the day I'd first met her, she was still attractive, and the house was certainly in better shape than it had been when she first moved in. Snapdragons and begonias bloomed around the front steps, and sprigs of a jessamine vine were beginning to crawl up one of the posts on the porch.

She was clearly surprised to find me standing at her doorway. "Mrs. DuBignon!" She caught her breath and added, "How nice to see you." I caught a glimpse inside the front room. The floors were scrubbed and the bubbly glass in the windows looked sparkling clean. Pretty though inexpensive curtains hung at the front windows.

"Good day, Mrs. Aust. I just stopped by to make sure you were all right. One of my servants seemed to think you might be reluctant to get out these days. I hope you're not sick." I tried to be friendly without seeming nosy. And I certainly didn't want to mention the gossip.

"I've just been tired of late, nothing serious, I assure you. It's...it's kind of you to call." Her face was flushed and her manner a bit brisk. "Won't you come in?"

"Oh, I can only stay for a few moments. How are Henry Charles and Eugenia doing in their schoolwork?"

"They're doing fine, though I must admit Eugenia is more studious than her brother. He seems to enjoy gazing out the window more than doing schoolwork." She gave me a nervous smile. "Nevertheless, he is progressing. They're...they're both doing fractions now and reading well. Eugenia has chosen to read *The Fair Maid of Perth* by Sir Walter Scott this spring, but Henry Charles, being a boy, prefers a book I have by Charles Dickens." She chattered on, her voice tense, and I thought she seemed rather nervous. "His penmanship leaves much to be desired, I'm sorry to say...but we're working on it."

"I trust you'll let me know if they cause you any problems or don't progress satisfactorily."

"Oh, of course," she said. "May...may I make you some tea?"

"No, no. I was just passing by. I do hope your fatigue will soon let up."

"Thank you. And I trust *you're* doing well." She was saying all the right things, but I couldn't help but sense her desire for me not to linger. Or perhaps that's just how I remember it, knowing now what discomfort she must have felt under the circumstances. I was beginning to feel uncomfortable myself and eager to get away.

"I'm just fine," I assured her, choosing not to mention the aches and pains of my fifty-five years. "I'm happy to hear that things are going so well." As I bade her goodbye and turned to go, I could feel her eyes on my back as I went down the front steps.

When I drove away in the carriage, with Samson at the reins, my mind was in a turmoil. I didn't know what to think. If she had been expecting at the time of her husband's death, she would have no reason now not to disclose it. But then, I had already figured that to be impossible. *Perhaps she isn't expecting at all. But what if she is, and someone here on the island is responsible? Surely none of my boys....* They were all too young for her—except perhaps Charles, but he had not been on the island. He hadn't even met her, as far as I knew. John Couper had learned his lesson and was far too humiliated by the incident with his cousin Fannie ever to approach another woman in such a way, and Joseph was happily married. That left only Henry Charles, who was just thirteen. *Ridiculous. Surely not one of the slave men. Then who?* Although the answer lay clearly before me, I refused to let my thoughts go there. And I wouldn't risk any accusation until after the child was born.

Needless to say, I did not invite Widow Aust and her daughters to that Sunday dinner. Nor would it ever again occur to me to do so.

CHAPTER 9

My head is pounding now and I feel sick to my stomach as I let myself remember. On January 24, 1840, Sarah Aust gave birth to a strapping baby boy, clearly not a mulatto but a pure white baby that she had the audacity to name Leonidas Henry Aust. Everyone who had seen the baby declared him to be the spitting image of my husband.

Rumors spread rapidly throughout the plantation. It was my daughter Eugenia who in all innocence brought me the news. She had heard about the birth from Julia, our kitchen girl, who had been her playmate when they were children. Now in their teens, they were still close and frequently confided in one another. There weren't many other people their age on the island, and the children all played together. It was not uncommon to find the two of them in the kitchen together, whispering their shared secrets and giggling. Sudie would have to shoo Eugenia out so Julia could get her work done.

"Mama." Eugenia was tugging at my sleeve. "Julia told me Mrs. Aust has had a baby. I guess we won't be having classes any time soon." They had not gone for lessons since well before Christmas. Henry Charles was delighted to have an excuse not to attend, but I think Eugenia rather missed them.

"I don't know, Eugenia. What do you know about the baby?" I asked, my heart racing at the news.

"Well, it was a boy, and she gave it a funny name...Leonidas Henry."

I caught my breath. "Leonidas *Henry*?" I repeated. "What does it look like? Does Julia know?"

"Just like any other baby, I guess." Her voice was jaunty, and I think she had no idea what she was saying. "Julia says it has blue eyes and a pointy chin, just like Papa's."

At those words, I slapped Eugenia's face. She looked at me in shock, and her eyes widened as her hand flew to her cheek. I had never hit her before, and I don't know what came over me. I just couldn't bear to hear those words. It was as though she had struck me first.

Instantly horrified at what I had done, I reached out to take her in my arms. "I'm so sorry, my darling. I didn't mean to. Please forgive me." But she drew back, her eyes filled with tears and revulsion, and ran from the room.

I covered my face with my hands and let myself weep at my cruel reaction, at the humiliation and shame of my husband's betrayal, and at the world in general. Life wasn't supposed to be like this. How could this be happening? All my pent-up anxiety, fear, grief, and rage poured out together. I must have sobbed for an hour, until I was entirely spent and felt compelled to take to my bed, where I covered my head with a blanket and remained for the rest of the day.

At sundown I heard the bedroom door open. "Amelia." It was Henry's voice. "What are you doing lying down? Are you ill?" he asked.

I lay silent and unmoving, my eyes closed, pondering whether it would be better just to lie here and die or get up and kill my husband instead. *Does he have no idea why I'm upset?* Henry's footsteps drew nearer, and I felt the mattress sink a bit as he sat on the edge of the brass bed we had shared for more than thirty years.

"What's wrong, Amelia?" he asked. I didn't answer. Then I felt him touch my shoulder. "Can I get you anything?" I lay still, ignoring his presence. He sat there for a long time, saying nothing. Finally, the mattress lifted again, and I heard the door close softly.

Later, Sudie brought up a tray of food and left it on the table beside my bed, but I never touched it.

When I awoke late the following morning, the tray was gone. In its place was another, with a plateful of toast, cold grits, a fried egg, two slices of bacon, and a glass of orange juice. I realized I was hungry. I sat up, drank the juice, and nibbled on a piece of dry toast. Then, about midday I got up, washed my swollen face, and put on some clothes, but I didn't leave the room.

Henry returned once again late in the afternoon. His face was stony when he entered the bedroom. "Are you feeling better?" he asked.

"Better than what?"

"What's the matter, Amelia? You seem put out."

"Put out? Put out? Is that a joke? How can you even ask such a question? You know perfectly well what the matter is." My voice was bitter. "I suppose congratulations are in order on your new son," I said, making no effort to suppress my sarcasm.

"You know about that?" he asked, obviously annoyed.

"Everyone on the island knows. For your information, it was our youngest daughter who told me."

"She said you hit her. How could you do that?"

It was like a punch in the stomach, his trying to put *me* in a position of blame, of needing to apologize. "Because I *wanted* to hit *you*," I said through my teeth.

"I don't know what you're so upset about. You cast me out of your bed more than ten years ago. And you didn't seem all that upset when Charlotte was born. Surely you didn't expect me to be a hermit for the rest of my life." I couldn't believe he was justifying himself.

"I didn't cast you out of my bed. I just asked for restraint. And your mulatto bastard was not the same thing. Of course I was upset, but you said it would never happen again, and at least that child won't be part of our children's lives. This is different. This is a white child who will grow up in the same world as my children."

"You cut me off from my marital rights."

"I only wanted to refrain from conjugal relations while I was still able to have children. Well, I'm not anymore. But the thought of having you touch me now, after you've been with that woman, makes me sick. And you, such an upstanding citizen in Brunswick! Hah! You know they won't have anything to do with you anymore. You're a cad. And what kind of whore is she? Carrying on with a married man right under his wife's nose."

"She needed loving. You didn't." His voice was quiet, determined.

My fury rose to a fevered pitch. I picked up a shoe and threw it at him as hard as I could. "Get out of my room."

His eyes blazed as he shouted. "Your room! This is *my* room too. And you're in *my* house. And while you're living under *my* roof, I'll hear no more about this." He stalked out and slammed the door.

As I'd predicted, news about the illegitimate birth spread quickly to the shores of the mainland and throughout the town of Brunswick. While a planter's mulatto child might go ignored and unmentioned in polite society, an extramarital affair that resulted in the birth of a white child was another matter entirely.

The atmosphere in our house was grim. All the children tiptoed around me and spoke in whispered tones to each other. I think they were bewildered as to what to do. They were all old enough to understand what had happened, but they just wanted it to be over. They wanted their old life back, their happy family. I'm sure they blamed their father, but they also wanted me to let go of my anger.

What was I to do? I had no income of my own and nowhere to go. I didn't want to leave my children, and I couldn't afford to support them. Then, one day almost two weeks later, Henry finally came to me and got down on his knees to beg forgiveness.

"It's over," he said. "I promise it won't happen again. Please forgive me, Amelia." He seemed sincere, but the animosity and tension that had prevailed for weeks in the household was still palpable. The older children had begged him to apologize and begged me to forgive him.

"Everybody makes mistakes, Mama," John Couper said. "I know Papa's was worse than mine, but you forgave me. And so did Fannie and Aunt Treyette." He evidently wasn't so sure about his Uncle Bernard and chose not to mention him. "Remember," he reminded me, "the Bible teaches us that to err is human, to forgive divine."

His sister Eliza frowned. "I don't think that's from the Bible, John Couper."

"Well, it's still a good saying," he argued.

"He's right, Mama. We can't go on living with all this anger. I know you're upset, and we all understand, but please forgive him, for the sake of your children." I knew she was right. Either I had to go away somewhere, banish their father from his own household, which I knew I could never do, or else come to terms with what had happened and get on with life—the family's life.

Within days of their persistent pleading, I relented and allowed Henry back to my bed, with conjugal relations, such as they were, no longer forbidden. They were perfunctory, rare, and unsatisfying for us both, I'm sure. Although I was well past the child-bearing age now, in truth, I no longer truly wanted my husband that way, nor, I felt, did he want me, but we went through all the motions of marriage. I'm still not sure why.

He certainly paid the price in terms of his Brunswick connections, for we no longer received invitations from the wealthy lawyers and businessmen of the town. And Charles Rinaldo, though he came over once at Henry's invitation to help repair a boat, confided to me on that occasion that his young wife had told him, in no uncertain terms, that this would be his last visit to Jekyl Island. She did not want him associating with "a man like Henry." There would be no more boat races for us. Henry was ostracized by every respectable household in the area, as was Sarah Aust, who didn't have many friends there to start with.

Whenever I had to go into Brunswick, which I rarely did, everyone was friendly and solicitous, but I felt their pity and unspoken dismay at the fact that I still lived with that awful man. I worried especially for the career of my oldest son, Charles, who had become a prominent lawyer in Brunswick and was planning to run for a seat in the state legislature to represent Glynn County the following year. He feared his father's scandalous behavior would affect his election. I was concerned for him more than for myself. I can only thank the good people of Brunswick who still considered my son an honorable man and elected him despite his father's misbehavior. After his election, Charles decided to move to the capital at Milledgeville, where he would not have to be reminded daily of his father's sullied reputation. At that point, with Charles no longer there to escort me to dinner at the Oglethorpe House, I had even less incentive to go into Brunswick.

Everything seemed to settle down for a while after that. There still was not the closeness between Henry and me that there had once been, but there was no longer palpable animosity. We both went about our normal lives with determined indifference, behaving toward each other, as best we could, as though nothing had happened, especially whenever the children were present. We gave each other perfunctory kisses at bedtime. And whenever he approached me with conjugal intent, I made no protest and allowed him his "privilege" until he was satisfied. I can't say how he felt about it all, but I performed *my* duty without protest.

A year went by, and there were no new rumors flying. No one reported seeing Henry's horse at the widow's house anymore, and the only new birth on Jekyl that year, except for those in the quarters, was that of Joseph and Félicité's second daughter, Josephine, on February 3, 1841. Now I had two sweet granddaughters to coddle and take my mind off that year-old bastard boy elsewhere on the island. Everyone seemed joyful at the birth of little Josephine, at least as joyful as we ever got in those days. While our family life may have lacked the luster of success and excitement we'd enjoyed in the 1830s, at least now it was calm, and we were still together.

Henry didn't go into Brunswick as much, for many of his business associates had severed ties or grown distant. Instead, he devoted himself mostly to the plantation and his family—the legitimate one. Despite our earlier concerns, cotton was still king, as they liked to say in Georgia, and while the prices fluctuated, it had once again become our most reliable economic resource. Although Henry kept his stock in the railroad company and other enterprises that had been promoted in the boom times, none of them paid very much, or so he said. Of course, I never saw the accounts.

I sometimes wonder what my life would have been like if I had never come to America but had remained in France. It would surely have been different, for France has suffered many upheavals since the big revolution. They beheaded the king but accepted an emperor. Then, when the Napoleonic wars were over and Bonaparte abdicated in 1815, the Bourbon monarchy was restored. After that came the July Revolution of 1830, when one king replaced another. It all seemed chaotic and rather senseless to me. Although there was a lot of violence in these later troubles, none of them seemed, at least from a distance, as bloody as the revolution of 1789. Nevertheless, they'd torn the country apart. At least political life here in America is less turbulent, and we Americans are able to settle our internal disagreements peaceably. I doubt I would even know my birth country now. Still, one can't help but wonder.

After all the unpleasantness, the whole family assumed that there would be no more contact between Henry and Sarah Aust. I'd wanted her banished from the island. The children too had thought it best, and I know that Joseph tried to persuade his father to send her away, but Henry overruled us all.

"I have shamed her," he said, "and I must bear the responsibility. Where could she go now? How could she earn a living? I can't afford to support her anywhere else. Think of her two little girls. And the baby."

"I'd rather not," I said dryly. The children made no answer.

"I must at least be a gentleman about my sins and help to support a child of my blood, even one born out of wedlock, as your mother once pointed out to me. Here at least they have a roof over their heads," he argued.

I didn't want another contretemps with Henry and finally let it go, but even though I didn't have to see the widow Aust, I resented her presence on the island every day of my life.

Then, three years later in May 1843, Sarah Aust gave birth to another son, a carbon copy, I was told, of the first one. It was the final blow. As soon as they heard about it, Joseph and Félicité came to the house to see how I was doing. Needless to say, I was distraught and angry.

"I just can't swallow my pride this time and live with him anymore," I said. I'm sure I was crying.

"Then you must come and live with us, Mama," Joseph said.

Félicité took my hand and looked me in the eyes with all sincerity. "We want you there. The children want you, and my mother will love to have your company. We all will." And so I accepted. Ordinarily three women in a household would not be a good idea, but Mimi and I were such good friends, and we both loved Joseph and Félicité. They were my refuge then, as they are now. A godsend in a barren world.

I packed my bags that very afternoon, and they drove me to their house in their carriage. Félicité kept her arm around me the entire way. They wanted me to feel wanted. I shall never forget their kindness. This time the children's anger was directed entirely at Henry. They were all old enough now to understand completely, and they knew the blame was his alone. They had at least tried to forgive him the first time, as I had, for I feared it was partly my fault. I had never told them of the years I had denied him what he called his "conjugal rights," for now it was no longer relevant. He had his privilege back, but still he betrayed me. This new birth was too much.

When it happened, I was thankful that Charles was safely away in Milledgeville, now engaged to the daughter of a wealthy and distinguished gentleman, the Honorable Seaton Grantland, who had just retired from the U.S. Congress. I prayed hard that this new scandal would not disrupt that engagement, and God answered my prayers. They were married on January 4, 1844, and Charles, no longer living in Brunswick and perhaps unwilling to push his luck any further given his father's growing reputation, decided to give up his political and legal career to manage his father-in-law's large plantation near Milledgeville. It's called Woodville. I was grateful that Charles's future now seemed assured.

So did Joseph's at the time. Despite whatever gossip there was, he was elected, again with the good will and sympathy of the people of Brunswick, to replace his brother in the state legislature as representative of Glynn County. As a consequence of his new position and, I suspect, his desire to distance himself from the embarrassing behavior of his father, he decided to move his growing family away from the island and settle in Brunswick. I came with them. Their home is my home now. I still long sometimes for the beauty and tranquil joys of the island, remembering the happy days I had there and the beautiful views of the marshes. But those memories were almost erased by the ugliness of all that happened later. My other children, four girls and my two unmarried sons, all grown now, still remain on Jekyl. I'm not sure where their father is living—with them or with that woman.

Then toward the end of May 1848, one more Aust baby, a girl named Rosalia, was born. Henry was apparently insatiable. He was out of my life by then, and I pretended only indifference to his carryings-on. I focused my attentions, instead, on a new grandchild on the way. On February 2 of the next year, Joseph's sweet wife gave birth to their only child not born on Jekyl, my youngest grandson, John Eugene. He's more than a year old now, toddling everywhere and quite a handful. As far as I know, Henry has never seen him. I can only assume that my husband has chosen to live with his illegitimate family now. I know my children no longer mention him whenever I see them.

As I let myself remember all these humiliations, I'm suddenly aware that warm tears are running down my cheeks. I swore once I'd never cry again for Henry DuBignon. Even now, I'm not sure whether I'm weeping for the past or for the present—for myself, for Joseph, or for us all. Everything is so confused, garbled, mixed up in my mind. It's hard to think clearly. My head is hurting.…I can't let myself remember anymore. Not just now.

The only thing I can do is acknowledge the misery of this world, knowing that, without a miracle, I am on the verge of losing my Joseph, the best and most thoughtful son any woman ever had. *Please God, give us that miracle. Make him well again.* I lean over to give him a kiss on his burning forehead and wrap our two hands together with my rosary. *Give us more time, Lord.* My mind goes naturally to the prayer I had prayed so many times as a child at mass. Now, appealing as one mother to another, I begin it in all earnest.

Ave Maria, gratia plena,
Dominus tecum,
Benedicta tu in mulieribus.

Hail Mary, full of Grace… Perhaps if I were a good Catholic, I should have been praying to the Virgin all along, not to God, who has already taken three of my children as well as my beloved brothers. It becomes almost automatic, as I pray that hypnotic prayer over and over.

I awaken with a jolt, aching all over. The oil in the lamp has burned low. It must be nearly morning, but it's still dark outside. I'd been holding Joseph's hand as I slept, hunched over in my chair. The rosary is lying on the bedcover between us. Suddenly I realize that his hand is cold. I begin to rub it between my own two hands to warm it up, but that doesn't seem to help.

I turn the lamp up a bit so I can see him better. *Oh my God! He isn't breathing.* In a panic I feel for the pulse at his throat. I can feel nothing. *Hail Mary, Mother of God…please.* I wait a few moments for that sudden wrenching gasp I've heard so often when he catches his breath again, but it does not come. *No. Please God, no.* A sob catches in my throat and my head is spinning. I hear a keening. Then I try to call out "Mimi," as I feel myself falling.

When I open my eyes again, light is streaming through the east window of the room, and I am vaguely aware of blue-flowered walls, the ticking of a clock, and the shape of a man sitting beside the bed I am lying in.

"Joseph," I whisper. "Joseph?" I try to say.

A man's voice answers, "Let's just worry about you now, Amelia." I've heard the voice before. It's Dr. Woodbridge, I think. "Mimi and Félicité are taking care of everything. Let's just get *you* well."

"Joseph?" I manage to say again, my voice barely audible.

"You did everything you could, Amelia, and now I'm sorry to say, you seem to have contracted the same winter fever he had. You need to rest. Joseph is at peace now, in a better place. He's not hurting anymore."

I hear a wailing. My mind is far away. *A better place…what place better than with his wife and children?*

Oh merciful God. My whole body is weeping. I have lost my Joseph. The world is black as night.

…voices in the room…Dr. Woodbridge?…talking with someone. Mimi? Félicité?…not sure…fuzzy words…*bleeding…mercury…*

…a woman speaking. *Mimi*? "…hope the cupping works better for her than it did for Joseph."…no energy to open my eyes again…hurts to breathe, someone moaning…hand behind my head, lifting…bitter taste…a sip of water…

"…tincture of opium to help the pain"…a man's voice…someone gently placing my head back on the pillow…hard to breathe…

Joseph. Félicité…Mimi…Joseph? Where are you? Must…must find you…

So tired…

ENTR'ACTE

MIMI

CHAPTER 10

Lord, have mercy. I don't know how any of us in the household were able to endure the pain of the weeks that followed my son-in-law's death. Félicité, broken-hearted, wept on a daily basis. Her eyes were swollen, and she was barely able to function. It was she, on the morning of April 27, who discovered the death of her husband and then saw her mother-in-law, Amelia, crumpled on the floor beside his bed. She was hysterical, screaming as I rushed into the room. The older children were terrified by the commotion and stood in the hallway, peeking through the open door. Little Johnny was crying, and the entire household was in an uproar. I had to pry Félicité away from Joseph's body.

"Oh, Mama, I didn't even get to say goodbye," she wailed as I held her in my arms.

"I know, my dear, but he knew you loved him, as he loved you. You must go and rest now. Let me take care of things. Please. Go and lie down."

Although I thought Joseph had probably been dead for several hours, I feared the air around him might still carry contagion. But my first thought was for Amelia. I was frantic to help her. It took not only me but also Beulah, our cook, and her daughter Rose, who cleaned and helped look after the children, to get her limp body to her bedroom. Then I sent Beulah out to notify the undertaker and Rose to fetch Dr. Woodbridge.

Once they were gone, I opened all the windows in Joseph's room to clear out the bad air, the miasma that the doctor said could cause the disease to spread. That's why he had wanted to keep Félicité out of the room. He didn't want *anyone* in there, for that matter, but someone had to look after Joseph, and Amelia had asserted her rights as his mother and insisted she take on the task single-handedly. I was fearful that the disease might have spread to her, but I hoped it was only a lack of sleep and exhaustion that had caused her to collapse.

The younger children were all crying then, while ten-year-old Mary and her sister Josephine, now eight, led their mother back to her room and tried to comfort her.

Joseph's mother was not able to attend his burial, for she was too ill. Dr. Woodbridge confirmed that she too had contracted the winter fever, so during the funeral, we left Rose to take care of her while we laid her son to rest on the island—with Henry's permission, of course—not far from his grandparents' graves. We buried him there because a plot at Oak Grove Cemetery would have cost money we weren't sure we could afford. We needed to be frugal now, for we didn't yet know what the financial situation would be. I had some funds saved, but I knew better than to spend them until we knew what provisions Joseph had made for his family.

It was I who took care of the funeral arrangements, keeping them simple, for I feared Félicité would be unable to bear up under more elaborate ceremony and would make herself ill again with grief. I wasn't sure I could cope if that happened, for Lord knows, how would I manage at my age with two sick adults and six children to care for?

Joseph's brothers and sisters, as well as his father, were present at the burial. When they learned that Amelia was too ill to come, her sons and daughters came to Brunswick and gathered around, making short visits to the room, covering their noses and mouths with handkerchiefs, just to let her know they were there and that they loved her. Henry never appeared.

She didn't last as long as Joseph had—dying on May 4, just one week after his passing. I don't think she fought it as he did, for Joseph had desperately wanted to live, while Amelia may have seen death, where she could rejoin her brothers and her four deceased children, as preferable.

I will miss her very much, for she was the best friend I ever had.

We had so many things in common—our French origins, our losses in Saint-Domingue, our grandchildren. We'd been together off and on almost from the beginning of our coming to Georgia. We were like sisters, having shared so many joys and losses almost equally. And in these recent years, ever since Henry had betrayed her so blatantly, we'd even lived together. I know how she suffered. Some things, I think, are worse than losing a husband to death, as I did.

As soon as Henry heard about her passing, he appeared at our front door, his chin high, his silver cane in hand, and announced, "I've come to bury my wife." He was wearing a black armband, and at his side stood the local undertaker.

"Where is she?" He hadn't wanted to face her while she lived, but now here he was, his usual imperious self, come to take control.

Beulah, Rose, and I had already bathed Amelia's body, dressed her in her best clothing, and laid her out in her own room, as we had done with Joseph. We didn't want to bring the bodies down to the parlor, as was the custom, for fear of contamination and bad air.

With somber expressions, the two men marched unceremoniously into the house, up the stairs, and down the hall, where I had told him her bedroom was located. I knew that Félicité wouldn't want Henry there, but she was in her room with the door closed, and I didn't see any need to upset her. Besides, if he planned to take care of funeral expenses, it would lift a financial burden from us, but I was certainly not expecting the showy funeral he would arrange.

When Henry got to the bedroom, he knelt down beside the bed where Amelia lay and crossed himself, the pose of a sad and grieving husband. *That hypocrite*, I thought. Then, after what I suppose he considered an appropriate period of insincere mourning, he got up to instruct the undertaker, loudly and in my hearing.

"I want only the finest," he told the undertaker. "A rosewood casket. Your best funeral coach covered with flowers. She loved flowers," he said, as though he had any idea at all what she loved and cared about. He talked about the French tradition of mourners following the hearse on foot, but the undertaker pointed out that the unpaved roads in Brunswick were rutted and often spotted with horse dung and that it probably wouldn't be advisable.

"Well then," Henry said, "we will follow the hearse in closed carriages to the dock. There I will arrange for boat transportation to the island. I know she would like to be buried beside Joseph."

Again, he sounded as though he knew exactly what Amelia would have wanted. I suspect that her greatest wish would have been to follow *his* casket to the graveyard, but I said nothing. He was taking over in his usual high-handed manner, and I had no choice but to step back. In a way it was a relief, for I'd had to make all the arrangements for Joseph's funeral, get the children dressed, support Félicité to the cemetery, and keep her from throwing herself on the casket. I was almost worn out, and my seventy-four-year-old bones ached. I could only assume that God was keeping me here because Félicité and the children still needed me.

Given the warm weather, Amelia's funeral needed to be planned rather quickly. Henry, determined it would be lavish or, as I thought, ostentatious, assembled a cortège of horse-drawn coaches to follow the flower-draped hearse to the docks. From there, a long line of boats also bedecked with blossoms accompanied the casket as it was floated through the tidal creeks toward the island. Boatloads of slaves followed after, singing mournful dirges that echoed across the water all the way from Brunswick. It was quite impressive, as he intended it to be.

Amelia's four daughters knelt and wept at her grave next to that of Joseph, still fresh from the week before, while her three remaining sons, dressed in their very best with hats in their hands, lined up with somber expressions. Henry just stood there stony-faced, trying his best to look appropriately sorrowful.

Before the month was out, he ordered two raised marble tombs, French style, to adorn the graves—both Amelia's and Joseph's. On hers he had words carved that touted her French origin and social virtues.

To know her was Sufficient to Esteem her.
Highly Educated in France,
Of which She was a Native;
Amiable and Courteous.
She bid adieu to a devoted Family
And a large Circle of Friends
Who prized her highly for her many
Sociable virtues, and respected her
As an Ornament of Society.

REQUIESCAT IN PACE

Following that, he added words that I suspect would have given Amelia a bitter laugh.

Ah lov'd one. Thro' this World's fierce strife
Thou were our friend and gentle guide
And dearly wert thou loved in life,
But dearer still since thou hast died.
And now we raise this Tablet stone,
To mark the place where sleeps in death.
As kind heart as Earth has known
As pure as E'er drew mortal breath.

Hypocrite to the end, I thought. I could only wonder how the world might interpret the lines: "And dearly wert thou loved in life, / But dearer still since thou hast died." I could only scoff that he had the audacity to proclaim his "love" now that she was gone, a love he certainly had not shown during the latter years of her lifetime. At least he had the decency to let Félicité decide the words that would ornament Joseph's tomb.

There is nothing left now to stop Henry, and we expect him to marry Sarah Aust within the coming year. We all assume it's inevitable sooner or later, save for the unlikelihood that he has finally developed a conscience.

PART II

SARAH

CHAPTER 11

Jekyl Island, 1850

Amelia is dead—finally. Henry dutifully buried her beside her son in that dreary cemetery on the north end of the island where his parents and three of the other children lie. At last it's over—all the secrecy, Henry having to hide his horse in the barn and sending my girls to the seashore with the little ones so that he and I could be alone. Most important of all, his duty as a good Catholic is done now. He has no more excuses, no more valid reasons why he cannot marry me and make an honest woman of me. I suppose, in a sense, it may be a bit late for that, but at least it will give our children his name and a legitimacy they didn't have before.

I know Amelia hated me, but I tried my best never to begrudge her years with Henry. She had, after all, become his wife before he met me. But I was the one he loved. I think he had grown tired of her years ago. When we were first together, he told me that he no longer made love to her. That part of their life was over. Still, he would never consider a divorce, even when they no longer lived together. Well, now he has no more vows to keep—not that he ever kept them anyhow. In any case, a widower, even a Catholic widower, has the right to marry again.

At the moment he is still "in mourning," and I haven't seen him for more than two weeks. He claims he needs to spend time with his grown children who have lost their mother. I don't think he is really mourning, but rather playing the role of a grieving husband to make some kind of show for his family and Brunswick society. But I doubt he's fooling anyone. Everybody with half a brain knows that he placed his affections elsewhere years ago. Now I want him home with me. No more pretense. No more shame. I'll soon be Mrs. Henry DuBignon. Lord knows, I've waited long enough. Ten years now. Twelve years since my husband George died. I hated every minute of being alone, and I welcomed the day Henry came into my life. I needed a man. Perhaps I didn't realize it at first, but I do now.

I still recall our first meeting. He was on the school board for Glynn Academy, and I noticed him right away when they interviewed me to be a teacher, for he was distinctive, quite different from the others. He was not tall, but he was slim and debonair in a French sort of way. He spoke with only the slightest accent, but there was something mildly flirtatious about the way he posed his hands on the table and cocked his head. And I could tell from the way he gazed at me that he was seeing me as a woman and not just as a potential teacher. I could feel myself responding, and despite my efforts to look professional, my eyes kept drifting back to him. All the other men there looked serious and a bit stern, but Henry wore a slight, appraising smile that looked almost naughty.

At the end of the interview, after I had described my qualifications, my fine English education—which I may have exaggerated a bit—my recent widowhood, and my need for the job, all the gentlemen stood. The chairman thanked me for my interest, informed me that they would notify me of their decision within a week, and asked that I write my address on the tablet he handed me. Three days later I received a polite letter from the board informing me that they had decided against my application and had chosen another candidate. I was at my wit's end, for I had no other respectable and sufficient source of income.

My husband George had died on a chilly January morning more than a year before, leaving almost nothing of value except his gold watch and a frock coat. He had tried to get ahead in Brunswick, once even running for public office, but nothing had worked out. To afford our rent, I had by now exhausted what was left of our meager savings, sold the gold watch, and was earning only a paltry sum as a seamstress, taking in piece work and mending. But there was never enough work to pay the bills, and I did not have the skills to be a true dressmaker. Needless to say, I was several months behind in my rent.

Decent work opportunities for women in Brunswick were, for the most part, limited to teacher or dressmaker. Even a milliner was a rarity in a small Southern town. The only alternative in Brunswick was menial labor of some sort, but the idea that I might work as a scullery maid or cook in the kitchen someplace like the Oglethorpe House was unthinkable. Anyhow, such jobs were mostly filled by free blacks or slaves who were allowed to hire out.

As for working as a domestic in a household, most families had slaves of their own they did not have to pay and would never have thought of hiring a white woman. Georgia was unlike England, where ladies' maids were essential among the upper crust and held reasonably high positions in a household. It explained why women here were so desperate to have husbands, but mine was gone forever.

Thus, when the opportunity opened up at Glynn Academy, I jumped at the possibility. I was fairly well educated and came from a decent family in England. My in-laws, though I never met them, had even brushed elbows with the nobility, or so George claimed, always referring to himself as George Butler Aust Esquire. He wanted people to know he was a gentleman. My parents, while they didn't associate with the gentry, would nevertheless have been mortified to see me working in a menial and demeaning position. Thus, I had little choice. Needless to say, my disappointment at the rejection from the Glynn Academy board was beyond measure.

The day after the letter arrived, informing me that I had not been chosen to fill the position, I heard a brisk knock on my door. When I opened it, there stood Henry, his broad-brimmed hat in his hand and the afternoon sun lighting the apologetic expression on his face.

"I take it that you have received the board's letter?" he said.

"Yes, it arrived yesterday morning. I must say I was surprised. I had thought that a well-educated English woman might be desirable in a town such as Brunswick."

"I argued vigorously for your hiring," he assured me. "I think you would have brought a new dignity to Glynn Academy."

"I had hoped so."

"But I was outvoted." He hesitated, but only for a moment. "A niece of a board member had also applied for the position." I knew quite well that such favoritism was common among those in power here as well as in England and that there would be no need to protest. Henry, instead of looking crestfallen or sympathetic, smiled warmly.

"Since that opportunity did not work out," he said, "I would like to propose to you an alternative position."

"An alternative? Yes, go on." I could not keep the hopefulness from my voice, even though I knew it was not good to appear too eager.

"I have two children currently enrolled at Glynn Academy. However, it takes a great deal of time and effort to get them from Jekyl Island, where we live, into Brunswick every morning in time for their classes. I considered your...qualifications carefully and wondered if you might be willing to come live on the island and serve as their tutor."

"I would need to live on the island?" I had no idea what it might be like, but I knew it would not have the amenities, such as they were, of even a small Georgia town like Brunswick.

"Yes, of course. I couldn't pay as well as Glynn Academy. I know they pay their female teachers $12 a month. I could pay you only $8, but I could provide you with a house of your own. We call it the Bernardey house, for the people who used to live there. You could stay there rent free."

I quickly calculated the savings. It was an enormous benefit not to have to pay rent, which would have taken almost half my salary at Glynn Academy. Perhaps it was worth the inconvenience of living on the island, and I certainly needed the job. I was on the verge of being evicted from my current rooms, for I had no idea where the overdue rents would come from.

"I have two little girls," I said. "Could I tutor them along with your children since they won't be able to go to school here?"

"Yes, of course."

"Then," I said, returning his smile and hesitating no further, "I would be happy to accept. When should I start?"

"As soon as arrangements can be made and it is convenient for you. And may I say, Madam Aust, that I am delighted."

He gave me one of those appraising looks I had noticed at the interview, and then he actually bent to kiss my fingertips. It was charming, though it made me feel a bit awkward. Still, I supposed it was the custom in France, where I assumed he'd been born.

"Well then," he said. "I must be on my way, but I do look forward to your presence on the island."

I nodded and smiled. "Thank you. I shall try not to disappoint you."

"Oh, I'm sure you won't," he said, returning my smile with one of his own and putting his hat on his head again. He nodded farewell and turned to leave. I stood at the door, watching as he made his way with a cheerful gait down the walkway and wondering what on earth I had gotten myself into. Whatever it was, I told myself it would feed my children.

When Mary, Fredonia, and I arrived on the island late one morning at the end of August, we were directed by the boatman to the DuBignon house. Some little boys I took to be children of slaves were playing near the landing, and I gave each of them a penny to see that our trunks were delivered to the place called the Bernardey house, as Henry had called it.

To reach our destination, we had to walk a mile or so farther along the hot, sandy road that ran alongside the river. There were not many houses along the way, except for the unpainted slave cabins that I could see bunched together in a little settlement among the trees a hundred yards or so off the road. They were easy to distinguish, tiny as they were. The big whitewashed house where the DuBignons lived stood in an open area beside the plantation road. There were several large live oak trees nearby, and in front of the house was a hitching post but no horse. I knocked on the door, and a heavy-set, middle-aged woman with maple-colored skin answered it. Henry was not there, she said. Only Madame DuBignon and several of the children. Amelia herself came to the door after a few moments.

"Good morning, Mrs. DuBignon," I said. "I am Sarah Aust, the new tutor for your children."

"Oh, do come in. We weren't expecting you until next week." I knew I had come early, but I needed to vacate our rooms as soon as possible to avoid another meeting with my landlady wanting more rent. In spite of my surprise arrival, Amelia was quite friendly and welcoming, though I noticed that she looked me over carefully. It was impossible to tell what she was thinking, but she seemed gracious and cheerful.

"And who are these young ladies?" she asked, smiling at my two little girls.

"This is Mary," I said, putting my hands and a bit of pressure on the back of my eight-year-old daughter's shoulders to remind her to curtsey, as she had been taught. "And the young one is Fredonia." She was only four, but she was smart and gave an awkward copy of her sister's curtsey.

Amelia nodded pleasantly at the girls, then said, "Let me introduce you to the two children you will be tutoring." She called out their names. A tall, lanky girl with long dark hair and a younger freckle-faced boy appeared at the top of the stairwell and ambled slowly down the steps.

"This is Eugenia, who is fourteen, and that is Henry Charles, who will be thirteen in November. They will be your pupils. All our other children have completed their educations," she said with a smile of satisfaction.

The two seemed docile enough, and I greeted them warmly. "I look forward to our time together," I said in what I hoped was a pleasant voice. They nodded mutely, clearly eager to get away.

"Would you care for any refreshment before I show you the house where you will be living?" Amelia asked.

Despite the girls' tugging at my sleeve, I smiled and replied,

"That's very kind of you, but we're eager to get settled and see the new house." I didn't want to appear too needy.

"Well, I'll at least have my cook pack a basket of food to take along. It will help you for your first day."

"That's very kind of you, but there's no need to go to any trouble."

"Nonsense. It's no trouble at all." I must say that I appreciated her kindness.

Soon the cook delivered a basket packed with food and covered over with a large red and white napkin. A coach driven by a dark-skinned man with bushy eyebrows was waiting at the front of the house. The girls perched on the bench behind the coachman, while I sat in the seat across from them. Amelia climbed in beside me. We drove another mile or two farther south, until we reached an unpainted two-story clapboard house, larger, of course, than the slave cabins but smaller than the DuBignon house. Still, it afforded much more room than we'd had in Brunswick. I was gratified to see that our trunks, which held our linens, clothes, a cooking pot, and a frying pan, along with a bit of crockery, were already sitting on the front porch.

The house had obviously not been lived in for quite some time and would need a thorough cleaning and airing, *but it will do*, I thought, thinking of the touches I could add here and there that would make it more homelike.

"I can send over a girl to help with the cleaning. It would already have been done, but I had no idea that you were arriving so soon. Perhaps I can also find some material you could use for curtains and such."

The house was sparsely furnished—a table with four chairs, two crudely made bedsteads, and a chifferobe. There was a dilapidated barn out back, and I thought perhaps I might find something useful stored there. But for now we would make do until the rest of our things arrived. At least we had a roof over our heads.

"Well, I'll go now and let you get settled," Amelia said.

As soon as she left, I set to work.

Henry dropped by that very afternoon to welcome me to the island and tell me that if I needed anything, I was only to ask.

"I think we'll manage just fine," I told him. "Your wife said she would send a girl to help me clean."

"I'll see to it that she is here first thing in the morning."

"I don't know how to thank you, Mr. DuBignon. Your help has come at a most opportune time."

"Oh, do please call me Henry," he said in a warm tone. "I hope we can be great friends."

I smiled and nodded. "I hope so too."

Then he tipped his hat and left the girls and me to spend our first night alone on Jekyl Island.

Not many days passed before he returned.

"Is there anything you need, Mrs. Aust?" he asked. Before I could answer, he said, "May I call you Sarah? It's such a pretty name, a biblical name."

"I suppose so," I answered, though I must say I thought it a bit forward of him to ask such a question. Ours was to be a professional relationship, I thought, but since he had asked me to call him Henry, I assumed it was the American way.

"Do you need anything?" he asked again. "Anything at all?"

"I'm sure we'll be fine."

He bent to kiss my fingertips again. "Well then, I'll be checking in from time to time," he said, with that roguish grin of his.

He was a puzzle of French and American ways, and I was still growing accustomed to this new country. But I *had* been here long enough to know that things were not as they were in England and that many of the old formalities had been discarded in this raw, new country.

Those first days on the island were difficult, what with having to beat layers of dust out of the old cotton mattresses on the bedsteads and sweep out the mouse droppings from years of neglect. Fortunately, the nights were still quite warm, so we only needed to gather firewood for cooking. The kitchen was separated from the house, connected only by the open-air passage that Americans call a dog-trot. We didn't have a dog, but that didn't seem to matter. Over time I had managed to set aside three dollars for a rainy day, funds I had refused to spend even for rent. I kept it in a tin box at the bottom of my trunk. I decided that the time had come to use it to keep us going until I received my first month's salary. It allowed me to buy eggs, vegetables, and an occasional chicken or fish from the slaves. Nelly, the girl sent over to help with the cleaning, knew all the island folk who had such things to sell and tried to bring whatever I needed each morning and collect the coins at the end of the day. I planned eventually to plant a garden and perhaps raise a few chickens of my own, but for now we depended on what we could buy with our meager savings. I hoped we could manage until lessons started.

In our earlier years in America, using whatever funds we had brought from England, we had purchased a few items of furniture, which I had left temporarily stored in the attic of my landlady in Brunswick, along with the promise to send back rents. Henry and one of his sons were kind enough to move them to the island for me, so little by little the house began to be livable. Among the items were a green velvet settee and two wing chairs that made the parlour come to life. In front of the fireplace I laid the only household item George had insisted we bring from England—a small oriental carpet his parents had bought many years ago on a trip to Turkey. He thought we should seek to live a gracious life, even in America. We had tried, but our lack of continuing funds took a toll. At least we had a little furniture. It was not easy, but after a few weeks, the old Bernardey house became a home, and my girls and I settled in with fair comfort.

We began lessons in early September. At first, when the DuBignon children came to my house, they sat in the parlour as we worked our way through an English grammar book I had brought with me. It soon became clear that the dining room table would provide a better location for our work. While the older children did sums and spelling on their slates, my little girls were learning to read from one of the two storybooks I had in the house. It was quite different from what I imagined a real classroom might have been. Although I had received something of an education, insofar as it was allowed for girls in England, I had no specific training as a teacher. I just tried to follow my instincts and draw inspiration from memories of my own education with my mother and an untrained tutor.

It was not a bad life, though I still missed George. Ours had been a sweet and growing romance. I was only seventeen when we'd first met. He was a clerk in the foreign office at the General Post Office, and his father was a man of higher rank there. We encountered one another quite by accident in the streets of London on a rainy September day in 1828. He was riding in a carriage that splashed my skirts as it passed. I was so startled that I tried to back away too quickly, stumbled, and twisted my ankle. I saw the carriage stop a few feet farther ahead, and George got out, paid the cabbie and motioned for him to move on. As I was brushing my skirt, he approached me and tipped his hat.

"I'm so very sorry, Miss. Are you all right? I saw you misstep when my carriage splashed you. I will be happy to have your skirt cleaned."

As I lifted my head, I looked into the face of one of the handsomest men I've ever seen. He had a strong jaw with a rounded chin and blond side whiskers. His eyes, which held a warm and sympathetic expression, were blue as the summer sky. To me he looked like Prince Charming. I had never had a beau before, though like all young girls I dreamed of one, and in my dreams he looked just like the young man who was being so solicitous to me.

"Oh, it's nothing. It will dry."

"Perhaps it will leave a splash of mud."

"I don't think so. The street is cobbled and should be well

washed after all this rain."

"Well, at least let me buy you some hot cider or mulled wine, something to warm you up. I feel terrible that my coach was responsible for your accident."

How could I resist such an invitation from so handsome a man? I was enchanted from the outset. It all began innocently enough, and I don't think he intended to be anything but kind, but after a glass of cider at a nearby pub, he suggested that we meet for tea the following afternoon.

"I can get away from the Post Office where I work by six o'clock and meet you at the tearoom of your choice."

I could tell he was of the gentry, and having tea with him seemed harmless enough. I didn't think my family would mind my meeting a real gentleman for tea in a public place. In fact, I doubted that my mum would even notice, for she was still besotted by her good fortune, as a recent widow who had just married a new husband. We now lived south of the Thames in the Southwark borough of London, while the General Post Office was on the north side of the river. They weren't terribly far apart by carriage. After that first late afternoon, my teatime with George became a weekly event. We met at first at a tiny, out-of-the-way tearoom on Staining Lane behind the former site of the old St. John Zachary Church, which had been destroyed in the Great Fire of London more than a century earlier.

Eventually, for my convenience, George said he'd found another tearoom in a hotel nearer the river and closer to where I lived. I guess it's safe to say that one thing led to another. He took his time, and many months passed before he suggested that perhaps we could take our tea in one of the private rooms of the hotel. By then I was completely smitten and would have taken tea with him in Hell if he'd asked me to.

As I said, one thing led to another, and of course we became lovers. It didn't take much persuasion from him to let our kisses become more intimate. The next thing I knew, my knickers were on the floor and George was on top of me, inside me, pleasuring me in ways I had never felt before.

I could hardly wait until the next time. We often met on or near Blackfriar's Bridge and sometimes took a romantic stroll along the Thames together. He would stop occasionally when no one was looking and touch my breast, whisper in my ear, and even kiss me lightly on the lips right there in public. He was a wonderful and romantic lover to the innocent girl I was at the time. He was always gentle and kind and unrushed. But I could hardly stand it until we were once again in the room he had rented for an afternoon, making frantic love. I wanted him so much.

CHAPTER 12

Finally, after one especially sweet afternoon of lovemaking, I suggested to George that I would like him to come to my home and meet my family—my mum and my new stepfather. Although George had not stated any intentions toward me, I felt that the time had come to raise the issue and inform our families that we were seeing each other with serious intent.

He looked sad and rather perplexed. "It would not do, I'm afraid, my dearest. If they saw me as a prospective son-in-law, as they surely would, they might want to verify my family connections, and they would soon discover that I have a wife."

"What?" I couldn't believe what I was hearing. "A wife? When did you plan to tell me? And are there children?"

"A boy, age six, and two girls, one who will be two on her next birthday and a baby girl. But my wife and I are not close," he protested when he saw the stricken expression on my face. "She and the children stay with her family much of the time. It is not a good marriage, but one that our parents encouraged. We were married when I was only twenty-one—much too young to know my own mind."

"But you still…"

"Very rarely, and only because she insists it's my duty. It's not like it is with us," he said, gazing tenderly into my eyes.

"I'm under twenty-one. Am I then too young to know my mind? Is this all a terrible mistake?" Despite my young age, I felt sure that I would love George for the rest of my life.

"No, no. It's different for young women. They mature much faster. And now, I too know what I want more than anything in the world. And it's you. I don't want to live without you. I just have to figure things out."

How can a woman resist words like that? I didn't make a scene, for I didn't want to lose him, and things went on for a while as they had been. Then, in early September 1829, not long after my eighteenth birthday, I began to suspect I was with child. Frantic as I was, I suppose I became a bit petulant.

"You must divorce your wife at once and marry me," I told George. "Or else I shall have to tell your parents. I will need support, and I'm sure my own family will cast me out." I wasn't sure of that at all, but it could have happened.

His face went white, and I could see his growing sense of desperation.

"Whatever you do, don't let my parents know," he said. "I'll take care of it."

I didn't want to tell my mum either, for she would know that I had been lying to her all these months. She thought I was meeting a lady friend once a week for tea. She never suspected that I had lost my virginity and was carrying on a love affair with the son of a distinguished gentleman.

"Everything will be all right," George assured me.

Each time we met, I wept over my plight, and each time he said the same thing. "I'm making plans for us. Don't worry. It will be all right."

"When?" I asked.

"Soon."

I didn't know whether to believe him or not, but I was trying my best to do so.

Then, in mid-January, he informed me that he *had* worked things out, though he didn't tell me how, and I thought it best not to ask. What mattered was that he said we would be married before the end of the month. I was glad, for I was getting anxious.

We were to be married by licence, which meant that we didn't have to post banns and wait the necessary three weeks before we could marry. I was glad about that, because by now I was sure I was in the family way and more than four months gone—maybe five. Marriage by licence was often done in such cases, but George said it was because I was not yet twenty-one. To marry by licence, one had merely to pay the necessary fees and make the required allegations that there was no impediment to the marriage. It meant, of course, that I would not have the romantic wedding of my dreams, but that did not seem to matter so much. All that mattered was that I would soon be Mrs. George Butler Aust.

True to his word, on Tuesday, January 26, George and I were married in a quick private ceremony in the chilly nave of St Stephen Walbrook in London. The only other people present were the rector and the two necessary witnesses, members of the choir who agreed to stand with us.

Only after we had made our vows did my new husband reveal to me that he had booked passage for the two of us to go to America. He would need another week or so, he said, to work out a few details. In the meantime, we should behave as though nothing had changed, and we would depart sometime during or just after the first week in February.

"You mustn't tell anyone of our marriage or our plans," he said to me after the ceremony.

"But why?" I wanted to share my happiness with my family. I felt sure my mum would have liked George.

"I don't want my parents to find out."

I protested that no one in my family would tell them, but he was insistent. "You'd be surprised how quickly news can spread. We can't take any chances. Go home to your family as though nothing has happened. You'll stay there until the morning of our departure. Then we'll depart in secret."

Since he had left his wife so recently, he was terrified that his parents would try to undo our marriage and block our departure.

"What will my mum think if I leave without saying goodbye? She will surely worry."

"We can send her a letter the day we leave London. You won't have to mention where we're going, at least not at first, but that will relieve her mind and let her know that you're safe."

I spent the Tuesday evening before our departure sitting in front of the fire of our small flat and chatting with my mother and stepfather. Before I went up to bed, I said my goodnights.

"I love you, Mum," I said, giving her a warm hug. I knew I would be sneaking out before dawn, and I had no idea when or if I might ever see her again.

"Get along with you now." She smiled and gave me a pat on the cheek, just like it was any other day. "You need your beauty rest."

The following morning, on February 5, a day I shall never forget, George abandoned his job at the Post Office without giving notice, picked me up at dawn in a carriage, and we began our adventure to America. It was the most exciting week of my entire life. I don't know what had possessed George to book passage for Savannah, Georgia, but it was an odd coincidence. My mother had a brother who had gone to America some years earlier and settled in that state in a region called Glynn County. We didn't hear from him often, but I think Mum would have been pleased to learn that I would be near a family member. Perhaps the booking was the first one George could get, but whatever the reason, we soon found ourselves en route to the port of Plymouth and on our way to Georgia, where we expected our first child to be born.

For me, the trip to Plymouth was an adventure in itself. I had never been on a long journey outside of London, much less on a seagoing vessel. Trains, which would have made our trip much faster, were not yet running from London to Plymouth, so George decided that we would take a mail coach rather than a private transport. He said it would be faster, cleaner, and roomier.

"But isn't your father more likely to hear of it and try to stop us?" I knew that George's father was a surveyor also employed by the Post Office, but George assured me that such a thing was highly unlikely.

"I know all about Royal Mail coaches," he said. "They're run by independent contractors. The only official Post Office employee is the guard, who will have no idea who any of the passengers are. The mail coach will be much more comfortable since it carries only four passengers, and it's certainly safer, for we'll have an armed guard."

Since he was making all the plans, I didn't object, though I knew it would be more expensive than an ordinary stagecoach. That concerned me somewhat, for I thought we should save our money for the unknown days ahead. Thrift, however, was never a part of George's nature. We both brought all our savings, though I had no idea how long the money would last. My contribution was paltry, at best. For that reason, I would have been willing to endure the twenty-plus hours in the regular coach in order to economize, but George had other plans.

"The faster we get out of London, the better it will be," he said. "While I don't want my father coming after us, we can make a holiday of it as well. It's our honeymoon after all. Even if we spend nights at inns along the way, we could still be in Plymouth in two days' time, three at most." The new macadam roads made travel faster and safer, he assured me, and there were many inns between London and Plymouth. I didn't care. I just wanted to be with George for the rest of my life. Even planning the trip was exciting—and, best of all, I got to be with my new husband day and night.

Once we reached Plymouth, we rented a room in the Barbican district near the docks to wait for our ship, which would sail soon, depending on the weather. The sight of Plymouth Sound was my first view of the ocean. I would wake up in the morning to the piercing cries of gulls and fishmongers. Then George and I would take our breakfast and stroll the cobbled streets of the waterfront.

Although the harbour was lined with rows of imposing houses four or five stories high, the briny smell and the stiff salt breeze made it clear that we were no longer in London. The area around the docks was rather seedy, full of drunken sailors, and George said it could sometimes be dangerous, so we took our supper early in the evening and went to our room, where as far as I was concerned, the greatest delights awaited.

Finally, on the day we were to sail, we arose at dawn and had our trunks sent on ahead. When it came time to board, we had to be rowed out to our ship, which was anchored a hundred yards or so from the dock. It was a sunny day, but the wind was brisk and the sea air cold. The innkeeper had told us it was probably the coldest time of year for sailing and wished us luck. "You may need it," he said.

Despite his warnings, the beginning of our voyage was fairly calm, but in mid-ocean we encountered several storms and stiff winds. And I have to admit, it was cold on the open water. "The worst sailing weather is in the fall, I'm told," George said, "and the cold will help with any seasickness." Who knows? Perhaps it did. Thank God, I was past the morning sickness stage of my early months. In any case, those weeks on the ship, once we had both recovered from our early queasiness, were still part of our honeymoon. We had left behind all our troubles and responsibilities and were as carefree and playful as children, wandering the deck on nice days and leaning out over the gray, uneasy waters of the Atlantic with the icy wind in our faces, making love in mid-afternoon in our tiny stateroom and speculating on our unknown future. I even enjoyed meeting other passengers, none of whom we knew before we boarded the ship. What I liked best was hearing my new husband introduce me as "my wife, Sarah." I beamed with pride.

It was a long trip, longer than I could have imagined. My belly was swelling as the baby grew inside, and I had to let out my dresses, but I felt certain that my child would not be born until we had safely arrived in Savannah. However, the winds slowed our voyage, and I had not counted on the delays caused by the stops we had to make at other ports. All told, we were aboard ship almost ninety days. Somewhere between New York and Charleston, I knew I wasn't going to make it all the way without giving birth. Needless to say, I was terrified, and George was frantic. Fortunately, there was a woman on board who claimed to be a midwife and who was willing to help. We managed somehow, and despite the pain, I gave birth to my first daughter, whom we named Mary Delora. George came up with the second part of her name. He said he derived it from a combination of Latin *de la ora*, which meant "by the seashore," and the French *de l'eau*, "from the water." I had no idea whether he was right or not, but I thought it was a pretty name. He chose it, he said, because she was born at sea.

We had no blankets, no clothes, nothing for the baby, but for a small price the captain allowed us to cut up one of the ship's blankets and two sheets to make the necessities to cover the child. As soon as we arrived in Savannah, which would not be long, we planned to buy all the necessary items. I had been totally unprepared for what it was like to care for a baby. Passengers in the neighbouring cabins complained about her crying at night, and so I nursed her more than I should have to try to keep her quiet. By the time we reached our destination, my breasts were sore, and I was eager to leave the ship, my daughter in my arms wrapped in her makeshift blanket, and settle into a quiet life.

After we deboarded in Savannah and acquired all we needed for little Mary, it did not take George long to conclude that the city was too large, filled with too many people who'd also recently come from England. Most of the more affluent Englishmen in the area had settled in or around Savannah or Charleston, and he was afraid someone might recognize him and notify his father. So he suggested that we make our way farther south to the smaller community of Brunswick, which was named for the ancestral home of King George II. It also happened to be the seat of Glynn County and the home of my uncle, William Dover Jenkins, whom I hadn't seen since I was a child.

"It might be nice to have a contact there," George said.

Brunswick was said to be a town that was booming at the moment, and it sounded perfect to us and as though it might be full of opportunity. When we arrived there, we located my uncle and decided to call on him in the hope that he might offer us hospitality until we could get settled. As it turned out, it was not a pleasant visit.

We reached his home in late afternoon only to discover that he was living with a common-law "wife," an attractive woman he called Peggy, who happened to be a mulatto slave.

I was rather shocked, but George was outraged. He insulted my uncle and his mistress in the rudest of terms. I won't repeat the vile things he said, for I am still embarrassed by them. It was a side of George I had not seen before. Most of his insults were hurled at Peggy, who had been nothing but affable and kind to us since we appeared out of the blue. I just stood there like a dunce, too embarrassed to utter a word.

My uncle looked at George in disgust. Finally he said, "I'm appalled by such language from a supposedly well-bred Englishman, but I can only assume you're nothing but an unlicked cub who knows no better." Then he turned to me and said, "It's good to see you again, Sarah, and to meet your daughter, but I'm sure you'll understand if we don't invite you to stay for dinner." Then he turned abruptly, offered his arm to Peggy, and the two of them walked out of the room without further ado.

A black servant brought George his hat and opened the front door for us to leave. Thus, my contact with my only relative in Glynn County was short-lived. Since no offer of hospitality was forthcoming from Uncle William, we had to stay in a hotel, using our valuable and limited resources, until we could rent our own place.

I soon discovered that, in Brunswick, George's attitude fitted right in. It seemed to be quite acceptable for a man to have a black mistress, but one didn't flaunt her in public or as a part of his household. I thought it hypocritical and chose to admire my uncle for his courage. Since then, however, I have seen no more of him. Someday, now that George is gone, I would like to mend our relationship.

At the time, however, I soon forgot about the ugly incident between George and my Uncle William. My days were filled with caring for Mary and trying to be a good wife. George found work as a clerk, though he was dissatisfied and thought it below his station. He even tried once to run for public office, without success. I didn't care. I was blissfully happy. We had little in the way of material goods, but none of that mattered to me. Our marriage was the most wonderful time of my life. I was a wife and a mother—all I ever wanted to be.

Like all men, George hoped for a son, but our second baby, a little boy we named Paul born two years after our arrival, survived less than a year. We were both heartbroken, but time is a great healer, and I refused to let myself dwell on it. Then, when Mary Delora was four years old, her little sister Margaret Fredonia was born. We had two beautiful little girls, one blond like George and the other with dark hair like mine. Life was good. I went about my days in a cloud of happiness, assuming it would last forever. Oh, like any husband and wife, we had little spats here and there, but none of any consequence. We would soon make up in the most delightful ways, and the little town of Brunswick seemed like paradise to me.

One thing I have been forced to learn in life is never to take happiness for granted. Snatch it where you can and enjoy it, for it will not last. Seven years and seven months after our arrival in Brunswick, George fell ill. I did everything I could for him, but he grew thinner and thinner until I thought he would waste away. Nothing helped. There were good days and bad days in the months that followed, but he only grew worse as time went on.

I lost him on Monday, January 22, 1838, just four days shy of our eighth anniversary. I was inconsolable. How the children and I survived the rest of that month, I'll never know. It was all so unfair. He was not yet thirty-eight years old, in the prime of his life when God took him away. For a long time, I didn't even want to live. Then, for the sake of Mary and Fredonia, I had to pull myself together and find some way to support them on my own. And that's how I came to meet Henry DuBignon and move to Jekyl Island.

CHAPTER 13

Henry visited often to check on us. He called late one afternoon after the children had been dismissed from classes and gone out to play. I was alone in the house, still having insufficient funds to afford a servant, when he appeared unexpectedly at the door.

"*Bonjour*, Sarah. May I come in?" Always before, he had come earlier, when the children were about or when the slave girl, whom Henry still sent twice a week, was in the process of cleaning and helping around the house. He knew the days she came, and he knew it was inappropriate for me to be alone with him. However, when he appeared at the door, I had no choice but to admit him. He was, after all, my employer, and I needed to stay in his good graces.

"You have made the house a home again, I see," he said, looking around the parlor. "It hasn't been lived in since Pierre Bernardey moved to Cumberland four or five years ago. During those days, this house saw a lot of life."

"Did he have a family?"

"His mother lived with him, and yes, he had a family…of sorts."

"What do you mean, a family 'of sorts'?" I asked.

"Well, he had a woman—a good-looking mulatto slave—and a little daughter."

"Oh." I could feel myself blush at the implications, thinking of the things that might have gone on here. Then I remembered my uncle and wondered if such relationships were more common in coastal Georgia than I had thought.

Henry looked at me intently. "This house has quite a past, and I trust that, with you here, it will have quite a future as well." He reached out and cupped my cheek. "You are a beautiful woman, Sarah. I hope you know that."

Oh, no, I thought. *Is he going to complicate everything?* "I…I don't know what to say."

"So beautiful," he murmured.

I took a step backwards and tried to collect myself. "My goodness, you're full of compliments today," I said, with a casual laugh and in what I hoped was a lighthearted tone, hoping to ward off his advances. "Thank you as always for stopping by. I think we have everything we need for now. The girls and I really appreciate the house you've entrusted to us." I hoped my voice sounded warm but professional.

His eyes narrowed a bit, and he drew his hand back to clutch the lapel of his jacket. Then he said, calm and quiet, "I'm glad to hear that, but please always feel free to let me know if I can do anything for you."

A sense of relief flooded my body when he left the house. I hoped that might be the end of it, though I doubted it would be. I had feared this kind of thing from the beginning and planned to do everything in my power to prevent its becoming a serious problem.

Needless to say, I wasn't surprised when he soon returned. It took visits over a period of several months, each with increasing familiarity—a brief touch of the hand, a lingering gaze, a verbal innuendo—for him to express his intentions more openly. I had put him off as best I could and for as long as possible. But he was wearing me down. What could I do? I have to admit that I missed the intimate touches I had enjoyed with George. Even though I thought of him as the love of my life, I was still young, not yet thirty, and my body longed for the kind of caresses I had known while he lived.

When George and I first met and became involved, I didn't know that he was already married, so I'm not sure whether it would have made a difference or not. But by the time he told me, I was already so in love with him that I would have committed any act or sin to keep him. But now I didn't have that excuse. I knew Henry's marital status from the beginning, and I had met his wife, who had been gracious to me and my children. Besides all that, he was old enough to be my father—in his fifties at least. He had children older than I was. I knew what he wanted, but I resisted and held him off as best I could.

My continued efforts to maintain a cordial but appropriate relationship did not seem to deter Henry in the least. He still came by on a regular basis, whether anyone else was at the house or not, often bringing small offerings—half a dozen oranges, a sweetgrass basket one of his slaves had made, or his latest copy of the *Savannah Georgian*. He knew I felt cut off from the world, and a newspaper was always welcome. Then, he took to "settin' a spell," as Georgia folk were fond of saying, and he began to talk to me about his family. How his oldest and most promising son had gone north to finish his education before returning to Brunswick to take up law. How his father's quarrel with his older brother Joseph had ended in the latter being disinherited. It came about, he told me, after his mother's grandchildren from a previous marriage arrived from France and disrupted their lives.

"Our father hated those children," he said, "and it was only after Joseph married one of them that Papa decided to disinherit him. I'm sure of that. It was that decision that came between my brother and me. He left the island then and never came back. After that, we lost touch, and I had to hear from a mutual acquaintance of Joseph's recent death. His wife didn't even bother to notify me."

I would listen intently. I have to admit that it was good to have an adult to talk with from time to time. The island was a lonely place, and I had a lot of time on my hands. I confess that I actually began to look forward to his visits.

He didn't make any attempts toward intimacy again until late one afternoon when he told me how his wife didn't want any more children and how painful that was to him. I know how much he loved his children, or said he did, and he looked so unhappy when he told me that his son Henry Charles, my youngest pupil, was to be his last. I gathered from his words that he and his wife didn't have marital relations anymore, and I felt sorry for him. To have that taken away, even while one's spouse still lived—it was unthinkable. He looked at me with such sadness and hunger, and when he got up to leave that afternoon, I could see tears in his eyes.

"It makes me feel less like a man," he said as we stood side by side near the front door.

"But Henry, you've accomplished so much in your life—not just your family but your wonderful plantation, your success in Brunswick. You're president of a bank and a member of the school board."

"Not anymore," he reminded me. "When I took my children out of Glynn Academy, the board felt I needed to resign."

"But you're still a vigorous man with many accomplishments." I put my hand on his shoulder in a gesture of reassurance. "You've done so well."

He reached out and pulled me closer. With his other hand, he touched my breast. "Oh, Sarah," he murmured. "If only—"

"Henry, the children!" I knew my little girls were upstairs playing in their room.

"What if they weren't here?" He leaned down to brush my neck with his lips.

I felt confused. "I…I don't know." He caressed me gently, and my body responded in spite of my knowing that I should push him away. Instead, I felt almost a sense of disappointment when he withdrew his hand.

"I'll leave now," he said in a husky voice, "but I'll be back." He tilted my chin upward and kissed me softly on the lips. "That's a promise."

I was trembling all over when he left, and I knew I no longer had the will to resist. I tried to think of George, to conjure up sweet memories of him, to drive away this surge of desire I couldn't shake off, but all I could think of was the touch, the promise, the warmth of Henry's hand cupping my breast. And I confess that, as I watched him mount his horse and ride away, I felt a confused sense of frustration. I tried to tell myself that it was merely for my inability to be strong, but even then I think I felt let down by his withdrawing so easily from the embrace.

I know I should have packed up my things right then and left the island. But where would I have gone? What would I do? I didn't fight it as I should have, but what would have been the point? I needed this teaching position. I couldn't afford to lose it, whatever it took, for I had no other prospects. And despite his age, I did find Henry attractive. In my heart, while I feared his next visit, I knew I would give in.

It was after class hours when he came by again, but still daylight. He probably guessed that my children would be out of doors taking advantage of the remaining sunlight, as they were most afternoons now. I was alone when he knocked. At first, I thought I might not answer the door, but he knew I was here. How could I not?

He must have realized that he had worn me down, for this time he strode in, closed the door firmly behind, and grasped my shoulders with his two strong hands.

"You're driving me crazy, Sarah," he said at once, fixing me with his dark eyes. "I want you so badly. Are the girls here?"

"They're outside playing." My voice was shaky, but I couldn't break away from his gaze. We both knew that they would probably play outside until dark, despite the winter chill in the air.

"Thank God," he breathed, and his lips sought mine with a hungry force.

He was kissing me as I hear only the French can kiss, deeply, thoroughly, his tongue exploring. Even through my skirt and petticoat, I could feel his stiff member pressing against me. What else could I do? I let myself melt against him. It had been so long, so long—nearly two years—since a man had desired me like that. I wanted him too. I admit it. I knew it was wrong, but my entire body was all at once on fire as it hadn't been since George's death.

He began to back me toward the sofa, kissing me the whole time. He was already starting to lift my skirt.

"No," I said. "Don't. The children might come in—"

"Upstairs then," he said, his voice heavy with desire. It was a command.

And so we went upstairs—the first of many times. And Henry showed me that he knew well how to please a woman.

That was only the beginning. Sometimes I would meet him in the forest, and we'd take long walks through the dim paths until we found a sweet-smelling bed of pine needles to soften our lovemaking. Once in the late afternoon, I even caught a glimpse of a deer peering curiously at us through the tangle of underbrush. On other occasions, we'd find the hollow of a sand dune to shelter us from view of any human habitation. Whatever was convenient. But most of the time, I could find a way to send the girls on an errand or some such, so that we could use the bedroom to avoid the pesky bugs in the forest.

Even given the irregularity of our time together, our years as a couple have not been fruitless. Only a few months after it all began, I discovered I was once again with child. When I told Henry, I hoped he would do what George had done—leave his wife to marry me. His only response was, "The Church doesn't allow divorce. I couldn't remarry if I left Amelia. Your George could do it because wasn't a Catholic."

No, thank God, for the Church of England had separated from the Catholic Church to allow for a divorce. Even so, I thought Henry's reasoning was ridiculous. "You do many of the things your Church doesn't allow," I pointed out.

"But I can always confess and be forgiven. If I were divorced, I wouldn't be allowed to take Communion. I could spend eternity in Hell. You can't ask that of me, Sarah. I'll take care of you and our son, of course. You needn't worry."

"What makes you think it will be a son?"

"I know you won't let me down," he said, making an effort to smile.

And of course, he was right. Thank God I was here on the island, where I had to face fewer people. In fact, I hardly ever went to the mainland anymore, for whenever I was there, people who'd known I was unwed and expecting a child or who later heard of my son's birth rudely shunned me. I don't think Henry even told Amelia about the baby until after he was born. It apparently created a storm in their household. Amelia, he told me, was angry and wouldn't even talk to him for a time, but eventually his children persuaded her to forgive him. Then, surprisingly, she decided to allow him back in her bed again. I guess she thought the only reason he had turned to me was because she had shut him out. But that wasn't the case. He loved *me*. I knew he loved me, not her.

When all that happened, I had to ask, "And do you make love to her again?" I hated the idea of sharing him with anyone—even his wife.

"Sometimes, out of duty," he confessed. I have to admit I was jealous. I recalled the same words coming from George. It was as though I had lived this moment before.

"But it's not like it is with you," he reassured me, looking earnestly into my eyes. "You're the one I think about constantly, and I look forward to those special moments when I can hold you again. It's you I desire," he said, pulling me into his arms and making an effort to demonstrate.

The memory of George gave me only momentary pause. That was then. This was now. I decided to be playfully coy about having to share Henry with his wife in order to let him seduce me all over again. I knew he wanted our relationship to be cheerful and not burdensome like the one he had with Amelia. I pouted seductively, then resisted with only a little tussle, letting him hold me down with a bit more force as his lips explored my body as a prelude to his lovemaking.

Three years later, when our second son William Turner was born, he told me Amelia was upset all over again. When she'd learned of Leonidas's birth, she had insisted that I could no longer tutor their two children and wanted me sent away from the island, but Henry had refused. He had no intention of letting me go. Although he no longer had tutoring services to pay for, he still provided for me and my children, as he had promised. I don't know what he told Amelia, but I do know that he loved me and wanted me always close by. He told me that he wanted to marry me more than anything and that he would when he could. Thus, I remained, but this time Amelia didn't.

She abandoned their home and went to stay with their son Joseph and his wife, who at that time still lived on the island. But then, when Joseph was elected to the state legislature to replace his brother, who had stepped down, he and his family moved into Brunswick, and Amelia went with them. That's where she was living when our daughter Rosalia Elisabeth was born. Their departure from Jekyl freed Henry to spend more time with me. We were almost like a real family, Henry and I, with our three children, and my two daughters born during my marriage to George. Everyone knew now of my relationship with Henry, as he began to spend more nights than not at my house.

Amelia's children who were still on the island lived a life totally separate from ours. Although Henry spent a week with them from time to time and tried to stay on their good side, it wasn't easy. Those children were all grown now, and I knew they resented me. They still do, but I rarely see them. Even then, I scarcely saw them and then only by chance on the roads, at the seashore or some such.

When I become their stepmother, I trust they will be more willing to accept me into their lives. The island is small, after all, and there can be little room for lifelong animosity. I am willing to forgive and forget all the past times if they are. I know they thought that what their father and I did was wrong, but it will now be made right. It's hard to believe, but we've been lovers for more than a decade now and have three children to show for it. The time has gone by so quickly. But things will be different now that Amelia has died. I will no longer be just an appendage in his life, for we will soon be man and wife.

CHAPTER 14

Two weeks later

The room was growing dark as the sun began to sink over the autumn marshes. It was well past teatime, but still I sat, sipping lukewarm tea and nibbling a biscuit. My baby, Rosalia, was asleep, and my two older daughters, Mary and Fredonia, were both outside with their little brothers, enjoying the sunset, no doubt. The girls had loved living on this beautiful island, as I had, and I assumed this was where we would stay once Henry and I married. I delighted in the perpetual breeze that swayed the gray moss hanging like an old man's tangled beard from limbs of the live oak trees. My girls, when they were younger, used to think it a bit macabre, but now they seemed to like its peaceful grace as much as I did.

As I gazed about, I took satisfaction in the fact that my house and small garden were well tended and tidy. I prided myself on making certain the beds were all made, the dustbins emptied, and everything was in its proper place. I knew I would make Henry a good wife. I hadn't seen him but once since Amelia's funeral, except when he came by to tell me he wanted to spend more time with his children as they mourned their mother. I looked forward to his return, for now there was nothing to block our way. *He is at last all mine*, I thought. *I just wish he would come home.*

Another week passed before Henry finally returned. I was delighted to see him and did my best to spoil him and cheer him up. I decided not to broach the question of marriage right away, but I didn't want a long delay either. After all, I had spent ten years in the shadows. Now it was time for him to make things right for me and our children.

Our life together had resumed much as it was before, though he continued on occasion to spend time away from our home at the other house with his grown children. Five of them still lived there with each other—the three daughters who had not yet found husbands, Eliza, Catherine, and Eugenia, as well as the two bachelor sons, John Couper and Henry Charles Jr., the youngest of the brood, the one finally named for his father. Those boys must have thought they were ready to be lords of the manor. Neither one of them had made any effort to marry and begin a life of his own, separate from that of their father. They just lived off his profits and whatever he paid them for their help on the plantation.

I tried to wait with patience, mentioning the idea of marriage on very few occasions, but by mid-November I decided to bring the matter to a head. Henry had had sufficient time, I think, to pretend to grieve. So one evening after the children were all in bed and we were enjoying some leftover pecan pie, and waiting for the fire in the grate to die down, I brought it up once more.

"I think the time has come, Henry, when we should wed. You're a free man now, and it's not a sin for a widower, even a Catholic widower, to remarry."

There was a long silence. He didn't look at me but stared instead into the last flickers of flame that were beginning to give way to glowing embers. Then he put down his fork.

"I know how you must feel, Sarah," he said finally, "but it's not proper for me to rush into another marriage before my wife is cold in the grave."

"Since when have you cared what's proper?" I asked. "Besides, it's been six months."

"It should be at least a year, maybe even two. I have to be concerned about my children now—not just myself. Think how they would feel."

"You have other children to consider as well."

"Yes, but they're too young to know the difference and suffer as my older children surely would."

"Leonidas is already ten, Henry. How long do you plan to wait?

Until he's fully grown?"

"Until I think the time is right. Now let's don't talk about it anymore. We're just fine as we are. No one is bothering us. I don't want any more pressure." He took the last bite of his pie and set his plate down with a clatter on the table beside his chair. "It's getting late," he said. "I'm going to bed."

After that I thought I could perhaps force the issue by telling him that I had decided to call my two boys by his name, Leonidas DuBignon and William DuBignon. They already knew he was their father. Rosalia, of course, would have his name as well, but it didn't matter so much in her case, for I knew that she would one day marry and change it anyhow. I had become almost obsessed with the issue of marriage, for I was already nearly forty and wanted my life settled once and for all. I was tired of living as a middle-aged mistress to a wealthy man. It was more demeaning now than when Amelia was alive. I couldn't count the number of times he said before her death, "Dear Sarah. How I wish you were my wife." Now he kept making up excuses for delaying our wedding. I was growing more and more depressed about it. *But what can I do?* I kept asking myself.

I had given a half-hearted thought of taking him to court on some kind of charge—breach of promise or some such. After all, I did have three of his children. But that would have been even more demeaning. And since he knew all the judges, I would probably have lost. I feared I might be driving him away with my too constant insistence, for he had been spending less and less time with me. Perhaps I had no choice but to let it go for a while and try to be content with the way things were. At least Amelia was out of the picture.

It was a warm morning in late October—the kind that makes you want to be outside and soak up the tranquility and soul-cleansing atmosphere of the island before the winter chill sets in. There is nothing more dazzling than driving through the wooded lanes, dimmed by live oaks and vines tangled among the trees, and then emerging all at once into the brighter world of the wide, sandy beach. I thought a day at the seashore would surely get my mind off the gloomy situation, so I decided to pack a lunch and take the children for a picnic.

"How does everyone feel about a day at the beach?" I asked.

"That sounds like fun," Fredonia said. The two boys were jumping up and down with the energy that only young boys have.

"Run down and tell Nina to get a lunch together while I gather up all the things the children will need," I told Mary.

"Can Nelly come with us?" Fredonia asked. Nina and Nelly were the two slaves Henry had provided to me after Amelia died. Perhaps they were simply my consolation prize, but I was grateful for them. Nina was our cook, and she clearly enjoyed her own cooking, as her rolls of mahogany flesh demonstrated. Nelly, only a slip of a thing not much older than my daughters, was still our cleaning girl.

"I don't see why not. She can help look after Rosalia."

When Mary returned from the kitchen, she told me that Nina was already hard at work preparing one of her delicious lunches. I noticed that my oldest daughter looked a bit pale.

"Are you all right, my dear? You don't look too chipper this morning. You've been very quiet."

"I'm getting a headache, Mum. Would you mind awfully if I stay here and lie down for a while? I can walk over to the beach later if I feel better."

I had once suffered from migraine headaches myself and hoped she wasn't afflicted as I was. I knew how painful bright light could be in such an instance, and the beach was probably the last place she wanted to be. I always worried when my children complained, fearful they might be coming down with one of those island fevers that were all too prevalent in coastal Georgia.

"Perhaps I should cancel the picnic and stay home with you."

"Please don't do that. I'd feel terrible if I spoiled your day. I'm sure it will pass soon. I just didn't sleep well last night. Now I'd like to lie down and rest for a while. I'm sure it will get better."

"Well, if you insist. But promise me you'll relax all day. No sewing or mending or anything that will strain your eyes or tax you in any way."

"I promise, Mum. I'll take care of myself." She gave me a weak smile.

I don't know how Henry could bear to lose four of his children as he had. Mine were the center of my life. So far we had been lucky in that none of us had been stricken with yellow fever or malaria or any of the illnesses so common in the area.

Despite my concerns about Mary, the younger children were still clamoring to go to the shore. I didn't want to disappoint them. Even little Rosalia, who was not yet three, was excited about getting to chase the seagulls and play on the edge of the strand, where her brothers would sometimes help her build sand castles. We all scurried about packing blankets and towels, pails and shovels, everything we might need for a day at the beach. Then, when we were all ready, I sent Fredonia to the kitchen to fetch the food. Nina followed her back into the house, beaming as she came in carrying a large basket.

"I'se fried some chicken and deviled some eggs, along with a few other su'prises," she announced proudly.

"I hope you included some of that chocolate cake we had for dinner yesterday."

"Yes'm," she said with a grin. "Reckon I ought to come along to put out the food and clean up when ya'll 're done eatin'?"

"That would be a help," I said, seeing the eagerness on her face.

She fetched her straw hat. I put on my sunbonnet, and we all set out on that sparkling October morning.

The children and I all squeezed into the buggy Henry had provided for our use, while the servants rode tandem on the mule that he had given Leonidas on his tenth birthday.

The tide was already going out when we arrived, and the beach stretched wide toward the sea. The edge of the shore was littered with whelk shells and sand dollars, a few stranded jellyfish, and a couple of horseshoe crabs The sun had already passed its zenith, so Nina and Nelly spread a quilt on the ground at once and started to set out the picnic lunch. By then we were all hungry for the chicken and deviled eggs, the sliced and roasted sweet potatoes, biscuits, figs and dried peaches, chocolate cake and fried apple pies. It was a feast.

After our family ate, Nina and Nelly filled their own plates and settled back among the dunes to enjoy their meal. When they were done, they packed up what was left and walked back toward the buggy to stash the basket out of the sun and keep the leftovers from spoiling. We had left the horse and mule tied in the shade to a tree limb near the edge of the wood where the beach began.

While we relaxed on the beach or walked on the seashore, Nina settled among the dunes, wearing her big straw hat and fanning herself. I rested for a while on the quilt to watch the children play and enjoy the sun. Then, carrying the sweetgrass basket Henry had given me, I strolled the beach for maybe half a mile, picking up shiny shells to line the windowsills at home. Fredonia and Nelly played along the water's edge with little Rosalia, while the boys romped about in and out of the sea, getting soaked and sandy. It was a lovely afternoon. I wish I could have held on to it and the good feeling it brought forever.

But about half past three a stiff wind began to blow, and I could see a dark cloud coming toward the island, with its threat of rain and lightning. It was time to try to make it home before the storm broke. We all raced toward the buggy, laughing, while Nina waddled behind us as fast as her legs would carry her. Then, the race was on, with me driving the buggy as rapidly as I dared and the mule trotting along behind.

By the time we reached the house, Rosalia had fallen asleep and the first raindrops were beginning to fall. I left Nina, Nelly, and the children outside to unpack and put the horse and buggy in the barn, while I carried my baby girl inside to tuck her in so she could continue her afternoon nap. I knew she would sleep a long time, for she was exhausted.

To keep from waking her up, I tiptoed up the stairs and toward my room, where she still slept in her crib. While the older children were taking care of the horse and buggy, the servants headed out to the kitchen to put away the food. The rain was beginning to pelt noisily on the tin rooftop.

Before I reached the bedroom door, I thought I heard muffled voices, but the raindrops were so loud that I couldn't be sure. I opened the door partway. The sounds of murmuring were clearer now. One of the voices was Mary's. The other one sounded all too familiar as well. I pushed the door wide open and stood there, shocked, looking down at the naked bodies of my oldest daughter and the father of three of my children, lying wrapped in each other's arms in the middle of my bed.

I gasped and almost dropped my baby girl, too stunned to speak. I think my heart may have stopped beating for a moment. They looked up at me, both together. Mary shrieked and leapt up, snatching her crumpled dress from the floor. Before she managed to cover herself, I had a clear view of her taut rosebud nipples, slick with saliva, and her sandy-colored pubic hair, tangled and viscous. Henry stood up as well but made no effort to cover himself and his stiff member, which was beginning to shrink under my enraged gaze. I knew it well. It was large for such a small man, and he was proud of it.

I stood there with my mouth agape until the words finally came. "My God, Henry," I sobbed. "How could you?" I looked at him and saw an old man in his mid-sixties, standing on one side of the bed, while my daughter, in her early twenties, stood on the other side in shock, her eyes filled with tears.

"How could you?" I repeated. He said nothing, just stared at me wide-eyed. "And you, Mary...oh, Mary." I groaned miserably, shaking my head. When I realized I was trembling all over, I laid Rosalia in her crib and grabbed a post of the big bed to keep from falling. Thank God the child had not awakened in the midst of this monstrous situation. I rubbed my eyes hard with my hands, trying to erase the scene I had witnessed, but it was etched in my mind. I will never forget the startled faces of my daughter and my lover, so close together, their pupils wide with desire, stunned with mutual surprise. I wanted to kill Henry DuBignon at that moment, more than

I had ever wanted anything in my life.

"Oh, Mum," Mary began, her voice tearful. "Mummy, I'm so sorry."

Henry just stood there, naked and silent, until finally and slowly he began to gather up his clothes. He wiped himself with his undershirt before he put it on.

"Get out," I said to him. "Get dressed and get out. I never want to see you again." My eyes were narrowed now, and my voice was full of suppressed rage. "And you, Mary," I turned in quiet fury toward my oldest daughter. "Go to your room and stay there." Clutching her dress to her bosom, she rushed from the bedroom, whimpering.

As for Henry, he took his time putting on his trousers and shirt, apparently gathering his nerve to speak.

"Sarah," he said finally. "I can't—"

"Don't say another word, Henry DuBignon. Just get out of my house." Even as I said it, I knew it was not my house but his, and that I was living on his charity. It humiliated me to think about it.

He could obviously see that I didn't want to have any kind of conversation with him, nor did he try to justify himself or engage in a quarrel. He just buttoned his pants and walked out into the hallway, down the stairs, and out the front door, leaving it ajar. I followed him and slammed the door behind him. Then I sat down on the sofa, dazed, and let myself weep out the great sobs that were rising up within me. I didn't care if Mary heard. I wanted her to. I wanted her to know how much she had hurt me with her wantonness.

A thought flitted through my mind. *So this is how Amelia felt.* I quickly brushed it away. *My own daughter. How could she?* But I knew how charming Henry could be when he wanted to, even now as an aging man. Mary was young, innocent, easily seduced, I suspected, like I had been by her father, but at least George had been handsome and not yet thirty, while Henry was three times her age. *And George had the decency to marry me.*

Then another fleeting thought: *Was it my bad example? Did she learn from me?* But I couldn't accept that. No, it was all his fault. *The bastard.*

The other three children suddenly burst in the front door, soaking wet and laughing. As he crossed the portal, Leonidas, the last of the three, was in the middle of a sentence. "We found Papa's horse in the barn, but he—" He stopped, suddenly silent as he caught sight of his brother and sister, standing stock still, staring at their tearful mother on the settee.

"What's wrong, Mum?" Fredonia asked finally. "Are you all right?"

I put my face in my hands and said, "I can't talk right now. Just go to your rooms and leave me alone for a while. I'll speak with you later."

Once I could weep no more, I sat there for a long time, staring into the cold grate of the fireplace and thinking of Mary.

Finally, she tiptoed down the stairs and came into the parlour. Her eyes were red from crying, but she had brushed her hair and tried to make herself look presentable.

"I'm so ashamed, Mummy. Can you ever forgive me?"

I stared coldly at her. "Was this the first time?"

Her face blanched, and silently she shook her head, ever so slightly.

"How long has it been going on? And where do you meet him?"

She had nothing to gain by lying, but I could see tears standing in her eyes.

"About four months. We meet different places…mostly at night after everyone has gone to bed. This was the first time here."

"In my bed." I felt numb, not knowing whether to let myself feel fury or grief. "My own daughter."

"I'm so sorry, Mum. I'm so sorry." A tear streaked down her cheek. "It just happened, and I didn't know how to stop it."

I could see her heart breaking. "Do you love him?" I asked.

She tearfully shook her head. "I don't know."

"Come here, Mary." She looked at me apprehensively, as though she were afraid I might strike her, but I spoke gently. "Come here and sit beside me." I patted the settee cushion.

She came with a cautious expression, looking for the first time into my eyes. I took her in my arms.

"Oh, Mummy. I'm so sorry." She was sobbing now.

"Shhh," I whispered. How could Henry DuBignon do this to my daughter? Well, I thought, this time he wouldn't get away with it. This time I *would* take him to court and accuse him of raping a child. I doubted that the courts would see her as a child, but that's what she was to me. My innocent daughter.

"How did it begin?" I asked. Then I thought better of it. She started to speak, but I put my fingers to her lips. "No, don't tell me. I'd rather not know."

This explained a lot about Henry's behavior of late and his reluctance to talk about marriage. No doubt he had watched Mary grow prettier over the years, with her blond hair flashing in the sunlight and her body developing into that of a tantalizing young woman. Perhaps he had just been biding his time, waiting like a scavenger for younger flesh. I supposed that's what I had been to him, younger flesh, back when it all began. But this time, he would not just walk away. This time he would take responsibility for what he had done.

I don't know how long Mary and I sat there holding each other, but when we finally went up to bed, we were both calmer, just trying to be mother and daughter again, despite lingering tensions.

It was about three weeks later when Mary came into my bedroom after all the other children had gone to sleep.

"Can we talk?" she asked in a soft voice.

"Yes. Sit down." She settled on the edge of the bed, where I was tucked in, trying to lose myself in an English novel called *Jane Eyre* that I had managed to have sent from Savannah.

Mary and I had been walking on eggshells around one another of late, and I thought a talk might do us both good. I had forgiven Mary, or at least tried to, but not Henry. His betrayal was unthinkable. Had it been one of the slave women, I would have been less surprised, but how could he do such a thing to my daughter? She did not have the experience to protect herself from his wily behavior. I remembered how, once he had made up his mind to have me as his mistress, nothing seemed to deter him. He wore me down, just as I suspect he had done with my daughter. I could forgive her, but not him.

"Mum, I need to tell you something." I could see apprehension in her eyes.

"What is it, Mary? I thought you had told me everything there was to tell."

"I've missed my monthly bleeding twice now. Do you think something is wrong?"

Was she so naïve? Did she not know what that portended?

I nodded soberly. "Yes, my dear. Something is very wrong. You're probably pregnant." I did nothing to soften the news and used the coarser word intentionally. I saw an expression of horror cross her face. "Have you felt nauseous in the mornings?"

She nodded almost imperceptibly and whispered, "Sometimes."

"And are your breasts tender to the touch?"

She sat still for a moment then gave the slightest nod.

I could feel my jaw clench. "Then it's almost certain. You're probably with child."

Her face blanched. "What can I do?" she asked. "Is God punishing me?"

"Well, that's one way to look at it. Another is that when you engage in such actions, pregnancy is a logical consequence," I said bluntly. Had I taught her nothing? I didn't know whether to laugh or cry. It was all so absurd. How could this be happening?

"What will I do?" she asked.

"You will have to take responsibility for your actions. And so will Henry." And I meant it. He would not do to my daughter what he had done to me. He may be in his mid-sixties, while she was more than forty years younger, but he *would* make it right, however much it might humiliate all concerned, including me.

CHAPTER 15

The next morning, I had Leonidas hook up the buggy for me, and I drove myself to the DuBignon house. There must have been an indomitable look on my face when I arrived, tied the horse and buggy to the hitching post, and marched up the front steps. I certainly felt indomitable. I knocked loudly. Henry's oldest daughter, Eliza, opened the door. When she saw me standing there, she tried to close it again, but I blocked it with my foot and pushed back. I was stronger than she was and far more determined.

"You are not welcome here." There was bitterness in her voice.

"I want to see your father. Now," I said.

"He isn't here."

"I don't believe you."

"He isn't here, I tell you."

"Well then, I'll come in and wait."

"No, I'll tell him you came by. You're not welcome here."

"I'll wait." I knew that if he was not in the house, he would come home for dinner. I brushed past her and made my way to the parlour. I had been in the house only once before, and that is where I'd waited while the DuBignon cook prepared food for our first day on the island. It was many years ago, but I remembered it vividly.

Eliza was over forty now. In fact, she was older than I was. Her hair was pulled back in a tight bun that made her look like the spinster she had become. Now that her mother was gone, she had taken on the role of lady of the house. She gave me one last venomous look when she saw that her words were ineffective and went to fetch one of her brothers. It was John Couper who appeared next.

"What business do you have here?" he asked.

"My business is with your father," I replied.

He looked nonplussed. I had no fear of him or any authority he might assume. He could not very well remove a woman bodily from the house. He wouldn't dare. His only weapons were words, and he knew it.

"Please leave at once," he said again.

"Why are you not working?" I asked.

He looked startled by my impertinence. "That's none of your concern," he answered. Then he turned on his heel and strode out of the room. I could hear him and his sister behind closed doors arguing about what they should do, but I sat stiffly in a Victorian parlour chair, resolved not to move until Henry returned.

I waited more than an hour before he finally walked in the front door. "Sarah!" he said. "I thought that was your buggy outside. What are you doing here?"

I sensed apprehension in his voice and rose to my feet. "I have come to give you an ultimatum, Henry DuBignon."

"Sarah, if it's about marrying you—"

"It has nothing to do with marrying me. I wouldn't have you after you have defiled my daughter. But she is with child—your child. And you will not do to her what you've done to me. You will not shame her and make her give birth unwed."

"What are you saying?" He looked aghast.

"I'm saying that you *will* make an honest woman of Mary." I moved closer until we were eye to eye, and I watched the color drain from his face.

He stared at me for a moment or two before he spoke. "Sit down now, and let's talk about this. The age difference would make it ludicrous, don't you think? Besides, how do you know the baby is mine?"

I slapped his face in fury, and he caught my arm. "Stop it! What's gotten into you?"

"You know very well that my daughter was a virgin before you…you violated her. You are also fully aware that she's never been with another man. I curse fate that it had to be you. You're not worthy of her."

"Sarah, be reasonable. Perhaps there is a midwife on the island who can—"

"Don't you *dare* suggest such a thing. You *will* marry her and provide for her and the child. Then, when this baby is born, you can go to hell for all I care. Your only alternative is to face a lawsuit. This one I could win, and you know it. Your name would be dragged in the mud throughout Glynn County. President of a bank! You couldn't be president of an outhouse after that."

At that point, Eliza, who could hear me lecturing her father, came into the room again.

"What's this all about, Papa?" she asked.

Henry just stood there, trying to come up with words to respond.

"He raped my daughter, if you must know, and now she's expecting a baby. He has no choice but to marry her immediately. Or else he will be very sorry."

"I didn't rape her, Sarah, as you well know. She was quite willing."

"My father has been very good to you, Mrs. Aust," Eliza interrupted. "He has provided for you for years. How dare you accuse him of such a thing and make demands of this kind?"

I gave a humorless laugh. "Good to me? How naïve you are, my dear. What a fool your father has made of his entire family, including your dear, departed mother."

At that, Eliza lunged forward and grabbed my hair. I shoved her backwards and she almost fell.

"Eliza! Sarah! Stop it at once, and act like ladies," Henry shouted, stepping between us. "This is my problem, and I'll deal with it. Now stop it!" Eliza and I stood there glaring at one another, but there was no more violence.

"Sarah, let's go out on the porch to talk," he said.

"Your horse is outside. You will follow me to *my* house, and we'll talk there," I ordered.

Henry looked toward his distraught daughter and nodded. "Perhaps that *would* be best."

He walked with me out the front door, while Eliza just stood there, wringing her hands. As I started to climb into my buggy, he stopped me. "Sarah, can't we talk now? I'm sorry this ever happened, but she was so beautiful. She reminded me of you when we first met."

"Ha!" I scoffed. "She looks nothing like me. She's blond like her father and has his features, not mine. If that were your excuse, you would have chosen Fredonia. She looks more like me, with her dark hair and eyes. No, you just lusted after that ripe, young flesh."

"I confess that I did want her," he replied. "But you and I both know she's too young for me. I'm forty-four years older than she is. Everyone would think it ridiculous if we wed. If you're going to insist on a marriage, I would prefer to marry you. She doesn't know anything about life or taking care of a home or anything of the sort. You and I, we're more suited."

"Don't try to play us against one another, Henry. I know you too well, and frankly, I don't want you anymore. I've already gone through the humiliation and scorn of having three children by you without the benefit of marriage. My daughter won't suffer the same thing. Once this baby is born, she can leave you for all I care, and I won't object. But you're going to go through with this and you *will* support her and her child. Now follow me." I climbed into the buggy and glared down at him. "Get on your horse. Now."

He stood there for a few moments, staring at me with indecision. Then he sighed with resignation and climbed on his aging mare. I noticed that Henry didn't mount so agilely as he once did. His hair was gray now, and his eyes were cloudy. He had become an old man who postured about, wearing a long cloak and carrying a silver-headed cane that, in his mind, denoted authority.

Do I really want to do this to my daughter? I wondered for a moment. But the alternative was public humiliation. I knew it very well, and I had no intention of letting her experience the shame I had felt. *She's already slept with him for more than four months. He couldn't be too repellent to her,* I thought. *But what of me?* I had given ten years of my life to this man. Did I want to give him up this way? He had just told me he'd rather marry me instead. A part of me was torn, but my anger as a mother won out, as did my disgust at his betrayal.

Once we reached my house, I called Mary to the front porch, where the three of us stood in uncomfortable proximity to talk it out. My face felt like stone as I confronted them both.

"Henry is going to marry you, Mary," I told her.

"When?" she asked.

"Tomorrow." I was giving him no time to make up excuses. She looked perplexed as she gazed from me to her future husband, unsure how to react. But I didn't see distaste on her face. At least I could spare her the dishonor I had suffered, and I felt I was doing the right thing. "This baby will not be born illegitimate."

Henry and Mary both stood there at first like mute children. My daughter could see, no doubt, that her life as a carefree young woman was over, but she had always been acquiescent, even as a child. She would do whatever she was told. As for Henry, he finally found a voice.

"Sarah, I will agree to this marriage because obviously I have no choice."

"That's right, Henry. You remember that. For you it's a matter of life or death." And I meant it.

"You don't have to threaten me, Sarah. I understand the situation, but I have one request. If I'm going to marry, I'd like to marry in the eyes of God. I've heard that there is a Catholic bishop in town, a former missionary recently returned from Africa. I'd like to have him perform the ceremony, but it will require some dispensations. Can you give me three days to see if I can work it out?"

"You know there is no Catholic church in Brunswick. If you think you can avoid this marriage by coming up with some stupid Catholic law, it isn't going to work, Henry." I didn't know what he was up to, and I didn't care. It could be a civil marriage as far as I was concerned. As long as it was legal.

"There's no church, that's true, but there is a mission. And he's a bishop. That's a good thing, because bishops can grant dispensations. Just give me time to make the arrangements. I swear we'll be married in three days."

It occurred to me that a religious wedding might compel Henry to take the vows a bit more seriously, at least as seriously as he had taken his vows to Amelia. For that reason, I gave in.

"I'll give you three days. But the wedding will be on Tuesday—three days from now—whether you've worked it out or not. You *will* marry my daughter. If you don't have your dispensations by Tuesday, you'll be married by a judge."

It was ludicrous that he would soon be my son-in-law. I would have no part in their lives, but I would find *some* way to survive with my other children. I would leave the island, move away someplace, though I had no idea how or where. The future was completely blank as far as I was concerned. But none of that mattered now. This marriage *would* take place.

On the early morning of Tuesday, November 23, four of the plantation slaves rowed us through the mists of the marsh creeks to the mainland, where I demanded that Henry rent a carriage to drive us to the Glynn County courthouse. When we arrived, court was not in session, and the courthouse halls were quiet and empty, except for one man standing just inside the heavy oak door. He wore a black ankle-length robe with buttons down the front and adorned with a red sash. He also had on a small red cap, a clerical collar, and wore a gold cross around his neck. This, I assumed, was the bishop in question.

"Thank you for coming, Father," Henry said, bending down to kiss the large purple ring on the man's right hand. As he introduced us, the bishop turned to Mary and me, gazing at us with what seemed to me a critical eye.

"Your Excellency, this is my bride-to-be, Mary Aust, and this is her mother Sarah." The bishop nodded politely.

"I hope you will excuse us for a moment, Father," Henry continued. "There's paperwork we need to sign in the ordinary's office before the ceremony. And then, as we agreed, I trust we will hold the wedding in the courtroom. I'm grateful for the dispensation all this required."

"Well, as you pointed out to me, Mr. DuBignon, the circumstances are, shall we say…somewhat urgent. I'm glad I was able to oblige."

"That's very kind of you. I'm sure," I said.

"I've recently come from a mission in west Africa, and I've seen quite a few rather unusual marriage circumstances. It's not uncommon when one is doing God's work in other parts of the world."

"Nonetheless, I'm very grateful." Henry seemed obsequious toward the bishop. I'd never seen him show such deference to anyone before.

The bishop nodded and said, "I'm glad I was here to help, and your pledge of assistance for the new church will go a long way to making it a reality."

I looked at Henry. So that was how he did it. I might have known that he would find some devious way to persuade the bishop to do his bidding. I have no doubt that he also told him his life depended on it. And perhaps it did. I *was* angry enough to kill the man. But who knew what, or how much, he had promised? I'd put nothing past him.

"If the judge is in," the bishop said, "you might ask him if someone from his office would be willing to witness the ceremony. And you, Mrs. Aust, can serve as the other witness." I gave a brisk nod, and we turned to go into the county ordinary's office.

I stood by while Henry paid the necessary fees for the licence. Then, despite raised eyebrows among courthouse staff, Henry strode directly into the judge's office, licence in hand, and in a few minutes both Henry and the judge emerged and turned to go toward the courtroom, beckoning Mary and me to follow. I was anxious to get it over with.

I stood through the ceremony, feeling caught in a bad dream, as I watched my daughter marry the father of three of my children. But I would not let the dream end until I saw the words on paper: "This certifies that Col. Henry DuBignon and Miss Mary Aust were duly joined in marriage this day the twenty-third of November A.D.

1852 by Edward Barron, Bp of Carinthia." They were now man and wife. It was on record, and no one could change or dispute that. I was satisfied. At least the determined mother part of me was.

It was a somber trip as we glided back through the tidal creeks toward the island, especially after I heard Mary ask in a plaintive voice, "Where will we live, Henry?"

He looked at her blankly. It was clear that he hadn't given it any thought. "Why, at Henry's house, of course," I said.

Henry looked at me as though I were insane. "With my children there?"

"She's your wife now, Henry. You have a home, and you will take her there."

"Sarah, you know that they will not accept her as a stepmother. I thought she would just live with you, at least for now," he said.

"She's your wife, Henry, and she belongs with her husband. You will take her to your home." I felt a sense of power I had never felt before, and it was sustaining me and holding off the other complicated emotions I knew would soon come. "I'll pack her bags and send them to your house as soon as we get back to Jekyl."

The rest of the trip passed in silence, except for the mournful songs of the black boatmen, who synchronized the strokes of the oars to the rhythms of their voices. I found them soothing, and I tried to think of nothing but the doleful chants and the chill in the air that portended the coming of winter.

Mary looked miserable, for both she and I knew what she would have to face at her new "home," but she too needed to learn that actions have consequences, and facing Henry's children would be hers. A carriage waited for us at the landing. I had the driver stop at the DuBignon house to drop off the newlyweds.

"I'll have her things sent over," I said, feeling only a tinge of guilt at Mary's stricken face as she watched me drive away. I looked back at her slumped shoulders as she walked up the front steps on

Henry's arm.

Fredonia, Leonidas, and William were all lined up on the front porch when I arrived home. "Where's your baby sister?" I asked.

"Taking a nap," Fredonia replied. "Where is Mary?"

"She's with her new husband," I replied in what I hoped was an indifferent voice.

"Did she really marry that old man?" Fredonia asked.

"Yes, she did."

Fredonia burst into tears and ran back into the house and up the stairs toward the room she had shared with her older sister. Leonidas and William just stood there, open-mouthed but silent. They looked at me, their eyes filled with questions they dared not ask. I don't know how much any of them knew, though I gathered from Fredonia's reaction that her sister had confided in her.

I didn't see Mary again for two more days. Then, on Friday morning she came running down the road, her face stained with tears and her hair disheveled.

"Please let me come home, Mummy. Please," she begged as soon as she reached the porch. "They're just awful to me. They call me vile names and spew out all kinds of meanness."

"They're your stepchildren now, Mary. Tell Henry that he must insist they show you respect."

"He's so ashamed that he doesn't even like to face them. We even have to eat our meals in a separate room."

"They'll get over it in time."

"How much time? I think I'll die if I have to live there."

"Henry is your husband now. You might suggest he find the two of you another place to live. You can't stay here. You're a married woman. Your brothers and sisters and I will be leaving the island as soon as I can make other arrangements." At the moment, I had no idea what they would be. But Mary must understand that this was her new life. "You should have thought of the consequences when you decided to let Henry take your virginity."

"Mum, I didn't encourage him. He just kept touching me…urging me to do things I didn't really want to do. He did it slowly, making me feel—" She was crying again. "Then…then one night he…oh, God! What have I done?" She broke down completely, sobbing now like a lost child.

I couldn't help but feel sympathy for my daughter, and of course I relented. "You can stay here tonight, Mary. But you and Henry must talk about all this. You must face facts. He is your husband now. You are his wife. You must take on the responsibility."

She reached toward me, and I responded as any mother would and opened my arms to her. But I was determined that Henry DuBignon had to deal with this problem and help her to grow up. After all, she was his responsibility now.

He didn't show his face until the next day. When he came riding up, I was already standing at the door.

"Is she here?" he asked.

"She is. And she was quite miserable when she arrived."

"Thank God. I was afraid she had— Thank God she's all right."

"Do you really care, Henry?" I asked archly.

"Sarah, I know I've made a mess of things. But I've talked to my children and told them that they have to be civil toward her. No more ugliness, and I meant it. I don't expect her to live with them forever. We'll find another place somewhere else, maybe even off the island. I'll be good to her, I promise. Looks like I've ruined everybody's life." I almost thought I saw a tear glistening in his eye.

Seeing even an ounce of remorse in Henry DuBignon was something new. Col. DuBignon, as he always wanted to be called, had thought he ruled the world—certainly the island—as he strutted about with his fancy cane. He'd always thought he could do whatever he pleased, with no consideration for anyone else. Now his deeds had caught up with him, and he had made everyone in his life unhappy. Was he really contrite? Who could tell? Any ounce of love I had ever felt for him seemed to have vanished.

"I'll take her back home now," he said.

I called Mary to the parlour to meet Henry. She came down slowly, apprehensively, but she came down. She was wearing a long-sleeved brown wool dress that she hadn't worn in years. She always said she hated it, that it looked so somber, but it must have fit her mood. Her dark blond hair was pinned up like a matron's.

"Mary," Henry said, "I'm sorry for the way my children treated you. They should know better. I can promise that they won't behave like that again. They may never love you, but they will be civil from now on, or else I will disown them. I think they understand that now. Come back with me, and let's try to make this work. I know I'm an old man to you, but I still have the vigor of a younger man and I'll do all I can to make you happy." He touched her arm. "Please?"

Mary looked at me, and I nodded. "You must go. You will have to face them sooner or later. Better now, I think. They've been chastened by their father." She looked miserable, but she did not question her duty.

After they left, I began to think of my own situation. My children and I certainly couldn't stay here. I needed help without question. But where could I find it? *Perhaps*, I thought, *it is time to try to reconcile with my uncle.*

I had no idea whether Uncle William would ever want to see me again after the way George had acted, but I wanted to make whatever arrangements I could before winter set in. It was rarely very cold in the area, but traveling on the water in December and January could be quite chilling, and I certainly didn't want to go through another winter on Jekyl. The thought was too depressing.

As a consequence, the next day I wrote to my uncle an abject and long-overdue apology for my husband's appalling behavior that day more than twenty years ago. I assured him that George had not spoken for me, and I did not share his views. I had seen mixed-raced couples on a few occasions back in England, but I had still been a bit shocked about my uncle's relationship because she was still a slave, though I didn't mention any of that in the letter. I did inform him that my husband had died many years ago and that I would have contacted him long before "had I not been so humiliated by George's snobbish behavior that I feared you would never want to see me again." Now, I confessed, I had fallen on difficult times and was begging him to consider letting us come to stay with him just until I could find a suitable situation. I chose not to explain all the complications and my relationship with Henry DuBignon, though I feared he may have heard rumors about it.

To make such a request was no doubt presumptuous of me, given how George had behaved. But this was *my* uncle, not George's, and I hoped that, as my mother's brother, he might be willing to help us. He was now a rich man. Four years earlier, I'd heard, he had inherited his uncle Thomas Dover's plantation of about nine hundred acres called Dover Hall. With it came seventy-two slaves and all the livestock on the plantation. I knew he could afford to take us in for a while if he had a mind to, but it was only with trepidation that I sent the letter.

He wrote back at once, expressing pleasure to hear from me. He had visited London, he said, in 1839, and at the time he assured my mother that he had seen me and that I was well. She was delighted, he said. The letter went on:

> *I did not explain to them that your husband and I had a falling out during our first visit and that I had not seen you since that first encounter. I saw no sense in worrying her further. At the time your mother was well, and I hear from her from time to time. I also assured her that, if you ever needed me, I was there to help. I am pleased to know that I can now be of service to you and your children. By all means, you are welcome at Dover Hall until you sort out your situation.*

His words made it clear that he did not intend this to be a permanent arrangement.

Then, he went on to explain that when he had inherited Dover Hall, he'd also inherited his "wife," Peggy, and their children. He'd sent them to live in Freetown, Massachusetts, where they were now free from the scourge of slavery. "*I visit them as often as I can and still love them with all my heart*," he wrote. I noticed that he called Peggy his "wife," yet, knowing the laws of Georgia, I knew they could not be legally married, at least not here. Nevertheless, he made it clear that in his heart he considered them to be loyally wed in the eyes of God.

Most important, to me at least, was that we would be welcome to come for an extended visit until I could figure something out. I wrote him back at once, expressing my thanks and indicating that we would arrive as soon as I could pack up our belongings. It seemed for once that things were going to work out for my family.

I didn't tell the children about our good luck right away for fear something might go wrong. That proved to be a terrible mistake, for I woke up only a day later and, to my shock, found Fredonia gone. She had left a note.

> *My dear mother, I can no longer stay here without Mary. It is far too lonely and depressing. I am going to be married as well—today—and I'll be leaving for Jacksonville with my new husband. You have met him. He is the young carpenter, Will Harris, we met in Brunswick two years ago. He is twenty-three years old and very handsome. He has even made arrangements for us to be married in a church by the Rev. Benjamin C. Franklin. I will contact you once we are settled.*

Will Harris? *Who was that?* I thought for several moments. Then I suddenly recalled a young man of that name we had encountered in Brunswick one day, where he and his father had been summoned from Jacksonville to help in much-needed repairs for the dock. It was specialized work that the town didn't want to trust to the local carpenters. As we climbed out of the boat from Jekyl, Fredonia tripped over a small but unexpected piece of lumber lying on the dock. It was this young man, this Will Harris, who had reached out to keep her from falling. I remembered him only because his sun-bleached hair and light blue eyes, as well as his rescue of Fredonia, had reminded me just a bit of my husband George. He was an attractive young man, but it seemed to me that the encounter was too brief to lead anywhere further.

Did Fredonia return to the dock during the walk she took that day, while I shopped for fabric to make a new dress? Where could she have seen him since then? Had he come to the island without my knowledge? Had they corresponded? If they had, I might not know, for it was always the girls who went to meet the mail boat. Had they made arrangements to meet again the few times we had gone into Brunswick since then? I had no idea. I could only accept the fact that both of my daughters had grown up behind my back and begun to make their own independent lives while my attention was focused elsewhere. I hadn't thought much about what they did during all those hours I had spent alone with Henry DuBignon. No doubt I had only myself to blame.

Fredonia was eighteen now, not an unusual age for a girl to marry. I could only hope she had chosen wisely and wish her well. At the bottom of the note, she wrote, "*By the time you read this I may already be Mrs. William Ewen Harris, Jr. I love him.*" I wished her good luck in my heart and prayed that she had found happiness.

I couldn't blame her for wanting to leave the island and start a new life somewhere else. That was my goal as well. Nevertheless, I would miss her terribly. My two oldest daughters, who had been my closest companions for so many years—both gone. Now, there was no one with whom I could share adult conversations. So much had to remain locked up inside. I knew I would miss them forever. It was unlikely, given the circumstances, that I would see much of Mary, and visiting Jacksonville was even harder, though not impossible. Perhaps I could stay in touch with Fredonia if she let me know her whereabouts.

Thus, with both my daughters now married, only four of us—Leonidas, William, Rosalia, and I—left the island at dawn a week later, savoring the rosy mist of sunrise on the water. By the time we reached Brunswick and started our long, fourteen-mile drive to Dover Hall in a rented buggy, the sun was high. Uncle William, who was expecting us, had seen us coming down the road toward sunset and was waiting on the big verandah, with open arms and a bright smile.

"Welcome, Sarah. I'm glad to see you again. So these are your children."

I introduced Leonidas and William, who at twelve and almost ten were, I hoped, old enough to be of use to him on the plantation. Then, I presented four-year-old Rosalia, whom Uncle William instantly dubbed "a little sweetheart" as he patted her dark curls.

He took us in and showed us to our rooms. Dover Hall was said to be one of the finest plantation houses in the county. Of its six spacious rooms, the boys would share one, while Rosalia and I would share another. Both were pleasant, sunny rooms with large windows overlooking magnificent live oak trees and nearby cotton fields. It was a quiet house, at least until my boys arrived, though Uncle William often complained about missing Peggy.

"Why did you send her away?" I asked. "Couldn't she have stayed here?"

"Her life here had no dignity. I didn't want to keep her a slave, which is how she would always be perceived in Georgia. As much as I miss her and our children, I wanted them to have their freedom. I hate slavery."

But he now owned many slaves and had freed none of the others. I said nothing, though he must have seen in my eyes the question I did not ask, for he nodded at me.

"I know," he said. "I inherited a lot of slaves. But running this cotton plantation, I have no real choice but to keep them. If I let them go, someone else would just enslave them. It's the only life they know. I treat them well, and most of them seem to prefer it here than any other plantation they've ever lived on. I hope they're reasonably happy. My overseer says I don't work them hard enough, but I want them to have good lives, at least as best they can."

"Have you seen your Peggy since they went away?" I asked.

"I have. She and the children can't come back to Georgia without considerable risk, but I visit them during the summer months."

"How many children do you and Peggy have?"

"She just wrote to me that she's expecting our ninth. I was there last summer." His voice sounded proud.

"How do you travel?"

"Most of the time I hitch a ride to Freetown with a friendly sea captain who lives there. He comes to Georgia each September and hauls loads of rice and cotton back up north in May. I go with him and spend the summers with my family. I stay as long as I can, but I need to be home for cotton picking. I've told Peggy that when I die, I want my body shipped to Freetown so that we can be buried side by side." Uncle William looked sad. "If I can't always live with her, at least I can lie with her in death."

"You must love her very much." I was envious that she could evoke such devotion in a man. "I'm so sorry about the way George behaved all those years ago. He was really not a bad man."

"Oh, he wasn't the only one. Unfortunately, we grew accustomed to such reactions. It was one of the reasons I sent Peggy away—so that she could live a dignified life. I didn't want my children humiliated every time a white person took offense. Needless to say, we didn't have much of a social life when she was here, though now I'm welcome in any plantation parlour in Glynn County, for they know she's gone and that I'm a rich man. Such shallow people."

"I understand how they can be. I'm sure you've heard rumors about my situation with Henry DuBignon." I knew it wasn't the same thing, but I was well familiar with judgmental people. I could only imagine what they were saying now that Henry had shown utter disregard for me by taking up with my daughter Mary.

"I've heard a bit of it, and I gather, given the boys' resemblance to the DuBignon children, that they are his. What happened? I thought you might marry him after his wife died," he observed.

"He decided he preferred my daughter instead," I said bluntly. There was no point in trying to dissemble. He would know sooner or later, and I thought it best to be honest.

"Good heavens! He's old enough to be her grandfather," he said. "I'm appalled. You are still a fine-looking woman, Sarah. He's an obvious philanderer. You're better off without him."

I was grateful that he didn't condemn me as so many others did and thanked him for his understanding.

"Who am I to judge?" he said. "I know what it's like to be condemned by people who don't know the whole story or understand the emotions and complexities involved. I'm just glad I can help for a while."

In May, six months after her marriage to Henry, I received news that Mary had given birth to a little girl named Virginia Elizabeth. Perhaps I should have been happy for my daughter's safe delivery and that I was now a grandmother. But my only satisfaction was in seeing Henry DuBignon deprived of another son.

CHAPTER 16

I was grateful to Uncle William for taking us in during our time of need, but I didn't want to be a burden. When he went north for the summer months before the cotton harvest to be with his family in Freetown, we stayed at Dover Hall and did our best to look after things. The boys were growing and could be increasingly helpful if they chose to be, though Leonidas seldom did, and William was his shadow. Then, when a letter from Fredonia finally caught up with me and she told me where she was living—in Jacksonville, of course—we began to make plans to visit her during some of the winter months so that Uncle William could enjoy his peaceful home for a period of time without three noisy children underfoot. Our stay had already stretched well beyond a year. I didn't want us to become unwelcome guests, and I hoped perhaps that our occasional absences might help him tolerate us a bit longer.

Fredonia was expecting her first child by then, and in 1854, she too gave birth to a little girl, named Frances Marguerite. They called her Fanny. I went to Jacksonville to be of help with her first childbirth and each time another child was born. It was while I was visiting for the birth of her second child, a boy I'm proud to say, that I met Willis Reddick.

Each day Fredonia would walk down to the dock to take a meal to her husband, who was working to replace rotting boards and shore up the pilings. Rosalia and I often went with her. We would all sit together, our feet dangling off the edge of the dock, to eat whatever Fredonia had prepared that day—boiled potatoes, pastries, and something she called "sandwiches"—meat between two pieces of bread. I taught her how to make Bedfordshire clangers, a treat I had learned from my mother ever so long ago. They were easy to transport, nourishing, and a change from Will's usual pot of stew or slices of bread with a chunk of meat.

One day while we sat there digesting our meal and watching the boats dance in the harbour, a fishing boat pulled up to the dock and Will called out, "Any luck this morning, Capt. Reddick?" The man certainly didn't look like a sea captain in his shrimp boat. I had always envisioned a captain as smartly attired, giving orders to his crew. But Capt. Reddick was disheveled and working alongside his two helpers instead of just giving them orders. I supposed "captain" was a label that people around here gave to the skipper of any boat.

"A pretty good haul, I'd say," the man shouted back.

"Come and meet my wife and mother-in-law and the rest of her family once you've sorted your catch."

"I'd say I'm far too smelly for such ladies. Perhaps later," he replied, "after I've had a chance to clean up."

As it turned out, Will invited Capt. Reddick to come to their house for Sunday dinner, with Fredonia's agreement. They were all too obviously trying their hand at matchmaking. Will said he thought I was much too young to remain a widow for the rest of my life. Or maybe he just wanted to get me out of the house. Who's to say? In any case, Capt. Reddick, a sun-wrinkled, middle-aged widower with no children, seemed to take a liking to me and began to visit on a regular basis during my stay with my daughter's family. And when I was preparing to leave, he asked if he might call on me in Brunswick sometime.

"I've been thinking about trying my hand at shrimping up around those Georgia islands. I'm already working in the waters off Amelia Island, and it's only a short distance up to Cumberland and Jekyl. There's plenty of fish in those waters, I hear, and the shrimping is good."

I assured him I had no objections and that I would be happy to see him again. I don't think my boys liked him very much. They usually vanished whenever he was about, but Rosalia, who followed me everywhere, looked forward to the visits of "Mr. Reddick," who almost always happened to find a peppermint drop in his pocket for her. He wasn't handsome and sophisticated like George, nor was he charming and persuasive like Henry. Certainly he wasn't wealthy, by any stretch of the imagination. He was just a simple fisherman, but he seemed steady and reliable. After all I'd been through, those qualities appealed to me at the moment. He didn't try to seduce me, which would only have been comical, and I suspect he had no inkling how to go about it.

When I returned to Dover Hall, Capt. Reddick did indeed come to call. He would sail his small boat up a branch of the Turtle River all the way to the dock at Uncle William's plantation. His appearances were fairly frequent during the mid-summer while my uncle was away. He was attentive in his awkward way. Under normal circumstances, I probably would not have been the slightest bit interested in such a man, but I was desperate to find another situation. I had promised Uncle William that our stay would be temporary, but it had stretched into years. We had already tarried far longer than I had intended to. I feared he was becoming weary of our presence, though he was too polite to say so. The boys were growing up. Leonidas was already seventeen and William fourteen. It was time they began to learn a trade, especially since their education hadn't been what I had hoped it would be.

Finally, in March 1857, Capt. Reddick got down on one knee like a young swain in the parlour of Dover Hall, and he asked for my hand in marriage. I wanted to laugh when his knee cracked as he knelt. But I managed to refrain as I agreed without hesitation to his proposal. He scrambled to his feet again, smiling broadly, and gave me an awkward kiss. I couldn't help but contrast that kiss with the first time Henry took me in his arms. In some sense, those two kisses personified the men themselves—Henry self-assured and well-practiced, a man who gets what he wants, and Willis inexperienced, self-conscious, and insecure.

"Let's go tell your children," he said.

The boys were outside throwing the new ball that Willis had brought to them on his last visit. He promised to try to bring them a bat as soon as he could find one, so that they could begin to learn the new game called "base ball" he had read about in the *New York Clipper*, a newspaper that arrived in Jacksonville once a week. The game was growing popular up north, he said. He was trying to do everything he could to make the boys like him, and he thought my sons might take to the game. In the meantime, he told them, until he could get them a bat, they could use a piece of wood. So far they just pitched the ball back and forth.

I called the boys to the porch to tell them the news. Reluctantly, they gave up their game and trudged toward the front of the house. "Mr. Reddick and I have something we want you to know," I began.

"We're going to get married," Willis blurted, and the boys looked at each other in horror. When Willis saw their reaction, he went on, trying to smile. "I want you boys to come work with me on the shrimp boat," he said. "I'll take you to Jacksonville and teach you everything you need to know, and you can have an occupation that will always put food on the table."

Leonidas brushed back an unruly lock of his dark hair, which had fallen over his forehead during their exertions. "I don't want to be a fisherman," he said. "And I don't want to live in Jacksonville."

"You'll like Jacksonville," Willis persisted weakly.

"I like Brunswick better," Leonidas said.

"You just like the place you know. I think you'll take to Jacksonville once you get to meet folks." He was trying hard, and I felt a sense of sympathy toward him over my son's sullen indifference.

"I don't want to meet them. I'd rather stay here," Leonidas said.

"Me too," William echoed.

"Don't be absurd," I told my boys. "You can't stay here. Uncle William isn't interested in taking care of two boys."

"I'm nearly a man," Leonidas said, "and I want to stay in Brunswick. It doesn't have to be at Dover Hall."

"And just where would you live?" I asked, irritated at their reaction.

"We could go live with Mary and Papa," Leonidas challenged.

"What makes you think they'd want you there?"

"He's our father, ain't he? He'd have to take us in."

"Yeah," echoed William.

"We could learn trades here just as well. I don't want to be a fisherman."

"How do you know until you try it?" I asked. It was Leonidas I had to convince. William would do whatever his big brother did. I tried every argument I could think of, but it was useless.

The boys made such a fuss about it that, in the end, I finally said in disgust, "Go and live with your father then, if he'll have you. What do I care?"

Almost immediately I regretted the words, which only hardened their attitudes. There was nothing I could do. They were old enough to defy me, and I knew that if I tried to force them to go with us, I would probably fail, and they would make everybody's life miserable. In the end, they wrote to Mary. She agreed without hesitation, sending her response to both the boys and me, saying, "Henry is surrounded by females and would be delighted to have his sons around."

They came to pick up the boys the day before Willis and I were to be married. Mary's firstborn, Virginia, a girl about four, sat between her parents on the buggy seat. A second child, Emily, who looked about a year younger, sat on my daughter's lap. And Mary was clearly expecting again, I noticed with disgust. The boys had seen them coming down the road and were waiting eagerly, their little bundles of clothes lying on the verandah. Rosalia was at my side, a miserable look on her face because her brother William was leaving. She saw him as her best friend and protector, especially from Leonidas, who often picked on her.

"Be good boys now," I said as the buggy approached. It was the first time I had seen Henry and Mary since we'd left Jekyl Island. They looked like a strangely assorted little family. Anyone who didn't know better would surely assume that Henry was Mary's father or even her grandfather. Mary and the two little girls didn't get out of the wagon, but Henry climbed down to help the boys with their small parcels.

"Hello, Sarah," he said in a conciliatory voice, giving me a half-smile. "It's good to see you again."

I nodded brusquely, not trusting myself to speak. He knelt down and gave Rosalia a hug. "I'm glad to see you too, sweetheart. You help your mother now, and I hope you enjoy your new home in Jacksonville."

Rosalia, by now a gangly nine-year-old, threw her arms around his neck. "I miss you, Papa," she said, her lips quivering in her effort to hold back tears.

He gave her an extra squeeze, then stood once more and looked at me. "I hope you'll be happy, Sarah. Let us hear from you."

I did not respond.

"I love you, Mum," Mary said, holding her two little girls close to her. "This is your grandmother, my darlings," she said to them. They looked at me with curiosity, and little Virginia gave me a tentative wave.

Suddenly I was very tired. I couldn't tell if it was the burden of anger I carried around or the stress of being in their presence. I tried to smile at the little girls—my granddaughters—but it felt forced, and I could find no words. I nodded my head toward them to acknowledge the introduction and gestured back with what I hoped looked like a wave.

I had thought that either Henry or Mary would tire of their forced marriage by now and go their separate ways, but I guess Mary didn't feel that she really had the option, for how would she support her two children, and another on the way? Henry obviously continued to enjoy her fresh, young flesh. She was still in her twenties, while I knew he would celebrate his seventieth birthday in August. An absurd couple. They were no longer living on the island. Henry had bought land on the mainland, at Ellis Point on the banks of Yellow Bluff Creek.

I couldn't imagine why my sons would want to go and live with them. Perhaps they thought that, given the hostile reaction of Henry's older children to his marriage to Mary, they could gain his favor and someday inherit Jekyl Island and all his wealth. He may even have promised them that. I can only guess. But they didn't know their father as I did. I was well aware that he frequently made promises he didn't keep. Perhaps they missed their big sister. Or perhaps they found me wearisome to be around.

I felt almost a sense of relief when they said goodbye and drove away. But there was a feeling of loss as well, as two of the people I had once loved most in the world disappeared down the sandy road with my precious sons, leaving me confused and uncertain. I did my best to refocus my thoughts away from Henry and Mary and what I imagined to be their happy little home. I thought instead of Willis Reddick—the man I had agreed to marry. Rosalia took my hand and led me back inside.

Our wedding day dawned bright and sunny. Clouds and rain would no doubt have better suited my mood. It was Sunday afternoon, April 19, 1857, a week after Easter. Willis had found an aging Baptist preacher by the name of John Blackstone to marry us in a little Brunswick church. I tried to think cheerful thoughts, how I would now have my own home again and a man by my side. At forty-five, I tried to consider myself lucky to have this fresh, new start. *I still have Rosalia with me*, I thought. *And adolescent boys are always difficult. I should be grateful not to have to deal with their willful ways.* But I knew I would miss them terribly.

I knew too that I felt nothing of the love for Willis I had felt for George and Henry, no real attraction or even affection. He was, I am ashamed to admit even now, only a convenience, a way out of a situation I knew could not last. Thank God, Rosalia came with me like a docile lamb to help me face this new life.

We made our move to Jacksonville without enthusiasm, and, as I had feared, life with Mr. Reddick proved to be as dull as ditchwater. It was a relief that he was gone on his fishing trips so much of the time. When he came home, he could never quite get the smell of fish off his body, no matter how much he scrubbed. When he was there, the little house just closed in on me.

I tried to take my mind off my situation by teaching Rosalia the things she would need to know when she married, like how to sew and cook. We would take long walks along the docks, remembering with regret the sunny beaches of Jekyl and even the quiet times at Dover Hall. Now we found ourselves amidst horns and boat whistles, busy streets where one had to be careful to avoid the piles left by passing horses or mules. The noise of building all around drowned out any sounds of the ocean or the wind through the palms. The Florida, Atlantic and Gulf Central Railroad was in the process of constructing a line to Lake City, and railroad workers came and went. I had hoped that soon a line would connect Brunswick with Jacksonville, but so far the only direct options were by stagecoach or the sea.

I suppose I should have embraced all the progress going on around me, but I missed the quieter life of the plantation and the island. The only consolation was being able to see Fredonia and her family fairly often. I adored her two handsome children, Fanny and the little boy they'd named Tommy.

We had no live-in servants, but Mr. Reddick allowed me to hire a cleaning girl to help out once a week. We got by. I kept telling myself that Jacksonville was a better place to start over than Brunswick would have been, for no one in Jacksonville knew about Henry DuBignon and me. As far as anyone here knew, before I married Willis I had just been a widow named Sarah Ann Aust with a daughter named Rosalia. It was a whole new beginning. All the rest was nobody's business.

I tried to be a good wife to Willis. I really did. For more than two years I kept a clean house and made an effort to feed him what he liked. He didn't talk much, and when he did he spoke of the weather and the size of his catch and what sort of fish might be most abundant at a given time of year. He had nothing to say of any interest to me. Inside I was dying of boredom and I missed my sons. At least he wasn't too demanding and seemed content to bed me once a week on Saturday nights in his usual methodical way. Once he was satisfied, he would roll over and go directly to sleep, his snoring loud enough sometimes to wake even the cat, who would walk across our bed in protest. Our lovemaking, if one can call it that, was perfunctory, unimaginative, workmanlike. Perhaps it would be better described as marital duty. In any case, Willis lacked the practiced ways Henry had always used to satisfy me as well as himself. I thought about Henry, sometimes remembering our happy times together and then visualizing his not-so-happy times with a certain malicious glee when I imagined his reaction to having daughter after daughter by Mary, who seemed incapable of giving him a son. There were three of them now, the third born not long after I married Willis—a sweet but sickly child named Camilla. And like clockwork, Mary was once again in the family way.

The malicious side of me hoped for yet another granddaughter, knowing how Henry always wanted sons. But I must also confess that the mother in me missed Mary and that I also began to think often about those little girls. It seemed cruel that any of my granddaughters should be Henry's daughters, for I longed to be some small part of their lives, as well as the lives of my two sons, who were becoming men in my absence.

Even so, I tried to hold out and keep my marriage vows to Willis, but after a couple of years I could stand it no longer. I wanted out of this marriage. I just had to get away from the fishy smell and the tedium. Had it not been for Rosalia, I think I would have lost my mind. I knew it would be hard to explain to Willis, for he was a simple man, but I tried to do it in as kind a way as possible.

We lay in bed one Saturday night after our perfunctory marriage ritual, and I caught his attention just before he went to sleep. "Willis," I said, "I need to go back to Brunswick for a while."

"Huh? What?" he mumbled, reluctantly rousing himself.

"I said I need to go back to Brunswick for a while."

"What for?"

"I just need to, that's all. Three of my children are there, and I need to spend some time with them. I'd like to get to know my granddaughters."

"Are you going to stay at Mary's house?" he asked, clearly surprised, for he knew the whole unthinkable story.

"No, I couldn't possibly do that, and we can't afford a hotel," I told him. It would cost at least a dollar or more a day to stay in one, more than thirty dollars a month. "I could rent a little house for a few months a lot cheaper," I said. I had worked out the costs carefully. A four-room house usually rented for no more than five dollars a month. Meats cost anywhere from ten to thirteen cents a pound, and flour was three cents a pound. I could even grow my own vegetables. We could manage on just a little with his help.

"How long do you plan to stay?"

"I'd like to have a nice, long visit." What I didn't tell him was that I didn't plan to come back at all, but I knew he wouldn't send me any money if I told him that. In a good month he could earn as much as fifty or sixty dollars, and I figured he could spare me a third of that to live on.

"Well," he said, "I reckon I could get by for a little while, but not too long, y'hear."

"You got by just fine before we married."

"I wasn't used to you then."

He finally agreed to send me twenty dollars a month, and in the spring of 1860 Rosalia and I went back to Brunswick. She was twelve now and growing more independent by the day. I think she too was glad to leave Jacksonville and return to a more familiar place. We stayed for a short while in a house Mary found for us not too far from where she lived, while I looked for something more convenient in town. In mid-summer, I found a little house on G Street and we moved in. I soon grew accustomed to life on my own again and rather liked it. I started calling myself Sarah Aust once more, feeling like I couldn't rid myself of Willis Reddick or the fishy smell I still imagined, until I rid myself of his name.

We saw Mary now and again. I had missed her, but I have to

confess that our relationship could never again be what it once was—just mother and daughter. To lose a man to one's daughter was a humiliating experience. And I always felt awkward around Henry. How do you cope with a man who has been your lover for ten years and who has left you, not just for another woman but for your daughter? It was in some ways humiliating to be back, but it was the only life I knew now. I was trying to make the best of living in a world that was both familiar and unfamiliar at the same time. Who was I now? Even I didn't know.

Willis wrote to me occasionally, short complaining letters wanting to know when I planned to return. Perhaps I would have gone back to him one day of my own accord, but I'll never know for sure, for only a year later, on April 12, 1861, war broke out and set off a powder keg of violence. Even if I had wanted to go back to Willis, which of course I didn't, I convinced myself that it would be dangerous to travel. I didn't want to return to Jacksonville, and the war would become my excuse.

CHAPTER 17

I hated the idea of war and had hoped it could be avoided, but I suppose it was bound to happen sooner or later. Most men around Brunswick were fire-eating rebels, convinced they could beat the Yankees easily if it came to that. Most of the women hoped it wouldn't, but the election of Lincoln in November of 1860 had made the conflict inevitable. People around here cheered when Georgia, with six other Southern states, seceded from the Union the following January. We were, they argued, a different region from the Yankees. The South needed its own country. We shouldn't have to abide by the same rules as folks up north where life was so different. They just didn't understand why we didn't do things like them and free all the slaves. But they didn't have cotton fields in New York and Connecticut, while in Georgia they were the livelihood of Southern planters.

I had never thought too much about slavery one way or the other, except when I was at Dover Hall. It didn't seem right to me that one could own people and compel them to work for no pay, but even though Uncle William didn't like it either, he had convinced me that plantation owners couldn't grow and harvest and bale the cotton without slave labor. It was our life's blood here in the South. I didn't have any slaves, of course. First of all, like most folks, I never could afford them, but I could understand why some people thought they were necessary, and they were a way of life in south Georgia.

Thus, when war finally broke out in April 1861 and Confederate troops attacked Fort Sumter, a Union stronghold in Charleston, to stop the Yankees from building up its fortifications, everybody around here went crazy with joy. People yelled and shot off guns and generally made fools of themselves when they learned the war was finally underway.

At first nothing much seemed to happen, though there would

soon be evidence of shortages and inconveniences. The whole town of Brunswick began to prepare for war. Soon, an army camp they called Camp Semmes, named for the colonel of the 2nd Georgia Infantry, was set up in the southern part of the town. A hospital was opened at the corner of Newcastle and Gloucester streets, though most of the early patients were brought in not for battle wounds but for cases of measles, which were sweeping the camp.

Some of the ladies in Brunswick organized a sewing association to make shirts and such for the Brunswick Riflemen and other regimental soldiers as they trained and waited for action. I wasn't asked to join, and anyhow I couldn't sew well enough to make such garments. Rosalia and I just kept to ourselves and waited to see what would happen.

Yankees soon began to patrol our coast, and people couldn't ship their cotton anymore, at least not without risk. Union vessels began to appear menacingly along the Georgia coastline not long after the war started. The barrier islands emptied out first. The people who lived there were terrified that the Yankees might come ashore as the British had in the War of 1812. After the islands along our coast were empty of residents, Confederate troops started building batteries and mounting big guns on Jekyl and St. Simons to guard the sound and keep Union ships from sailing into the Turtle River, which led into the entrance to Brunswick harbour.

It began to look like things were about to get heated up around here. The troops worked hard building those batteries. Even General Lee came down to inspect them and found them quite fine, but then, after all the work was done and before anything even happened, Lee ordered the troops stationed on the islands to abandon them and began to move them north to defend Savannah, leaving Brunswick completely vulnerable to the Yankees.

Not long afterwards there was a knock at my door. When I opened it, one of the neighbourhood boys stood there with an anxious look on his face. He didn't wait for a greeting before he spoke. "Miss Sarah, they're sayin' we gotta leave. Right away. The military's evacuatin' ever'one in Brunswick. They want ever'body out 'fore the end of the week. Mama sent me over to tell you. Please help spread the word."

"But where will we go?" I asked.

"I dunno. Wherever we can, I guess. Just inland someplace. We're headin' for Waynesville. My mama has a sister there we can stay with. I don't know 'bout ever'body else."

I immediately thought of Dover Hall, but then remembered that it didn't belong to Uncle William anymore. He had died not long after Willis and I were married, and the plantation belonged to someone else now. He had left me and my daughters $50 each in his will, and I had hidden mine and Rosalia's away in a secret pocket that I kept underneath my skirts, saved for a day when we might need it desperately. I had used part of it to help pay for an old mule and the small wagon we needed to get around. But I thanked God that I still had almost half of it left.

I wondered whether people out in the county were having to evacuate as well or whether Mary and her family would stay. They lived quite a way outside of town. But even if they could stay, would they want to? We'd all heard terrible stories about the Yankees and how they would steal everything in sight, rape women, and kill children. I suspected that Mary would want to get her daughters as far away as possible, but I couldn't be sure.

Rosalia and I packed up what we could carry in our little wagon, mostly blankets, as much food as we thought wouldn't spoil, and extra clothes. I knew we couldn't take much, because the only mule I had been able to buy with a portion of Uncle William's legacy and my meager accumulated savings was old and not worth much. He could get us around Brunswick, but I could only hope that he was strong enough to pull us in the loaded cart all the way to Waynesville, which was the closest place of refuge, lying near the border of Wayne County. If necessary, we could walk part of the way. It was about twenty miles or so, and I knew we'd have to stop and rest the mule fairly often. Still, I hoped he would get us far enough away so that the Yankees couldn't find us.

As we left Brunswick, people were in a rush, almost a panic.

Some of the women were crying or trying to comfort wailing children. Everyone seemed afraid, for we had heard stories of how the Yankees were virtual devils and would destroy everything in their path, burning houses, defiling churches, and doing whatever mischief they could. We didn't know whether these stories were true or not, and none of us had any idea what we would find when we returned to Brunswick, if we were ever able to go back.

I guess some folks made the trip by train since our railroad line ran that way, but there were a lot of people, black and white alike, on the dusty road to Waynesville, while others headed for more distant places like Tebeauville or Waresboro. Some were on horseback, some walked. Others were driving wagons, pulling carts, carrying loads on their backs or, in the case of the slaves, on their heads. I could never figure out how those slave women could balance such big loads on top of their heads. Alongside these came a few rich people in shiny carriages, followed by huge wagonloads of fancy furniture and all sorts of trunks and boxes. I felt sorry for the horses that had to pull so much weight. A few people even led cows and goats. Everyone carried away whatever they could in whatever manner they could.

Most people were in family groups, but some traveled all alone. One old woman in a sunbonnet plodded along by herself, a faraway look in her eyes and a sewing machine tucked under her arm. Nearby was a young man, barely out of boyhood, also alone, with a knapsack on his back and carrying a banjo. While I saw maybe a dozen or so like them, most folks were in family groups, with more women and children than men. A majority of the men, I guessed, had probably enlisted in the new Confederate Army, as both my sons had, joining up with local groups like the Glynn Guards and the Brunswick Rifles, who stayed behind to defend the town. Most of the men and boys on the road were too old or too young for the army.

After a couple of miles, the hurried pace slowed to a determined trudge. I thought surely the town must be completely empty of citizens by now, for I swear they were all on the road. Brunswick wasn't a big town, with only a little over 800 residents, black and white combined. But with everybody leaving at once, the road still seemed crowded.

Rosalia and I didn't make it all the way to Waynesville that day. The old mule just gave out in midafternoon and refused to go a step farther. We had no choice but to stop and let him rest. After we tethered him to let him graze and gave him some water from a nearby creek, we were able to find space in an empty barn loft to sleep for the night, along with a few other people, though some stumbled on, even as dusk was falling. We huddled together, my daughter and I, as best we could to keep warm, and I was grateful for the blankets we'd brought. It was still chilly at nights, for it was not yet spring. What we lacked in comfort, though, we found in safety from the Yankee invaders. I couldn't imagine where everyone would stay when we got to Waynesville, especially if we had to be away for a long time.

The town, the seat of Wayne County, was located near the Old Post Road, so its citizens were used to travelers. Even so, I knew there would not be enough places to house everyone and that prices would be high. To reassure myself, I patted the hidden pocket in my skirt that held Uncle William's money. It would take care of us for a while, but I had no idea what we would do when it was gone. I even considered the possibility, just for a moment, of trying to make it back to Jacksonville and Willis, where at least we'd have shelter, but I couldn't be certain that the Yankees weren't threatening there as well. And I was sure our old mule wouldn't hold out for such a long trip.

At the time we could only wonder what happened back in Brunswick after the town emptied out, with residents taking everything they could carry. We would learn later that once it was deserted, the Confederates themselves had set fire to the harbor and the railroad station to keep Union troops from using them. They might have burned the whole town had the Yankees not moved in so quickly, but by the time they got there, the Southern troops had deserted it, leaving the docks and station still ablaze. As we'd left, we had no idea how long we would be away or how long this war would last.

When we finally got to Waynesville the next day, it was already teeming with people. I could see a few soldiers here and there about the town, which contained a regimental hospital that served the 4th Georgia Cavalry. Everyone was milling about, trying to find a place to stay for who knows how long. People sought shelter where they could—with relatives, in empty sheds or barns, even in makeshift tents in an area where a refugee camp appeared to be taking shape.

We were luckier than some, for I found a boarding house where the landlady agreed to provide a small room for Rosalia and me in exchange for our help with the extra cooking and housekeeping required by the influx of so many new and unexpected guests. It was clean but crowded, and I could see by the harassed look in the landlady's eyes that she was overworked and hassled. She was about sixty years old, I think, probably attractive in her younger years, with graying hair pulled up in what was obviously a hasty braid on top of her head. As she brushed back the few strands that had escaped during the busy morning, she seemed glad for our offer of help and relieved that it was just my daughter and me, with no man to put up with.

"I reckon y'all will do. I shore need somebody," she said, gesturing around at the parlour, where a few people were sitting in sullen silence, their belongings stacked beside them as they waited for a room.

We all hoped that our stay in Waynesville would be brief and that we would be able to return to Brunswick before long, since the message that informed us about the fires at the dock and railroad station also indicated that the Yankees had not harmed the town. But only a short while later, a scout arrived with another dispatch, indicating that some of the soldiers who had first withdrawn to the interior, I think it was the Wiregrass Minute Men, were sent back into Brunswick on March 18. Somewhere on the riverbank between the town and Fancy Bluff, they had spotted a small group of Federal troops who appeared to be gathering oysters. When our soldiers challenged them, they rushed back to their boat and rowed for their lives to get away. Our boys said they thought they killed two or three of them with their sharp shooting, but then a Federal gun boat and the flag ship got into the fray and started shelling Brunswick from one end to the other. We heard there was not much left of the town now. Who knew what we would return to? I hoped the report was an exaggeration, but we couldn't be sure. We just went day by day, with news trickling in, never certain how reliable it was.

As we settled in for a longer stay, I decided to write to Mary and Fredonia to let them know where we were, though I had no assurance that they would receive the letters. Someone needed to know, and the rest of my family, except for Willis and my two boys who had joined the army back in December, were there with Mary and Henry.

The months went by slowly. It grew harder to feed all the people in the boarding house. So many supplies were scarce, if they could be had at all. One of the first things we ran out of was coffee. It was almost impossible to find, and what little there was to be had sometimes cost as much as $100 a pound. We learned to improvise and tried making coffee out of all sorts of things—acorns, beets, cornmeal. As long as it looked like coffee, people didn't complain too much. They were already growing used to the hardships of being refugees.

We got news from various sources, especially from the wounded returning to the hospital in Waynesville. We held our breath every time we heard about another battle. The months went slowly by, and when the long year ended, we were still in Waynesville. At first our soldiers seemed to be doing well and winning victories, though the names of the Confederate dead kept coming in, but by July of 1863, things began to change dramatically when the Confederacy suffered a big defeat at Gettysburg. The folks in Waynesville, those of us who had fathers, husbands, brothers, and sons in the war, were upset by the news, and as the names of the dead and wounded began to reach us, there was much weeping and moaning. We all worried about our boys and men off in the battles. I had no idea where Leonidas and William were and could only hold my breath in fear as I read the lists of names posted at the railroad station. But I was relieved not to find their names on any of the lists.

Only a few months later, in mid-September, I received a most unexpected letter—from Henry himself. "Dear Sarah," it began. I had recognized his handwriting even before I opened it, knowing it could only contain bad news. I was not mistaken. The letter was a plea for help.

> *We have much sickness here at home—scarlet fever, I think. I wouldn't bother you, except that we need help. Mary is ill as well as two of the girls. I don't know what to do or how to tend to all these sick folks, and I thought perhaps you could find it in your heart to come to Ellis Point and help out your daughter and granddaughters. I wouldn't ask, except I don't know where else to turn. There are no doctors left in Brunswick. Please come. I remain, your devoted servant, Henry DuBignon.*

I must confess that I had mixed feelings about the letter. Here was Henry, daring to turn to me for help. But I didn't think long about it before I decided that I must go to them. Mary *was* my daughter, after all, and I guess a mother will do most anything for her child. If she needed me, I would go. I hated to take Rosalia into a house of sickness, but it would probably be a good thing to get her away from all the tempting young soldiers. Besides, I was sick of waiting on strangers at the boarding house.

Evidently, because they lived so far outside of Brunswick, Mary's family had not been compelled to evacuate, and I know it would have been hard with so many young children. I explained the situation to my landlady, who was not happy to lose my help, but she knew I wouldn't be hard to replace, given the swell of needy people in the town.

"Don't expect me to keep your room for you. I'll have to hire somebody else to help out," she told me.

"I understand," I said. It gave me pause to realize I might not have anywhere to come back to if the situation with Henry was intolerable, but even after all that had happened, Mary was still my daughter, and I had to go.

CHAPTER 18

The railroad tracks back toward Brunswick had been torn up by now because the army needed the iron for military purposes, so there was no chance of taking the train. Once again we had to rely on our old mule who, after such a long period of relative idleness, had grown older, lethargic, and more ornery. Since Mary and Henry lived four or five miles west of town, it wasn't quite as far, but it still took a great deal of effort with that mule. He balked several times at pulling the little cart and refused to take another step, and then, once, I mistook the road and wasted three hours before I realized my mistake. It took almost two full days for us to get to their house on the edge of the marsh.

When we arrived, Henry rushed out to greet us. I could hardly recognize him. His beard was entirely white now, and deeper wrinkles had settled around his eyes, which looked red, like he'd been crying or maybe from lack of sleep. He looked older and thinner and shorter than I remembered.

"Sarah, thank God you're here. I think Mary may be a little better, but Camilla and Agnes seem worse. I appreciate your coming."

"I don't know as I can do much, Henry. You said there weren't any doctors left in Brunswick, but Dr. Woodbridge is in Waynesville. He and his family evacuated with the rest of us, and they're living there with his brother. I spoke to him, and he's willing to come if you send for him."

"Why didn't you bring him with you?" he grumbled.

"I don't have the means to pay him, and I didn't know if you'd want him or not. You deal with it. Now let me go in and see to Mary and the girls."

The house had a terrible smell, in part because it had not been properly cleaned in recent days but mostly from the acifidity bags the girls wore around their necks. I had smelled them before. They were a common medical preventative among slaves to ward off a sickness. The smell came from a combination of the sulfurous odor of boiled root of asafetida dipped in turpentine. One of the bags even hung around Henry's neck, and he had one ready for Rosalia and me. It was revolting, but since everyone else was wearing them, I put mine on despite the stink. Rosalia protested at first but finally relented and hung it around her neck like the other girls.

Mary was still weak, but Henry was right. She had already begun to recover by the time I arrived. Her eyes lit up when she saw me. "Thank you so much for coming, Mum." Tears that I took to express both relief and helplessness, maybe even a tinge of regret, stood in her eyes, but she gave me a brave smile. Although her fever was gone, she still suffered from a fading rash and general weariness.

"I have no idea what to do for the girls," she told me.

"Don't worry, my dear, I'll take care of them." And then, when I told her about Dr. Woodbridge, an expression of hope crossed her face.

"Oh, Henry," she said, and only then did I realize he was standing right behind me. "Please send for him at once."

Henry volunteered to fetch the doctor himself. He left early the next morning, looking almost thankful for an excuse to get out of the house of sickness, even for a little while. I was glad to see him go. It was awkward, to say the least, being there with Henry and his new family. Though I knew he would come back, the brief absence would give me time to prepare myself and talk with Mary in private.

When he was gone, Mary reached for my hand. "I'm sorry for everything, Mum. I know this is not easy for any of us. But I hope you can forgive Henry, at least for now and for my sake."

"You're asking a lot, Mary," I said. "It's complicated." And it was. I didn't know what I felt for Henry anymore.

"I know it's hard, but I can still hope."

"Are you happy with him, my dear?" I asked.

"I don't have much time to think about happiness. I'm too busy with my girls. And I've been with child almost the whole time we've been married. I don't get much time in between to think about it one way or the other."

"He is insatiable, isn't he?" My voice sounded cold, even to me. "That's the condition he kept Amelia in until she finally turned him away. I suppose that's why he came to me—any port in a storm."

"Are all men like that?"

"No, not all," I said, thinking about Willis.

Almost as though she were reading my thoughts, Mary asked, "Why did you leave Mr. Reddick?"

"He leads a very dull life, Mary. To be truthful, I didn't love him."

"Like you loved Henry?" she asked, without thinking. She drew a quick breath and put her hand over her lips, but it was out in the open, and I could think of no response. She saw my stunned reaction and said again, "I'm sorry, Mum. For everything."

I patted her hand. "What's done is done. Now I'm going to check on the girls." I rose quickly so that she didn't see the tears springing to my eyes.

By the time Henry and Dr. Woodridge rode up the next afternoon, a cloud of dust in their wake suggesting they had come in haste, Agnes had already begun to feel better. Her chills had ended, and her fever had dropped to almost normal overnight, though her skin still felt sandpapery from the rash. She was sitting up in bed, chattering away and asking for something to eat.

Camilla, however, was sicker than ever. She was only six years old, small for her age. She had always been puny, Mary said. She'd been the first one to get sick, and now it seemed the illness had gone to her lungs. She coughed constantly and had trouble breathing. Still suffering from fever and teeth-chattering chills, she had begun to complain of pain in her chest and aching muscles. Already thin as a winter sparrow, she grew frailer by the day and seemed to have no strength left in her little body.

"I think it may have turned into pneumonia or maybe pleurisy,"

Dr. Woodbridge said after he had examined her, cupped her back, and bled her, which only made her weaker. "Its persistence is not a good sign. Keep her warm. Be sure to give her the thirty grains of calomel and the chokeberry juice I prescribed, and try to get her at least to drink some broth every day. She needs nourishment. If she feels strong enough to sit up, put her in a sunny window or even outside if the day is warm. The sunshine will do her good." His face looked grim. "I'm afraid there's not much more I can do."

Mary was crying softly, though she said nothing in response. I put my arm around her and she turned to me, burying her head on my chest as she had done when she was a little girl.

Although it was moving toward late afternoon, the doctor declined to spend the night, not wanting, I think, to expose himself any further to the sickness, or perhaps it was the smell in the household. He seemed eager to get away. His horse was a fine-looking animal, but there was no way he could make it all the way back to Waynesville before nightfall. I suppose he had made arrangements to spend the night somewhere else along the way.

"I'll send along my bill," he told Henry as he mounted his steed. Henry nodded.

"Well, he wasn't much help," he muttered as soon as the doctor was out of hearing distance, looking at me as though it were my fault. A week later, when he received Dr. Woodbridge's bill for $23.30, he was outraged. "He charged twenty-two dollars just for coming from Waynesville," he grumbled. "I don't mind paying for the treatment and medicine, but a dollar a mile is ridiculous. I won't pay it."

"It was a two-way trip, Henry. Maybe you should have discussed the cost before you asked him to come," I said. I no longer hesitated to disagree with or correct Henry, trying instead to think of him as my son-in-law. After all, I thought, a mother-in-law should have some authority when she is called in to help. I didn't care what he thought. Or maybe I just wanted to irritate him.

As the days went on, Mary still struggled to regain her strength. She was too weak in her condition to care for Camilla—or any of the other girls, for that matter. I was grateful that Rosalia kept the healthy ones occupied much of the time. She was almost sixteen now and like a mother hen with the girls, who adored her. She became their unofficial schoolteacher, lining them up every morning for whatever she had decided to teach them that day. Sometimes it was a song, sometimes sums, sometimes spelling. They had varying degrees of success, depending on their ages, but teaching seemed to come to her naturally.

Henry stayed outside and away as much as possible. The all-female household seemed to get on his nerves, or perhaps it was just me. In any case, the responsibility of caring for the sick and making sure the housework was done properly all fell to me. I was in charge. It was all Mary could do to nurse and change her new baby girl, Valeria, born only the year before. There were five little girls now, all too young to be of much help. Virginia, at eleven, was the oldest, and Emily was nine. The other three, even younger, were quite a handful, but I was their grandmother, after all, and Rosalia and I had come to help.

It was during that time that I came as close as I ever would or could to forgiving Henry DuBignon. I could see that he loved his little girls in his own undemonstrative way, and that this was hard for him. Perhaps, I thought, he does have some feelings after all. That thought was probably premature, because I would learn, only after the war was well over, that during that same year he had betrayed Leonidas and William and signed over Jekyl Island to the sons and only unmarried daughter of his first marriage—Eliza, of course, the only one never to find a husband. I suppose he didn't think the island was worth much by then because nobody could live there. It was still in the hands of the Yankees. I'm not sure why such a thing would even cross his mind at that point in time. Maybe his other children were pressuring him. I don't know. All I know is that any love I once had for him had given way to…what? Indifference? *Hatred* would be too strong. He didn't deserve such a powerful reaction. Let's just say I learned to tolerate the situation and turned my focus elsewhere—to my sick granddaughter.

All any of us could think about was Camilla—with her frail little body, pale skin, and so much pain in her blue eyes. Her thin brown hair splayed out on the pillow like fading petals, ready to fall. It was clear that she was growing worse and sinking daily. Finally, as the cooler weather set in, she slipped away one night while most of the household slept.

When I awoke, it was quiet throughout the house—too quiet. I suddenly realized that no one was coughing and got up at once to check on Camilla. Her small body was already cool. She had been dead for several hours at least. She had simply stolen away in the night to a place where she could finally find peace and a release from pain, for she had suffered terribly. I woke up the household, and we spent the rest of the day mourning for the child and preparing for her burial. We laid her to rest in a little cemetery just across the creek that belonged to one of the neighbours, a man called Colonel Burnett.

By then Rosalia and I had become accustomed to our unusual living situation, and even though the illness was no longer a threat, we made no move to return to Waynesville. Nor did anyone suggest it. I knew there would likely be no place for us to stay, and Mary would probably still need my help, for by this time she was expecting again. I could hardly believe that Henry had insisted on conjugal relations when she was barely well enough to walk. But then, he was Henry. I think he was growing desperate to prove he could father another son.

By the late summer of 1864, it was obvious, even to me, that the South was losing the war. Repeated reports of so many dead and wounded had dampened Confederate hopes, and all the bluster had gone out of those who had been so eager for the war to start.

Sherman had by now invaded deep into Georgia and was on the outskirts of Atlanta. The battle started there in late July, but the city didn't fall completely into Union hands until early September.

Not long after we received news of Sherman's capture of Atlanta, Mary gave birth to yet another baby girl, Gertrude Louisa, on September 16. I must confess that it gave me a sense of smug satisfaction to be the one to bring the news to Henry. He was waiting outside.

"You have another fine daughter," I said with a bright smile. His shoulders slumped perceptibly, and he just nodded with resignation before he went to the birthing room to see the mother and child. It pleased me to know that my two boys, Leonidas and William, were likely to be the last sons he would ever have, assuming baby Gertrude would be his final child since he was only two years away from his eightieth birthday. Surely he wouldn't be able to father any more children, though one could never be sure with a man like him. Mary was only thirty-four and no doubt still fertile.

Following the fall of Atlanta, we heard that Sherman was marching toward Savannah, leaving havoc in his wake. He captured the city just before Christmas. It was a sad time in Georgia that holiday season, but at least the war seemed to be winding down. After that, things began to happen quickly. Our soldiers were said to be starving, with some deserting. Yankee blockades and raids kept supplies from getting to them. Things went from bad to worse until it all came to a head in April, when we learned of General Lee's surrender at Appomattox. Even so, about a week later, we heard that fighting continued in places and that Columbus was under siege. That same day, news arrived of Lincoln's assassination. It was all happening so fast, but one thing seemed certain. The war was coming to an end and the enemy had won.

Shortly thereafter, I received a letter from Fredonia. It was written in late August of the preceding year and had been a long time in arriving, for our mails had not run regularly for quite a while. Her husband Will, she said, had joined the Confederate Army as a private in Company F, nicknamed the Cow Boys of Duval County, as part of the 3rd Florida Infantry shortly after the war began. Now, she wrote, "*I am broken-hearted to tell you that my dearest husband is dead. He was wounded in the left foot on August 7 during the battle of Atlanta and later hospitalized. Thinking it was not too serious, they released him from the hospital a week or so later, but he died of infection on August 27.*" He'd left her pregnant and with four children, the youngest of whom was only three years old at the time of his death.

In the same letter she also informed me that my husband Willis was dead. He'd apparently had a stroke or a heart attack while he was at home alone, and no one had found his body for nearly a week. I felt nothing, except perhaps a tinge of guilt that I wasn't there with him, but there was nothing I could have done anyhow, and I'd have probably died of boredom myself by now. But I *was* his widow and sole heir, and Fredonia seemed to think there might be property to be settled—his small house, at least. It was clear that I needed to return to Jacksonville, not only to comfort my grieving daughter and see whether I could be of help to her but also to claim whatever Willis might have left me.

Once we were assured that a kind of uneasy peace was restored, I felt ready to make my trip. Before I left for Florida, I wanted to pay a visit to Leonidas and his family, for I didn't know when I would return. Both my boys had served in the Confederate Army. Leonidas had enlisted as a private and ended the war, after serving all four years, at the same rank. I wasn't surprised. I expect his heart wasn't in it, for less than six months before the war started, he had married a young bride named Sarah Jane Higginbotham. Evidently he had regular leave from the army to visit his wife, for before the war even ended, they already had three children—all boys. He had returned to Brunswick after the war, and they lived not too far away.

I was happy to see him alive and well and to meet his wife and their three sons: Thomas, Alfred, and two-year-old Gus. It was apparent that his wife, Sarah Jane, was expecting again.

"Have you heard from your brother?" I asked.

"He mustered out in Tallahassee, and I think he plans to stay there for a while," Leonidas said.

"Why would he do that?" I asked.

"He's been courting a girl there. Says her name is Charlotte Kindon, though he calls her Lottie. Says she's a fine lady and very pretty. I think he's planning to ask her to marry him."

"Well then, perhaps when I go back to Florida, I could visit him there or get him to come and visit me."

"Maybe," Leonidas said. "But it's a pretty long way over to the panhandle."

"Maybe there's a train that connects the two," I suggested.

"Maybe."

Sarah Jane didn't say much during my visit. She was too busy trying to keep an eye on her three little boys, all of whom were still under six and busy fellows, to say the least. Somehow I gathered that all wasn't blissful in their house, but I didn't want to pry.

Leonidas told me that by the time William had mustered out of the army, he'd made the rank of 4th sergeant. He laughed. "Reckon he was a better soldier than I was, since I was still a private." They'd both served in Clinch's Cavalry. "Maybe I should've stayed in the infantry where I started."

It didn't surprise me that William made a better soldier than Leonidas. He's always been a good boy, the responsible one, once he learned to stop following his brother around like a puppy and trying to do everything he did. My oldest son, on the other hand, had never been one to follow orders or honor requests. He was always the one I found hardest to handle, for he had a defiant streak that made him strain against any restrictions. In any case, I was glad to see him and meet his family before leaving for Jacksonville once more.

Since there was still no direct railroad from Brunswick to Jacksonville, my best choices for travel were stagecoach or ship. I decided to take the latter, which would take me a single day. I would go back to Jacksonville and claim whatever inheritance Willis had left me. I tried to feel sad for him, but if I'm truly honest with myself, his death was more a relief than anything else.

CHAPTER 19

My early days back in Jacksonville were busy ones. During those first months, it behooved me to become Sarah Reddick once more and set about claiming Willis's estate. For a simple fisherman, he had accumulated remarkable savings, still a modest amount but more than I had ever expected, and thank God, it was all in U.S. currency, not in Confederate dollars. I inherited his little clapboard house on the east end of Beaver Street as well. It was run down from wartime damage and neglect, but it was a welcome respite for me after being cooped up so long with my daughter in one room of the Waynesville boarding house and then at Mary's, where I had shared a room with Rosalia and two of the girls. Here I had my own room, and Rosalia had hers. We had a small parlour as well as a kitchen with a dining area big enough for a round table with a few chairs, though one wall had been badly damaged during the Union occupation. Nevertheless, the house was mine, mine alone—the first thing I had ever owned all by myself—and I was proud of it, even in its run-down condition.

I fixed it up as best I could to make it livable, but there was still a lot that needed doing both inside and out, and the porch sagged like a tired old man. It would require considerable repair, and the kitchen wall needed rebuilding. Even as it was, I did what I could to make it homey, painting the bedrooms and parlour a sunny yellow to make them more cheerful. I even planted flowers, starting with easy-to-grow pentas, spiderworts, and lantanas, around the front of my house, which Willis had always left bare. Little by little, I planned to make it into the home I had always wanted.

Fredonia lived not far away, so I saw my widowed daughter and her children fairly frequently. She was still broken-hearted from losing her husband, but those five children, two boys and three girls, kept her busy. I had known the three oldest before the war when I left Willis, but there were two more little girls now, Louisa, already four years old, and Wilhelmina, whom they called Willie Mae. Born three months after her father's death, she was now a bright toddler. They were a handful, but I liked having the little ones about from time to time, as long as I didn't have to tend to them myself and could just enjoy them like a grandmother should.

For once, I could welcome a new year—1866—with cheerful anticipation. We were at peace again, and for the first time in my life I was living on my own terms. I was content, in spite of all that needed doing. Rosalia was my only concern. She would turn eighteen on her next birthday, and she had long since begun to catch the eye of members of the male gender. Many of them had fought in the war and come back, some whole, others wounded and maimed, and still others who had been too young to fight and were rapidly growing into lusty young men. I was anxious to keep her pure until she found a husband, but my task was becoming harder, for she was a pretty young girl, straining to be a woman.

Overall, that first post-war year passed quickly as we all adjusted to the changes in our lives. Then, early on a Saturday morning in December, I received a telegram, the first I'd ever gotten. I was outside, pulling winter weeds from around the lantanas blooming beside my porch, when the messenger boy arrived.

A telegram always brought bad news, and I opened it with trepidation. It was from my son William. "*Father is dead. Funeral Monday. Mary wants you at burial*," he wrote. "*As mother of three of his children. I think she needs you. Urgent.*" The length of the telegram made me realize how important he thought it was for me to go.

Henry's death was a shock. I tried to focus on Mary, left now, like her sister Fredonia, a widow with five young children to support—the oldest just fourteen. I knew it would be hard for her. But my thoughts kept turning to Henry. I won't say that I was sorry to hear of his death, but I can't say that I felt nothing either. It was hard to imagine the world without him. He had seemed somehow indestructible, a permanent fixture, the barrier that stood between Mary and me. I had never actually thought of him dying, assuming, I suppose, that he would just grow older and older and live forever. But it was just like Henry to abandon his wife and children at a time when they were all trying to get their lives back together. It was as though he had decided to avoid all the hard work ahead and take the easy way out.

They buried him in the old Burnett cemetery at Ellis Point, just across the creek from where he had lived with Mary and the girls—the same place we had buried little Camilla. It was a tranquil spot, right on the edge of the marsh. It reminded me of the view of the marshlands from Jekyl Island, where nothing disturbed the peace but the rustling of the sea grass, the sound of the birds, and the shifting of the tides—a good place to spend eternity.

Like many funerals for old people, there wasn't a lot of grief—at least not the kind expressed in weeping and moaning. Mary said his death wasn't totally unexpected. He was, after all, eighty years old and in failing health, growing more decrepit ever since little Gertrude was born. My daughter looked sad, but she certainly didn't shed any tears for him, unless she did so before I arrived. Though she never said it, I think she must have felt a certain liberation now that he was gone for good and she would never again have to endure his nightly rituals and unquenchable appetite for his own physical satisfaction, if he were still capable of it. It must have been repulsive to her by now—all that wrinkled, flabby flesh.

I suspect there was a lot of joking about him in the community—the old man who had betrayed his wife, jilted his mistress to marry her daughter, and then fathered all those little girls, pop, pop, pop, one after another. He was insatiable almost to the end. I can only imagine what people said about him because, of course, they never said it to me.

Nobody came to the funeral except family and a couple of nearby neighbours. There'd been a time when Henry was a big man in the community, and half the town might have turned out to mourn his death and pay their respects, but now almost no one came. None of the children from his first family showed up either, though I'm pretty sure they were notified. I think they were all embarrassed to have their names associated with his, for there's no doubt he was viewed as a man without honor, if anyone ever thought about him at all. And to think, he was once the highly respected president of a bank and a member of the board for Glynn Academy. Now he'd become just an old man with a bad reputation—a joke in the community. Even our sons remembered him with a certain levity.

"You got to hand it to the old man," I overheard Leonidas say. "This was one way to keep from signing that damned loyalty oath the Yankees demand."

"If anyone wanted a loyalty oath from my father, they're out of luck. Loyalty was not his strong suit," William said, chuckling. "But you're right. He picked a good time to go." They were all disgruntled to learn that they had to sign the oath to do business in this former Confederate state now run by those Reconstruction Yankees they called "carpetbaggers."

"The war didn't seem to bother him much," Leonidas said. "He just carried on—and I do mean carried on, fathering one baby after another—at his age! Not many eighty-year-olds leave behind a two-year-old daughter. Imagine." He sniggered. "Nothing but girls. Good thing he didn't have a plantation to worry about anymore, like in the old days."

"When did the plantation ever stop him?" William asked.

When their wives approached, they both resumed the mourning faces they were supposed to be wearing. I remember it vividly—all of it.

There was a short graveside service, and before they lowered the coffin in the ground I saw that water had begun to seep into the bottom of the grave. I didn't doubt that there would be more, for the day was cloudy and threatened rain. It held off until everybody was back at the house, sharing all the food my daughters had prepared. Henry's children spent the rest of that rainy afternoon telling stories about their father, until the skies cleared and the brothers and their wives rounded up their little ones to head back to their own lives, leaving Mary, Rosalia, and me to clean up the mess they left behind.

I said I remember it all. I do recall the events, but it's hard to remember what I thought about that day. Or even what I felt. I think I went through most of the day half numb, just watching everyone else's reactions. Although Mary was solicitous of me, the others scarcely noticed, as though my feelings were unimportant. And maybe they were. I have to confess that I'd shed a tear or two when I first heard about his death—not that I was sorry he was gone. My sorrow, or better still my regret, was for what might have been, for the time I had wasted on that man, and for the embarrassment my children and I had to go through when he took up with Mary. It all came back to me in a rush. But it was a truth I could never forget, one I would carry with me for the rest of my life.

The next day, Rosalia and I said our goodbyes to Mary and the girls and returned to Jacksonville. I was glad to be home, but Rosalia was more restless than ever. While we were in Brunswick for Henry's funeral, William had invited her to come to Tallahassee sometime for a nice long visit. She liked his wife very much. Lottie was ten years older than Rosalia, who saw her as a figure to emulate. She could have chosen worse; Lottie was a pretty young woman, still in her twenties, with a good-natured charm that had attracted Rosalia's favorite brother and made him adore her. She was a compelling embodiment of what, in my daughter's view, the ideal woman should be.

Back in Jacksonville, I was intent on resuming the necessary repairs to my house and at first paid little attention when Rosalia and Lottie began to exchange letters. They corresponded for a full year. Then, in early March of the next year, 1868, Lottie informed us that she was expecting a baby and would love to have Rosalia come for a visit before the child was born. I was reluctant because I knew I would miss her terribly, but she wanted desperately to go. William had always been her favorite big brother. He had looked after her when she was a little girl and had not teased and pestered her as Leonidas did. And she was thrilled that his wonderful wife liked her so much and wanted to see her.

"Please, Mum. I'm so tired of Jacksonville. They tell me that Tallahassee is a really nice place, and it wasn't even occupied by the Yankees. Everything is just as it was. Besides, I think Lottie can use my help while she's expecting," she begged.

How could I say no? She was old enough to make her own decisions now, and they did seem to want her to come, both Lottie and William. Besides, it would give me the free time to focus entirely on my repairs without having to worry about watching over Rosalia.

"Well, as long as your brother is willing to keep an eye on you and keep you out of trouble, I suppose it would be all right."

Little did I know that William had already picked out a man he wanted her to meet. I received her letter telling me about him only a month or so after she had left for Tallahassee.

> *Dear Mum, I have met the most wonderful young man. His name is Duncan Cameron Cook, and he works with William in his grocery business in Tallahassee. He's tall, handsome, and brave. He fought in the war, serving with the 10th regiment of the Florida infantry and did very well. He enlisted as a sergeant and was promoted to second lieutenant before his discharge. Isn't that something? He's a few years older than I am, but still in his twenties. William says he's a steady and reliable man, and he's certain you will like him. You can be sure that William is watching over me like a hawk. Even so, I'm having fun here, but don't worry—not too much. I'm not sure when I'm coming home.*

I wrote to William at once to make sure that the young man was an appropriate suitor. He responded promptly, assuring me that both he and Lottie found Duncan entirely suitable. They had introduced him to Rosalia especially, thinking the two of them might make a good match. He also let me know that he was making certain that everything was entirely proper. "*You would surely approve of our watchfulness. Please don't fret. She's in good hands.*" I could only hope that William's taste in men for his little sister was as good as his own taste in finding a bride for himself.

Judging from Rosalia's enthusiastic letters, the romance was blossoming, and she was very happy in Tallahassee. I began to worry that she might marry there and not come back to Jacksonville at all, but since Duncan had not yet asked her to be his wife, I couldn't very well bring it up.

Lottie's baby, a little girl named Florida, was born in mid-July, and Rosalia finally announced she was coming home.

"Well," I said, when I met her at the railroad station, "you decided to come back."

"I had no choice," she said. "William and Lottie are moving to Brunswick."

"My goodness, why?"

"William has decided to move his grocery business to Brunswick. But it's all for the best, because guess what?" She was smiling broadly. "Duncan is going to start a new grocery business here in Jacksonville. He's going to be his own boss. And guess what else?" She arched her eyebrows coyly.

"What else?" I wanted to know.

"We're engaged!" She took off her left glove to display her finger, adorned with a gold ring set with a small sapphire.

"That's wonderful, my dear. When do I get to meet Duncan? And when is the wedding?"

"He's coming to Jacksonville next week to find a suitable place for his business. He says Jacksonville is growing now and that business probably has a good future here. As for the wedding, we haven't set a date yet, but we want to wait until it's a bit cooler. Oh, Mum, he's just wonderful. You're going to love him!"

"I hope so, my dear."

And I did. When I finally met Duncan Cook, I was more than willing to concede that William and Lottie had good taste. He was a most pleasant young man, well-mannered, and, as Rosalia had insisted, quite attractive. I was almost as enthusiastic about him as she was. He looked like a gentleman I might have chosen for her myself. And best of all, he assured me that he adored "Rose," as he called her.

"Isn't it wonderful, Mum?" For her, all of life seemed wonderful these days.

"It is indeed. Have you set a date yet?"

"Not yet," said Duncan, "but in the early fall, I suspect."

"Why don't you wait until November? It's my understanding that the people who live in the house beside mine are moving away in October, and the house will be available for rent. Perhaps you could plan your wedding to coincide with their departure, and the two of you could live next door."

"Do you think that's a good idea?" Rosalia asked.

"I think it's a wonderful idea. I could help you set up housekeeping, and I would be nearby if you needed anything."

The dear boy was entirely in agreement. He suggested his twenty-eighth birthday, November 6, as a date for the wedding, until he realized it fell on a Friday.

"That might not work too well, Rose," he said. "The weekend is usually the busiest time at a grocery store. It might be better to wait until the beginning of the next week." So they decided to set their wedding date for November 9.

Rosalia seemed to have her doubts about living next door to her mother, but she was willing to agree to almost anything to keep the peace. "I'm sure we won't live there forever, Mum, but I suppose it would be a good beginning."

That little house is where their first child was born fourteen months later. I was not surprised when they decided to call him William, naming him after the brother who had introduced them and encouraged the marriage.

What more could I want? I had part of the family next door, my own little home in good shape once more, and no complications. But I might have known that such good fortune would not last. I should not have been surprised, for it was the pattern of my life—to find contentment and, after a few short years, have it slip away. Nothing ever lasts—except the past filled with sorrows I can't forget.

CHAPTER 20

Jacksonville, 1877

The change wasn't long in coming. And now, here I sit, alone, on the front porch of my little house, just watching people go by on the street outside. It's a hot day, and most men are in their shirt sleeves or work clothes. The women are wearing sunbonnets or wide-brimmed hats to keep the sun off. None of the ladies in my part of town carry parasols, though I can imagine them prancing about with their dainty little sunshades over in fancier parts of Jacksonville like Springfield or Riverside.

I don't mind the sun so much. The older I get, the more I appreciate the warmth. Besides, my porch is shaded and there's a slight breeze. It's certainly better than being cooped up inside on a hot day. This little house is my refuge now, no longer the oppressive cage it was when Willis was alive. But now he's gone, Rosalia is married, and it's just me and my cat Pearl. This is how we spend our time, sitting on the porch or doing whatever else I can find to help me get through one more day.

It's hard to believe that more than a decade has passed since Henry's death. Much has changed in my life since then. Three months after Rosalia's marriage, Fredonia up and married again—a man named John Conrad. It didn't last long, and I hardly knew him. Then, three years ago she found a third husband—this time a Jacksonville painter named Charles Cumberland. She still visited me from time to time, but not nearly as often as when I first moved here. Her life was full of social activities and her own little family. Even that is over now. Vanished. I miss her, but I can't let myself think about that. Not yet.

I miss Rosalia and Duncan as well. Like William and Lottie, they have gone to live in Brunswick. I well remember the day Rosalia came to inform me that they were going to move. I had just hung new curtains in my living room, and I was eager to show them off.

"Well, what do you think?" I asked her.

She eyed the ecru lace curtains that now hung at the windows and nodded, "Very nice." I was quite proud of them, for I had never been able to afford lace curtains until the lace began to be made by machine and not just by hand. I'd sewn them myself and thought they looked quite splendid. The little cottage still needed some dressing up, and I had been getting it just the way I wanted—even painting the outside and planting more flowers around the sides of the house. I was pleased with myself and with the way everything looked.

"Mum," Rosalia said, "I've come to let you know that Duncan has taken a job as a railroad watchman back in Brunswick. Maybe he can help William with his grocery store too. We're going to be moving there in a month or so."

"Why on earth would you do that?"

"Well, railroad work provides a steadier income than selling groceries, where prices fluctuate drastically and there is such rapid spoilage. Duncan and I have talked it over and we've decided that this is for the best. He thinks the future of the railroad is a bright one."

"You're not moving there just because William and his family went back to Brunswick, are you?" I thought maybe she wanted to be closer to her favorite brother and his family. She was always partial to him, and he and Duncan were friends. I suspected that was where she'd got the idea.

"Well, of course that's a factor."

I could only hope they weren't making a mistake, but they were determined. All my DuBignon children are in Brunswick now. Leonidas never left, except for military service. He and Sarah Jane already have eight babies, losing only one, and I'm sure there will be more. I've heard from others that he and his wife don't get along too well and that he drinks too much and hangs out with other women, but, nevertheless, the babies keep coming. He's working as a butcher now, I hear. I haven't seen him but once or twice since I returned to Jacksonville, though I pray for him daily to mend his ways.

When William and Lottie moved, it didn't affect my life at all since they lived in Tallahassee, which is farther away from Jacksonville than Brunswick. They didn't visit that often anyhow. But I knew I would miss Rosalia and her little family terribly.

"What about me?" I asked her. "I'll be left here all alone."

"You can move too if you like."

"And leave the only true home I've had since I left London so many years ago?" But nothing I could say would dissuade them.

During the years since Henry died and Rosalia moved away, I've become an old woman, and events of the past year haven't helped a bit. I'm almost seventy now. I feel it in particular this afternoon, for the more recent past is weighing heavy on my soul. I try not to think about it because it brings pain and grief that I'm not quite ready to face yet. But I can't forget for long, no matter how hard I try. Pearl is nudging at my ankles and beginning to purr, trying, I think, to comfort me and stop the warm tears sliding down my cheeks as I let myself remember.

Mary and Fredonia are both dead.

There. I've said it. I keep telling myself it can't be true. Not both of them. They died just three months apart: Fredonia in March and Mary in June of last year. Both of my daughters from my marriage to George are gone. They were my only connections to that happiest part of my life, the only other ones who could remember him. Even their memories were dim, for they were so young when he died. I still can't believe I lost them both in the same year, so close together. It's more than God should ever ask.

I hadn't even begun to recover from Fredonia's death when I learned of Mary's. They were only in their early forties. Why were their lives so fragile, and yet mine goes on and on? When you outlive your children, you know you have lived too long.

It's hard to take comfort in those I have left when they're all so far away and I almost never see them. I feel that my family has abandoned me. I can't deny it. The only one I can still even pretend to visit is Fredonia, who lies buried in the old Jacksonville City Cemetery. They say she knew she was dying, although she was only forty-two, but she never told me. Perhaps she didn't want to worry me, but I wish I'd known so we could have said our proper goodbyes.

Then just three months later, Mary was gone as well. The news arrived by letter on July 3. She had passed away from a fever of some sort. A yellow fever epidemic went through coastal Georgia last year, killing lots of people, though I'm not sure if that's what caused Mary's death or not. Once again the letter came from William. Not a telegram this time. How well I remember the shock of that afternoon.

> *She died on June 21. We couldn't delay the burial because of the heat. We laid her to rest in that same little cemetery where my father is buried. I'm sorry to have to be the bearer of such bad news, especially when the loss of Fredonia is so recent.*

I think I would have collapsed at that point, but there was no one here to look after me, so I had to bear up and keep going. Pearl was my only comfort.

The sun feels good on my shoulders, though I long for rain to water my flowers, which are beginning to droop a bit in the heat. I'm getting too old to be out there with a heavy sprinkler as often as I should. Now is the time I need grandchildren nearby to help out. Although both Mary and Fredonia left me with plenty of grandchildren, they're almost like strangers. Most of Mary's daughters were married by the time of her death, and I presume they're all still in Brunswick, though I can't be sure. I can only assume Fredonia's children are living in Jacksonville, though again I'm not certain. She left them in the care of someone I do not know, and I never see them.

As for the rest of my grandchildren, there are so many I've lost count, and some of them I haven't even met. Sometimes I can hardly remember all their names. Yet despite my large and growing family, I remain alone here except, of course, for Pearl, who is purring as I stroke her back.

At least my children with Henry DuBignon are still alive, though none of them uses his name anymore. Rosalia goes by her married name, to be sure, but my two sons both decided they didn't want to be DuBignons any longer either. Strange as it may seem, William and Leonidas recently decided to take William's middle name—Turner—as their legal surname. Although William had never met the favorite cousin for whom I had named him, someone I haven't seen since I left England so many years ago, that's the name they chose. They went to court two years ago to change it legally. I don't know for certain why they did it.

From what I've been able to piece together, Henry's youngest son from his first marriage, Henry Jr., was named executor of their father's will. He was evidently having a lot of financial problems at the time and was trying all types of shenanigans to hold on to his part of Jekyl Island. During that time, Mary took him to court, accusing him of mismanaging his father's estate. She and the girls weren't getting the financial support they were entitled to. I don't know if my boys even got the paltry $50 their father had left them in his will. He'd left me $50 as well, but I didn't want his pity money. All I know is that it may have been Henry Jr.'s financial mismanagement and his other legal problems that so upset my sons.

Or it could have been the birth in 1875, the same year they changed their names, of a mulatto grandson born to the family of John Couper DuBignon and his black mistress, Sylvia, one of his father's former slaves. They named the boy William DuBignon, just like my son. Maybe my William was offended and decided to make the change. Whatever the reason, it was his idea first, and Leonidas followed along. Their father had referred to them in his will as William and Leonidas Aust, but they didn't want my last name either.

No one ever sits down and explains the reasons for anything to me anymore. I hear things only piecemeal. Then, I have to put together any fragments I hear and try to figure out what's going on. I suppose they either think it's none of my business or that I am too old to understand. But I know more than they think.

I don't see any of them very much anymore. Sometimes, on increasingly rare occasions, I receive a short letter or a brief visit from William or Rosalia, never Leonidas. I think it's so no one can say they completely neglected their mother. After Fredonia died, Rosalia came to see me once and suggested that I should move back to Brunswick.

"It's really hard for everyone to get down here to Jacksonville to see you," she said. "Now that Fredonia is gone, we're all thinking it might be best if you just moved back to where the rest of the family lives."

I had given it some thought, but I knew it would be costly and a lot of trouble. And I wasn't eager to return to the place where I was known as Henry DuBignon's old mistress, discarded when he married her daughter instead.

"I'm too old to start all over again, Rosalia."

"It surely would make everything easier on us."

That, of course, was the main reason they wanted me to move back—to make it easier on them, to save them the trouble of having to go out of their way to visit their mother once in a while. And I knew what it was like when I went to stay with them. I would spend more time mending and cooking than I did talking to my children or getting to know my grandchildren.

The worst of it was that I would have to sell my little house here in Jacksonville, which would be hard for me to do. It's the only place that's ever been truly mine in my whole life. And I am proud of the way I have fixed it up to suit me.

"I manage here just fine," I told her. "I have no rent to pay, and I'll get along with the modest savings Willis left me, especially now that prices have gotten more or less back to normal."

No one ever mentions Willis. It's almost as though he never existed. I've often wondered why I ever married him. My rational excuse was that I'd been at Dover Hall with my uncle too long, but I think it was mainly to prove to Henry that another man still wanted me and to escape all the humiliation he'd caused. He'd made a fool of me, using me all those years and then seducing my daughter. Willis could not have been more different. Sometimes I think he must have been the world's stingiest man to have saved all he did on what he earned, but of course I'm grateful to him now.

"Well, you could come visit us, instead of our having to come here," Rosalia said. "It's easier for you to get away since you don't have any responsibilities."

"Well, I have Pearl. Now who would look after her?"

Rosalia glanced with annoyance at the cat nestled in my lap and sighed.

"Besides," I said, "it's hard at my age, and the older I get the harder it is. There's still no direct rail line from Jacksonville to Brunswick. You have to change trains at places like Tebeauville and then wait for another train there. It takes a long time, and it's just a nuisance."

"It's not Tebeauville anymore, Mother. They've changed the name to Waycross. I've told you that before. Remember?" Rosalia informed me with condescending patience. I know she's getting exasperated when she calls me "mother."

"Waycross—that's such an ugly name. Why on earth would they do a thing like that? Tebeauville sounds much nicer."

"Mother, you're just trying to change the subject."

"It wouldn't hurt you and your brothers to take a day or two once in a while to come see me. You're younger, and it's easier for you."

"We all have busy lives, Mother."

"Well, then..."

She finally just shrugged and said no more about it

The problem with living here all by myself is not so much that I have few friends and no family. It's that I have too much time to remember the past. I've outlived everyone involved in this melodrama of my life, and I'm the only one left to tell the tale, which no one in my family wants to hear. For them my life is embarrassing and irrelevant. My children don't like to talk about it, and some of my grandchildren are horrified to think that their father is also the father of three of their grandmother's children. They just want to forget the peculiarities of our family, but unlike them, I'm doomed to remember, and those memories close in on me sometimes, demanding my attention.

Henry's been gone for almost eleven years now, and I think, during all that time, Mary and I were the only ones ever to visit his grave. I helped her once or twice to pull weeds around the small granite stone that bears only his name and the dates of his birth and death. It's such a tranquil and beautiful spot, isolated from the turmoil of the world, a resting place that varies only with the rising and ebbing tides of the marsh. It's ironic, I suppose, that as Mary and I worked together around his resting place, we were still doing him service in a way. We both knew him intimately. We had shared him as a mother and daughter should never have to do, yet he separated us. There were so many things we'd shared, but we could never talk about them, for they divided us more than they connected us. There is so much that will never be said, now that Mary is gone. We tried to live, I suppose, as though it were forgotten. But we both knew it never would be—not by us.

I hate it that my memories of Mary are so entangled with those of Henry, for it makes me sound like a bad mother—the way I waited breathless with anxiety and then rejoiced every time she gave birth to another daughter. His last sons were mine, and I hadn't wanted him ever to forget that. It was my sons—not his daughters by Mary—that would carry his name into the future. Or so I'd thought until they disavowed it, hoping, I guess, that everyone would forget the truth.

Now I just want to live out the rest of my life and let my remaining years go by without upheaval and drama. I don't want to move back to Brunswick and get caught up in all the family's problems. I don't want to live there in the shadow of my bitter past. I prefer to stay here and let the empty days come and go. It rains or the sun shines. It's hot or cold. It doesn't much matter. I sit on the porch, gazing at whatever or whoever happens to pass by. My eyes are too dim now to read. I think I've even begun to talk to myself as I relive those early days back in London with George, remembering our wild rush to America, Mary's birth on the ship, my love affair with Henry, and my children born on the island. Here, without others to remind me, I can remember only what I choose to remember and ignore the rest. At least I try to. Those early memories all seem more vivid to me now than those strangers who are my grandchildren.

There are times when I feel ready—even eager—to let go of this world, times when I can't think of any particular reason to live on now that the good parts of my life are over. One day, when I was in such a mood, I wrote it all down in a little poem I call "Lines to my Children," to try and tell them how I was feeling. I don't know if they'll ever see it or, even if they do, whether they'll care, but one of the verses in particular expressed my thoughts:

> Let me go, for earth has sorrows,
> Loss and pain and bitter tears.
> All its paths are dark and dreary,
> All its hopes are fraught with fears.
> Short lived are its brightest flowers,
> Soon its cherished hopes decay;
> Let me go. I fain would leave it
> For the realms of endless day.

Along with that little poem I recorded one single request. I'd like to be buried in that peaceful little Burnett cemetery on the edge of the marsh and just be forgotten. Yes, I know it's where Henry is buried, and Mary lies there now as well, but somehow it seems appropriate that the three of us should share the same fate in the spot that reminds me so much of Jekyl Island, where it all happened.

Other times when I'm contemplating our lying there together for eternity—the three of us—I decide I don't want us to be forgotten. I want all the world to see our graves and learn our story. Perhaps that is an important reason for me to live on. Maybe that's why God has left me here. Since I'm the only one left who was part of what happened, perhaps it's my duty to preserve it all.

Henry once said that, if he had to marry again, he'd rather marry me than Mary, but I don't think he ever regretted that marriage—except for what it did to his reputation. He certainly got his money's worth, so to speak, but I have to laugh when I remember how much he always wanted sons and how Mary gave him only daughters instead. I thought it fitting that it should be so, after using women for his own pleasure all his life. It must have galled his masculinity to see that he couldn't father sons any longer. I saw it then as I do now, as retribution—God's judgment—to surround him with only females for the rest of his life. I can't help but see the humor in it, bitter though it is.

Since I'm the only one left to keep the truth, it's up to me to tell the tale as I see it. I don't know what lies ahead, but I can't help but think that I have been left here for one reason only—to shape the story and determine how the future judges Henry DuBignon. I smile just to think of it.

EPILOGUE

Outskirts of Brunswick, Georgia, March 12, 1957

It was six a.m. on Tuesday morning when the first bulldozer rolled onto the old Burnett property. The wrecking crew had finished its work the day before, and all that remained of the aging frame houses that once stood there was rubble. Now it was up to the bulldozer operators to push the scattered debris into either large piles ready to be hauled away or smaller piles to be shoved into the creek and out of sight. A backhoe and a front-loader waited on the edge of the property to help remove any additional debris or obstacles that might hinder the new development.

All the heavy machinery was busy by nine o'clock, and a wood grinder had been brought in to remove any remaining limbs of the felled trees. The demolition overseer had marked any trees that were to remain with a yellow ribbon—mostly massive live oaks draped with Spanish moss that would add character and charm to the ranch-style brick houses to be built in the new subdivision located alongside the marsh creek. The oaks would add considerable value to the lots they graced. Families destined to buy them would surely be willing to pay more for plots of land shaded by the stately trees that would live for hundreds of years and no doubt outlast the houses themselves, as they had outlasted the wooden houses that preceded them. They were a kind of status symbol in the South, adding both dignity and a sense of tradition to the property. Everything else, the supervisor said, had to go. By the end of the week, the land-clearing crew was expected to have all the detritus removed and the land smoothed to make way for the construction crew that would start Monday morning.

Just before noon, Everett Richards turned off the motor of his bulldozer, his eyes fixed on something that looked like a raised gray stone near the edge of the creek. He wanted to make sure it wasn't something that would damage the tracks or the blade of the bulldozer. He jumped down from his perch atop the heavy machine and waded through the tangle of undergrowth to get a closer look. Not just one, but six or seven granite stones dotted the area. Tombstones, he guessed—some broken, all dirty, leaning, and mostly illegible. Something told him he'd better check with the supervisor and see what he should do before moving on.

He turned back and walked with a steady gait toward the silver, bullet-shaped trailer that served as construction headquarters, where he hoped to find Superintendent Perkins and see what he wanted done about the little cemetery. There were only about half a dozen graves there, and the small markers were overgrown with vines and too damaged to read, obviously long neglected. Richards suspected that anyone who had lived here before and might have tended them had long since sold out, died, or moved closer to the Liberty shipyards where they had probably worked during the war years. Who knows? The cemetery was filled with weeds so high that they almost completely shielded the tombstones from view.

He found Perkins sitting at a table inside the trailer, chewing on the last of his sausage biscuit.

"Hey boss, what do you want me to do about those graves over by the creek?"

Perkins swallowed and took another swig of black coffee before he answered. "What graves?"

"There's an ol' cemetery over yonder."

"Shit," said Perkins. "The developer never mentioned that."

"Maybe he didn't know it was there when he bought the place. It's hid pretty good by weeds and vines. Don't reckon nobody's been out there for a long time."

"Did you notice any of the names on the markers?"

"I couldn't say for sure. Can't hardly read 'em. One of them looked like the last name started with a D, but I couldn't make out the rest."

"Shit," Perkins said again. "Let me take a look." He followed the bulldozer operator toward the creek. By the time the waterway was in clear sight, the supervisor shrugged. "You're right. I can hardly see 'em. It's pretty obvious nobody cares."

"What should I do?" Richards asked.

"Just bulldoze 'em into the creek. I never saw 'em, did you?"

Richards blinked at him for a moment, a puzzled expression on his face. Then, seeing the supervisor's stern eyes fixed on him, he shook his head. "No sir. Never saw 'em."

"And you don't mention it to nobody, you hear," Perkins said. "Nobody."

"Yes sir," Richards said with a nod. As Perkins walked back to the trailer, Richards climbed once more onto his bulldozer and cranked it up. It rumbled beneath him as he approached the ruined graveyard. The first stone toppled easily, and the second, already leaning sharply to the left, followed suit. They were all fairly small.

As he leveled the ground and pushed the stones toward the tranquil waters that cut through the marsh, he couldn't see them as they toppled into the water one by one and sank to the murky bottom of Yellow Bluff Creek, each splash drowned by the sound of the motor. It was high tide now, and he wondered whether the stones might be visible when the tide went out. Probably not. The plough mud at the bottom was soft, and it was likely that the granite's weight would disturb it just enough for the silt to resettle over the stones and obscure them from view.

He reckoned that any bodies buried there had long since deteriorated. The water level had no doubt seeped into the coffins and rotted anything inside. He hawked and spit over the side of the bulldozer.

"So long, buddies," he said, with a salute toward the creek. "Guess your time on earth is over. Nobody'll ever know you were here."

At the end of the workday, Richards parked the bulldozer alongside the other heavy equipment near the silver trailer, went inside, and punched the time clock before getting into his rusty blue pickup. He started the engine to head for home, hoping Agnes would have supper ready by the time he got there. As he turned left onto highway 341, he glanced back with satisfaction at the parcel of land he had helped clear. It was smooth and bare now, save for the live oaks, ready for next week's builders. He smiled with satisfaction as he roared down the highway toward suppertime.

AUTHOR'S AFTERWORD

When I started the first draft of this book, I was relying in part on information I had gathered for one of my earlier books, *Jekyll Island's Early Years* (University of Georgia Press, 2005), from various repositories in the United States, Mauritius, and Brittany, France, as well as stories I had gleaned from family members and whatever local or online records I could find. For this current book, however, I was curious to explore further the second generation of the du Bignon family (who wrote their names at various times as du Bignon, DuBignon, and even Dubignon) and to learn more about the wife of Henri du Bignon, Anne Amélie Nicolau, as they would have spelled their names back in France, as well as about the entire Nicolau family before they came to America. Since relatively little is known about them, this book required further research in the place of Amélie's birth, Bordeaux, France.

The results of that research compelled me to toss the earlier draft and begin again, for I discovered that much of the information concerning the Nicolau family, available in sources consulted in the United States and mostly derived from family lore, was inaccurate or incomplete. As I have ascertained, even Amélie's tombstone in the du Bignon cemetery on Jekyll Island contains incorrect information. The following facts were gleaned from records held in the Archives de la Gironde in Bordeaux.

The parents of Amelia (as she came to be known in Georgia) were Etienne Nicolau and his (presumably) second wife, Jeanne Petit, who were married on 24 July 1769 in the Bordeaux parish of St-Rémy, when Etienne was thirty-four years old. Jeanne Petit was the daughter of Thomas Petit (deceased at the time of the marriage) and his wife, Jeanne Matias. Amelia's father, Etienne, described in the parish records as a *menuisier* or master carpenter, died at age fifty on 18 August 1785, only four months after her birth on 4 April.

(Amelia's tombstone records her age as sixty-three, when she was in fact sixty-five at the time of her death in 1850.) She was baptized by a vicar named Père Loubère that same day.

Like her father, her godfather was a carpenter, Joseph Peyssy, and her godmother is listed as Anne Nicolau, also said to be "sister" of the baby. That, plus the fact that Pascal Nicolau was her half-brother rather than her brother, allows me to conclude that her father Etienne had been married before. (Pascal lists in his will, probated in Glynn County, Georgia, another brother named Cadet and a niece, Arial Richard, who may have been the daughter of his sister Anne.) It may seem odd that a family would choose to give their daughters the same first name, but another example in the history behind this novel is that the three Grand Dutreuilh sisters all have Marie and Félicité as part of their names, which has resulted in the frequent confusion of the three sisters.

The other children of Etienne and Jeanne Nicolau were Bernard (born 21 July 1776), Jacques (born 20 February 1779), and Joseph (born 30 March 1782). Jacques never came to America; however, there was a Jacques Nicolau listed among the planters on Saint-Domingue (modern-day Haiti). Apparently, Joseph also went briefly to Saint-Domingue, since a passport to Cap Français, one of the country's major ports, was issued to him on 13 July 1802. These connections to Saint-Domingue may explain why some family members to this day believe that the father of the Nicolau family was also a planter on Saint-Domingue who was killed during the Haitian uprising. Clearly Joseph's visit was brief, for he obtained a second passport, this one to come from Bordeaux to America, on 23 February 1804, the same day a passport was issued to his sister, Anne Amélie. Jacques's fate in Saint-Domingue is uncertain, but there is no evidence to suggest that the other Nicolau siblings ever saw him again.

I have found, thus far, no record of the date Bernard first arrived in Georgia, but he purchased Marengo Plantation on 9 January 1804 from a man named John Elliott, paying $1900. Marengo bordered the lands of David Jeffrey on the east and those of John Fox on the west. If he notified his brother and sister at once, his letter would have arrived in time for them to apply for passports by the date of their recorded applications.

A crossing of the Atlantic at the time usually took about six to seven weeks, if all went well. That would place their arrival in America at the earliest in mid-April. However, chances are good that they would have waited for warmer and calmer spring weather before sailing. A letter from Aaron Burr to his daughter, Theodosia, written at the home of John Couper on 31 August 1804, indicates that Amelia arrived "about three months ago from France." That would place her arrival approximately in late May or early June, if he is correct. It is also Burr who records the story of the drowning of her brother Joseph.

We can assume that Burr's visit to the Couper plantation lasted at least a week, since he was still there (or there again) at the time of the hurricane that struck the coast of Georgia the following September 7 and 8. My fictional account of the hurricane is based largely on another letter of Burr in which he describes the event to Theodosia, as well as on other eyewitness accounts.

The fact that Amelia gave birth to at least eleven children is attested by a letter of Henry written on 31 May 1827 to his father's agent in France, René Peltier, in which he says, "I have had eleven children, eight of which survive. I had the misfortune in 1824 of losing my eldest daughter Louisa, aged sixteen, a charming and favorite child.... I have also lost a little boy of seven and a girl of six." Unfortunately, he fails to name these last two or give the dates of their deaths in the letter. Since the letter was written in 1827, given their ages, the oldest could not have been born after 1820. I think that the most likely time for their births (though not the only possibility) is between 1814 (the birth of his son Joseph) and 1819 (the birth of his daughter Sarah), when there is an unusual five-year gap with no new recorded babies. Rather than completely ignore that the two children existed, I have imagined their births and names in my fictional account as Bernard, born in 1815, and his sister Anne, in 1816, both family names. That would place their deaths (assuming they died in close temporal proximity of something contagious like yellow fever) in the vicinity of 1822. In short, during the first eighteen years of their marriage, Amelia, with eleven live births, was pregnant most of the time, a situation not particularly unusual in an era before birth control.

Readers may notice that, in my earlier book *Marguerite's Landing* (Twin Oaks Press, 2016), I chose not to mention the existence of these two unnamed children, since they played no significant role in the life of their grandmother of the eponymous title and since we know virtually nothing about them beyond the information contained in their father's letter. I could once again have chosen to ignore their existence. However, the deaths of two children who survived six and seven years must have been difficult for their mother, and I have decided to include them in this book. I beg the reader's indulgence for this discrepancy.

George Butler Aust, the first husband of Sarah Ann Maccaw, was born on 18 April 1800 to his parents, Leonard Aust Esquire and his wife Harriet. (The Esquire after his name denotes high but non-specific social standing in British usage.) Leonard was a surveyor of the General Post Office and was in part responsible for getting his son an appointment as a clerk at the Post Office when he turned eighteen. A nobleman, Lord Chinchester, nominated him upon the recommendation of both his father and Sir Francis Freeling, who would himself eventually rise to the position of General Post Office Secretary.

Three years later, in May 1821, young George Aust married a woman named Jane Faith Evans. He had held his job at the Post Office for about twelve years when he became enamored of Sarah Aust. The two were married on 26 January 1830 at St. Stevens, St. Benet, London. Ten days later, on 5 February and without giving notice, George "absconded" from his job at the Post Office to set sail with his new wife to come to Georgia. The marriage was apparently bigamous, for no record has been found of a divorce between George and his first wife. He left behind three children from his first marriage—a boy named George Thomas Butler Aust, born 1

August and baptized 25 August 1823 at St. Leonard, Shoreditch, London, and two daughters, Jane Sarah Maskelyn Aust, born probably in late February and baptized on 10 March 1826, and Augusta Mary Aust, born 21 August and baptized 10 September 1828. Both baptisms took place at Camberwell, St. George, Southwark. Church records also reveal that Jane Faith Aust, listing herself as a widow, later married a man named Joseph William Inch on 19 August 1832 at St. Botolph, Aldgate, London.

The marriage of George and Sarah and his sudden departure from his job without notice appear to have been surreptitious. They arrived in Brunswick in 1830, the same year Sarah gave birth to their first child, Mary Delora. Some family lore contends that she was born at sea, most likely during their voyage to America. Other stories allege that a second child, Paul, was born in 1832, though I have found no documented record of his existence. If he existed, he evidently died very young. A second daughter, Margaret Fredonia, was born in 1834. George died on 22 January 1838, just shy of his thirty-eighth birthday, leaving Sarah a widow with two daughters to support. His obituary in the *Brunswick Advocate* lists him, like his father, with the honorific Esquire after his name. It ends enigmatically with the words, "Let the finger of silence rest on the tongue of malevolence and detraction."

Sarah's parents, who lived in London, were Michael Foreman Maccaw and his wife, Sarah Jenkins. Sarah Ann was their third child, born in 1812. At the time of her marriage to George Aust, Sarah Maccaw was still in her teens, while he was almost thirty years old. She was a parishioner at St. Mary's Newington and apparently lived in the Newington area of London south of the Thames, while George worked at the General Post Office north of the river. It is probable, given the suddenness of the wedding, their clandestine departure from England, and the family source mentioned above, suggesting that their first child was born "at sea," that Sarah was already pregnant at the time they left London.

There is evidence that Sarah's younger brother, William Dover Maccaw, born in 1821, came to Savannah prior to the Civil War, where he married a woman named Susannah Dupont. He died in that city in 1871. Since we have no record of any interactions between him and his sister in Georgia, though there may have been some, I have omitted any mention of him in the book, which already contains many names and complex relationships. I have chosen not to add one more.

Surprisingly enough, there is a sparse paper trail for Sarah after her liaison with Henry DuBignon ended and his marriage to her daughter Mary began. Thus, the later chapters of Sarah's life, including the time spent at her uncle William Dover Jenkins's plantation, Dover Hall, are purely speculative and based largely on the fact that there was evidently some contact between the two, given the fact that Jenkins remembered Sarah and her daughters with fifty dollars each in his will. Despite her large number of descendants, I was unable to uncover any firm information about the details of her later life, other than census data.

The one important record we *do* have during this time is Sarah's marriage in 1857 to Willis Reddick of Jacksonville. It is documented in Glynn County court records, as are the marriages of both her Aust daughters. Presumably, after her marriage, Sarah and her youngest daughter Rosalia lived in Jacksonville, where her second daughter Fredonia also lived. Fredonia's husband, William Ewen Harris, is listed in census records as a carpenter, but there is no mention of Willis Reddick's profession. I have chosen to make him a fisherman in order to give him a reason to sail to Brunswick. Only three years after their marriage, Sarah is recorded in the 1860 census as living once again in Brunswick, under the name of Sarah Aust, with only her daughter Rosalia. Census records of 1870 indicate that she later returned to Jacksonville and retook the name of Sarah Reddick, though there is no further information about Willis Reddick. No family record or official document discovered thus far indicates the date of Sarah's death (usually given as "about 1885") or the place of her burial.

The marriage of Henry DuBignon to Mary Aust was actually performed by Edward Barron, bishop of Constantia, who had recently returned from a mission in Guinea. Upon his return to America, he was assigned a role as missionary priest to various areas, one of which was Florida. I have no explanation as to why he was in Brunswick on that particular day, though I have surmised that it might have been in connection with the Catholic mission in Brunswick, which did not yet have a parish church. He died in Savannah of yellow fever two years later.

Many of my readers will likely be aware that, in 1886, Jekyll (spelled Jekyl until 1929) Island would become home to the famous Jekyll Island Club, where the nation's wealthy elite—bankers, businessmen, and industrialists like J. P. Morgan, William Rockefeller, and Joseph Pulitzer—gathered to winter in their own self-created and exclusive Eden. The club lasted until 1942 and the coming of World War II.

However, fewer readers might be aware that Dover Hall, the plantation of Sarah Aust's uncle, William Dover Jenkins, was purchased in 1916 by a syndicate of major league baseball owners and interested parties, with the expectation of turning it into an important training camp for their ball clubs. Instead it became Dover Hall Club, a winter resort for relaxation, hunting, and fishing for such baseball luminaries as Babe Ruth, Ty Cobb, and Gene Tunney. The club no longer exists. On another topic concerning Dover Hall, it is interesting to note that, at his death in 1858, the body of William Dover Jenkins, Sarah's uncle, was indeed shipped to Freetown, Massachusetts, where he lies buried beside his beloved Peggy in Assonet Cemetery. Matching tombstones mark their graves.

I trust that readers will have noted that this book is a sequel to my earlier novel, *Marguerite's Landing*, which tells the story of the first generation of the du Bignon family (as they spelled their name at the time), who settled on Jekyll Island to escape the French Revolution. It is my intent to write one more novel in this series, focusing on family members of the third generation, the last to own and live on Jekyll Island, which in 1886 would become the possession of the famous millionaire's club mentioned above. I hope readers will be interested in the entire saga of this fascinating family. Certainly its members were never dull.

ACKNOWLEDGMENTS

As with all my books, I owe a debt of gratitude to the many people who helped in my research efforts or who shared their knowledge and/or historical documents to make this book as accurate as possible within the limits of historical fiction. I am especially grateful to Dr. Carole Nivet Rathier, my research assistant in Bordeaux, France, for helping me to locate important documents concerning the life of Amelia Nicolau and her brothers before they came to America. I am also grateful to Professor Florence Buttay of the Université Bordeaux Montaigne for having recommended her. The results of those newfound documents are incorporated into the story and also elaborated in the Author's Afterword.

For invaluable English sources on the backgrounds of the Aust family, I owe my thanks especially to Peter Smith from Kent, England, who alerted me to information gleaned from British records that I did not previously have. These sources led me on to discover yet other useful materials.

On this side of the Atlantic, I have benefited enormously from the work of Amy Hedrick, who has put together an amazing collection of Glynn County records and made them available to the public on her website Glynngen.com. It was she who first enlightened me about the relationship between Sarah Aust and William Dover Jenkins, her mother's brother in the Brunswick area. I am thankful to Amy not only for generously answering my endless questions but also for making so many helpful historical records easily accessible to the general public. In addition, I appreciate more than I can say the various exploratory field trips she and I have taken together, including to the sites of Dover Hall and Marengo Plantation as well as those of the last home of Henry DuBignon and the Burnett Cemetery. She also passed along the story of what allegedly happened to any remaining tombstones there.

For helpful information about the Aust-DuBignon families in America, I am especially grateful to Dr. E. Lynn McLarty of Tallahassee, who has graciously shared many of the documents he has collected over the years. He has been arduous in uncovering not only useful genealogical information but also family letters and documents such as the bill from Dr. Woodridge for his treatment of Camilla DuBignon during the Civil War. Such details help a book of historical fiction come to life.

Wherever I can find a DuBignon descendant or someone else who is familiar with Brunswick history or the families involved, I glean whatever information I can. In this context I appreciate the generosity through the years of Bunny Cowan, Elizabeth DuBignon, John Hunter, the late Polly Kitchens, the late Doris Finney Liebrecht, Susan Peterson, Angela Meyers, and Buddy Sullivan. The segment of the poem penned by Sarah Aust is from the collection of the late Spencer Popwell. It is factual that she indicated after the poem her wish to be buried in the Burnett Cemetery. I am also grateful to Father John Sims Baker of St. Rose of Lima Catholic Church in Murfreesboro, Tennessee, for answering questions concerning the plausibility of the Catholic marriage I have described in this book.

Finally, as always, I thank staff members at the various repositories where I have worked, especially those at the Jekyll Island Museum, who have always been of enormous support to me in various projects over the years. I also thank Mimi Rogers at the Coastal Museum on St. Simons Island for her help with the John Couper papers, as well as the past assistance of the Georgia Historical Society in Savannah with my work in the DuBignon family collection and the papers of Charles Rinaldo Floyd.

On a personal note, I have also benefited from the various comments from members of my writers group in Murfreesboro, Tennessee, as well as from friends and readers who have made helpful suggestions concerning earlier versions of this book, among them Michelle Adkerson, Vicki Brennan, Ron and Emily Messier, Karen Pratt, and Margaret Ordoubadian.

Finally, I would like to thank Marc Jolley, Director of Mercer University Press, and Marsha Luttrell, Publication Assistant, for their help and interest in this book, as well as Kelley Land for her excellent editing. These various people have helped enormously and have my sincere gratitude. Any flaws that may remain are mine alone.

QUESTIONS FOR DISCUSSION

1. Both primary narrators are "truth keepers," aware that their stories may be forgotten with their deaths. How do their roles differ, and why does each feel compelled to be the keeper of *her* truth for as long as she lives?

2. Alongside the theme of preserving "truth" that runs throughout this book is that of deception. How does the willingness of each character to live with or confront deception affect your view of them? Do you think we all live with some form of deception, either self-deception or the deception of others?

3. Do you think women tend to feel a greater urgency to be truth keepers than men?

4. With which character are you most sympathetic? Why?

5. Discuss Amelia's decision to have no more children and the impact it has on her marriage. Do you think she is justified in her decision? In your opinion, does that decision justify her husband's subsequent actions?

6. Did the sudden discovery after Sarah's picnic on the beach with her children surprise you? Why or why not? What do you think of Sarah's reaction?

7. Why, in your view, would a man in his prime and at the moment of his greatest success conduct himself as Henry did? How does his power and success impact his life?

8. Do you think Henry truly loves any of the women in his life? Do you think they love him?

9. How does the coming of the Civil War impact the lives of the people in the story?

10. Do you think Sarah does the right thing in forcing her daughter to marry? Discuss the relationship between Sarah and Mary after her daughter's marriage. Were you surprised at Sarah's willingness to respond as she did to the letter from Henry requesting her help?

11. Does it seem strange to you that as they age, both Amelia and Sarah seem compelled to remember the past? Do you think that tends to be true of all people as they grow older? Do some people prefer to remember the past not as it was but as they have imagined it to be?

12. Although Henry is an important focal point throughout the book, the author does not let him tell his own story. Do you think his version of the truth would differ from the truths of the two women in question? If so, how?

FAMILIES OF HENRY DUBIGNON AND BIRTH DATES OF HIS CHILDREN

Henry DuBignon—Amelia Nicolau. m. 1808

Maria Louisa	Charles Joseph	Eliza	John Couper	Joseph	[Bernard?]	[Anne?]	Sarah	Catherine	Eugenia	Henry Charles Jr.
1808	1809	1810	1812	1814	c. 1816?	c. 1817?	1819	1823	1825	1826

Henry DuBignon—Sarah Aust (no marriage)

Leonidas Henry	William Turner	Rosalia Elizabeth
1840	1843	1848

Henry DuBignon—Mary Delora Aust married 1852

Virginia Elizabeth	Emily Amanda	Camilla	Agnes Sarah	Valeria Marie	Gertrude Louisa [aka Garland]
1853	1854	c. 1856	1859	c. 1862	c. 1864

Henry DuBignon- Margaret (free woman of color)

Charlotte
mid-1830s